REVENGE BOUND

HEIDI JOY TRETHEWAY

TATTOO THIEF

BOOK THREE

Text copyright © Heidi Joy Tretheway

Tretheway, Heidi Joy.
Revenge Bound. (Tattoo Thief #3) / Heidi Joy Tretheway.

Summary: When a vengeful ex-boyfriend posts naked photos of Violet online, a stalker haunts her. The man who wants to protect her—Jayce, lead guitarist for the rock band Tattoo Thief—is the one whose fame could cause her photos to go viral.

ISBN-10: 1499786778
ISBN-13: 978-1499786774

[1. Romantic suspense—Fiction 2. New Adult & College—Fiction.] I. Tretheway, Heidi Joy. II. Revenge Bound. III. Tattoo Thief, Book Three.

Editor: Jim Thomsen
Copy editor: Cynthia L. Moyer
Proofreader: Amy Duryea
Cover design: Heidi Joy Tretheway
Cover photo: Artem Furman

Published by Heidi Joy Tretheway: www.heidijoytretheway.com
Printed in the United States of America
First printing, 2014

For my parents: encouragers, cheerleaders, believers.
Even when I write naughty books.

PROLOGUE: VIOLET

The Internet is full of naked pictures of pretty girls. Curvy girls splayed on beds. Busty girls gripping their breasts in ecstasy. Blondes getting pounded, pistoned, defiled. Brunettes taking the money shot, the deep throat, the back door.

Any Google search will find you these images. And one of them might be me.

I'm the redhead. The one with her back arched, her eyes wide, her mouth open with desire. The one with her legs spread and her arms tied tight above her head.

I'm the one shot with her own camera and uploaded for the world to see.

And now I'm the one with the secret.

CHAPTER 1: VIOLET

I've never been so thankful for the oily smell of Chinese food and the subtle whiff of socks.

"I thought you weren't coming home until tomorrow?" Neil lounges in our living room with his feet up and a half-empty takeout container beside him.

"I missed you, too." I muster a little sarcasm for my roommate and drop my overfull camera gear bag at the entry beside my suitcase. My eyelids are leaden with exhaustion. "I waited at the gate forever to get on standby."

"You look like shit. Long flight?"

I snort. "Don't sugar-coat it, Neil. Tell me what you really think." My phone pings and another text shatters me.

When I fuck you, I'm gonna pull that pretty red hair of yours until you scream.

My breath hitches and my shoulders begin to shake. I can't keep ignoring these texts. My legs refuse to take two steps into the living room and I collapse, gulping for air.

"Violet! I'm sorry!" Neil springs off the couch and reaches for me but I recoil.

I pull my knees to my chest and my phone slips through my fingers and lands with a clunk on the floor. "Don't touch me. Don't even touch me." I want to curl into a ball and sleep until I can wake from this nightmare.

Neil takes a step back. "What happened to you?" He picks up my phone and glances at the screen, his jaw hardening when he sees the message.

"Is this from Brady?" he demands. "That asshole. I thought you dumped him before you went to Europe."

I try to control my breath against sobbing hiccups. I thought I was all cried out, but turning on my phone after the long flight slammed me back into the reality of the past several days.

Each text is more poisonous than the last.

"We did break up. But I've been getting these texts."

Neil waits for me to explain. When I don't, he nudges me. "From who?"

I shake my head. "I don't know. It's not Brady's number."

Neil sits quietly at my side, then reaches a tentative hand to my shoulder. When I don't flinch, he cups my elbow and pulls me up off the floor and to the couch.

He goes to our kitchen and pours a few fingers of gin for each of us. I hear the refrigerator door open and close and I know he's adding olives, making his martini dirty and mine muddy, just the way I like it.

He places a drink in my hand and clinks my glass, even though I'm too numb to make the gesture. "I'm glad you're home, Vi."

I take a sip and my shoulders convulse, a sob shaking my chest. I hear another ping and Neil leaps for my phone, tilting the screen away from me as he reads it.

He shakes his head.

"Another one?" I ask.

"Yeah. But this one's from a different number."

I let out a faltering breath.

"How many have you gotten so far?"

"Twenty. Thirty. I lost count." My cheeks are hot with embarrassment but I trust Neil. After what happened with Brady, he's the only one I trust.

"How do they have your number?"

I shrug, totally at a loss. I wanted to believe it's a wrong number, but the text about my red hair says otherwise.

I finally gather the strength to go to my room and unpack. Neil lurks in my doorway.

"Vi? I was planning to go out tonight, but the girl who stayed in your room, Stella, she's supposed to come by and pick up her stuff. Are you going to be OK here without me?"

I nod and he hangs at my door for a moment longer. He enters my room and picks up my phone from the top of my dresser. "Shut this off and get some sleep, Violet."

I promise him I will.

***

I drag my rear out of bed to answer the knock at my door. I didn't mean to fall asleep—I need a shower, some non-airline food in my stomach and a change of clothes.

"Hi! I'm Stella. I brought you this." A too-chipper pixie with a cherry-brown bob thrusts a wine bottle into my hands.

"Thank you?" I squint and my fuzzy brain threads this girl's name together with why she's here. When I left on my trip, Neil said a reporter at his newspaper needed a place to stay for a while. Of course I had to let her have my room; Neil's always taking in strays. That's how I ended up being his roommate.

I open the door wider for Stella, who is followed by a curvy brunette and a well-muscled guy. "Is Neil here?" Stella asks.

"He went out for a drink with some friends." I watch the guy hoist Stella's stuff and as he turns, he's weirdly familiar. "Wait. Are you an actor?"

"Uh, no." The guy shrugs and lugs Stella's stuff toward the door.

"I recognize you. Are you one of Neil's friends?"

"Never met the guy. Sorry."

"Huh. You just look really familiar." I sway and grab the back of a chair for balance. The time change and long hours waiting in Charles De Gaulle Airport drained every ounce of my energy, but the more texts I got, the more I just wanted to come home and hide.

Now that I'm here, I feel better. Barely.

"Hey, you're probably tired. We'll just grab this stuff and get out of your way, OK?" Stella points to a pile of bags and boxes in the living room.

I nod and watch them shuttle the bags out.

Stella returns for the last few things. "What's your number?"

"For what?" I blurt. Right now, my phone is my enemy.

"For your phone? I'm going to text you my phone number in case you find something in your room that Neil forgot to pack for me. Can you text me and I'll come get it?"

"Oh. Sure." At least that's one message that won't be from an unknown letch.

"Thanks. And welcome back."

CHAPTER 2: JAYCE

There are some temptations too good to resist.

Boobs on a platter, for instance. Give me a handful—or more—in a push-up bra and I'm a happy man. I'll have some of that tonight, and maybe the next night if she's hot and willing.

They almost always are.

Hot stage lights fade and I bow and wave to the audience with my band mates. Tyler, Gavin, Dave and I hold our positions as the curtains close and the backstage lights come up.

"Fuck yeah!" Gavin high-fives Dave triumphantly. "Tattoo Thief's back!" He runs down a corridor and I know exactly who's waiting for him—his new girlfriend, Beryl.

Tonight my band played hard. It was a last-minute gig and we're pretty rusty. Gavin, our lead singer, is the "King of Wing," coming in cold after more than two months traveling the world and never answering *one* of my fucking emails.

Who freezes out their friends like that?

Temptation, in the form of two busty blondes, squeals from the wings. The girls watch me wipe down my guitar and pack it away in its case.

I had to fight hard to back Gavin tonight. We did it acoustic, so we didn't have big sound or the energy of a massive crowd as cover, just a few hundred fans at the Rockwood Music Hall. Thank God we didn't make too many mistakes. It's the smallest show we've played in more than a year, but this first step back into performing is why Dave urged us to take the booking.

And with almost no practice, Gavin agreed. A small part of me wishes we had sucked tonight. Maybe that would make Gavin pull his head out of his ass and take the band seriously again.

But tonight, I'll cut him some slack. He's back, he's happy and healthy. He's got a girl.

Don't think I'm jealous. I've got dozens. I could call pretty much any number in my phone and I'd be hitting that tonight.

I'm high from the adrenaline as I stride toward the green room after our show. Shelly and Teal's heels clomp behind me and I could have either of them tonight. Maybe both, if they're down with it.

I fucking love being a rock star.

***

Change of plans. I tell Shelly and Teal to go home. I call them a limo to ease their disappointment and tell them I'm going to help Tyler.

He's helped me more times than I can count, so I've got to help him haul the shit in his loft around so a girl he's been whining about for the last week can stay with him.

That could be interesting. Stella's a firecracker. I wanted to hate her for posting Gavin's song on the Internet without permission, but I also think she could be good for Tyler. I watched them together when she came to apologize, and she was the first girl I've seen who didn't look at him like prey, like he was fresh meat to be devoured.

Tyler's a gentle soul, but I know how to handle girls—keep it fun, keep it casual, and always keep it no strings attached. I put it out there from the beginning, and the girls who are into that stick around. The girls who want more go find some poor sucker who will give it to them.

I won't. I've seen too many guys burned by clingy girls who want more, including Tyler.

Shelly and Teal follow me out to the limo and they pout, giggle, and smear lipstick on me.

I wink. "I'm not wiping it off, I'm rubbing it in," I lie, and shut the door behind them.

I turn back to the stage side door where a guy in a button-down shirt is smoking. "Nice set."

I slow my stride. "Thanks, man."

"So, what's next for you, Jayce?" The man's tone is casual, aloof, as if he doesn't really care how I answer.

"What do you mean?"

"From what I can tell, you put your guitar in storage while Gavin was gone. Don't tell me that doesn't make a musician like you itch just a little bit."

I take a step toward the guy, trying to get a read on his expression beneath the slanting streetlight. "We're back now. That's what matters."

The man takes a long drag on his cigarette. "No, what matters is taking it to the next level. You've got a lead singer who flaked out on you, and then released a song without you. I smell a solo career for him, and maybe it's time you think about one, too."

The way the man lays out the facts gets my hackles up, so I deflect. "The only thing I smell is smoke."

The man dips into his back pocket and extracts a red embossed card from his billfold. "You're going to want to give me a call."

My hand moves automatically and I take the card. He nods, flicks his cigarette into the gutter, and walks away.

CHAPTER 3: VIOLET

The halls that usually stream with rowdy, pubescent junior high school kids are eerily quiet as I walk to the principal's office. My footsteps echo off bright green lockers and I hesitate at the frosted glass door.

It's summer break. I shouldn't be here.

"Come in, Violet."

He must have heard my footsteps, so I enter. Principal Dash sits behind a gray industrial desk, his thin, pasty face lit by a computer monitor.

"Sit down."

I obey, wondering again why he called me, less than twelve hours after I got back from my trip, for "an urgent matter we must discuss in person."

"Do you know why you're here?" He cocks an eyebrow and inspects my chest as if I have a stain on my blouse.

I glance down, my dark red hair sliding forward on my shoulders, but there's nothing. "No—I, ah, is this about the teaching assignments?"

My heart flutters with hope—is it possible the school got funding for a full-time art teacher? That's what I studied to be, but in my first year out of college, the pickings were slim. I was lucky to get a part-time assignment teaching art. The other half of my time is spent teaching sex ed to seventh- and eighth-graders.

I learned long ago how to roll a condom over a banana without snickering.

Mr. Dash frowns. "Yes and no. I'm sure you realize that teaching is not a lifestyle choice that's for everyone. We expect our teachers to live by a certain standard, even when they're out of the classroom."

I nod my head vigorously. I'm carefully neutral on Facebook, nonexistent on Twitter. I don't want a thirteen-year-old student to come across some half-drunk pictures of me at a bachelorette party and forward them to every other kid's phone.

His frown deepens. "That's why it pains me to see certain … images of you online."

Images? My heartbeat quickens. "What do you mean?"

"I realize you have a life outside of work, but what you're making public is not appropriate for our students. We have enough controversy over our sex ed curriculum. If more parents find out about these pictures, we'll have all-out war." He rotates the monitor to face me and my jaw goes slack in horror.

It's undeniably me: my flame-red hair tumbling across my breasts, my nipples peaked and lips parted, my hands bound tightly above my head.

An erotic and terrifying moment that my boss somehow found online. I want to die.

Dying would be sweet release compared to the toxic flood of acid through my veins. This is worse than the texts, far worse, and I open and close my mouth but no words come.

I have no excuse, no explanation, no way to make this photo anything less than what it is—career suicide.

Mr. Dash's lips thin and he shakes his head, scrolling down the web page to reveal two more images, each more damning than the last. "I'm sure you understand why I'll need to change the teaching assignments for the coming year. You won't be teaching."

"Not sex ed?" I whisper, my eyes clouded with tears as I cling to the thin hope that I might salvage the part of my career that I care about.

"Not at this school," Mr. Dash says. "I'll do you a favor and I won't write this up as the reason for termination. But I can't give you a recommendation, either. This—" he waves his hand at the monitor "—is totally irresponsible. Considering your background, it's not something I ever expected from you."

Mr. Dash's disdain pinches his face, and I shrivel in my chair with shame as tears stain my blouse. "How did you ... how did you find these?" I'm desperate to figure out how these got online, but deep in my gut, I know.

"I got an email with this link. I'd guess it was a concerned parent, but who knows how they found these? You'd better hope, as I do, they don't forward them to the PTA president."

My chest heaves and I feel the first sobs build. *Keep it together, Violet.* I force my gaze away from the haunting photos on Mr. Dash's screen and meet his stern, disapproving look. There's nothing to say. Nothing to make this right.

"Stop by your classroom and pick up anything personal. You're dismissed."

***

I wish I'd had the courage to get the link to my photos from Mr. Dash, but the shock of them left me horrified and just ... empty. I feel like I'm rushing to the scene of a terrible accident, not knowing how bad it will be, but desperate to find out.

I perch my laptop on my knees in my living room, unsure where to begin. A porn site? There are thousands. I try searching "naked redhead hands tied" and get dozens of pictures with varying degrees of bondage, from playful neckties to intricate *shibari* knots.

None of them are me.

Then I type the words I'm most afraid will yield a result—my own name, Violet Chase. I pray for boring Facebook profile photos and my student art projects.

The first page of results is clean—nothing more scandalous than my fine art photography. My portfolio includes plenty of back-lit nudes, all of them tasteful and none of them me.

I click to the second page of results and hear Neil's key in the door. I turn to him and he smiles hello, but then his face drops with a glance at the screen behind me. "What the hell is that?"

I turn and immediately zero in on the photos Mr. Dash showed me.

It's me. Tied up. Ready. Willing.

My stomach lurches and a sick wash of sweat prickles on my back. I don't even bother answering Neil; I just click on the picture as he hovers over my shoulder. The site is called *Sexy Bitches* and I scroll down through three pictures of me in bondage.

"Jesus, Violet." Neil's voice rises with alarm. "When did this happen? How?"

"Brady," I whisper. That's the only answer that makes sense. "He got revenge."

My hand freezes over the trackpad.

There's my name.

And my phone number.

And my address.

And the name of my school.

"He did this? He took these pictures and posted them?"

My head bows in shame. "He must have," I choke out. "I mean, he grabbed my camera when we were, you know … it wasn't like I could untie myself and grab it back."

"But that's your *name*." Neil's voice rises. "Any creep looking at this could find you, they'd know our address—"

His voice halts and I know he's just drawn the connection I made on the train ride home from the school. "They're sending the texts, aren't they?"

I nod, believing it must be true. For the fifth or fiftieth time today, I bow my head in shame and let the tears fall.

Neil pulls me against his chest in a hug and his soft hand strokes my arm. To most people, he's a jerk—abrasive, self-centered, hypercritical and very, very gay. To me, though, he's my slightly slobby roommate and a caring guy.

If he likes you enough to let you in.

When my sobs abate into a cottony, snot-clogged voice, I tell him the rest. "My principal found out. He called me down to the school this morning. He fired me."

"God, Violet, I'm sorry." Neil tucks a curled finger under my chin and forces me to meet his hazel eyes. "But you're stronger than this. This won't end you. I already gave your resume to my editor to try to get you some freelance photo gigs during summer break."

Neil's hopeful note is too weak a ray of light to shine into the darkness I feel. But I appreciate the gesture, and I gather the strength to go to my room.

The nudes on my wall—what used to be my favorite kind of photography—stare back at me and accuse.

CHAPTER 4: JAYCE

Even with my shirt off and the windows open, Tyler's loft is a sauna without air conditioning. It makes playing that much more intense.

I dig into our latest song, adding depth to Gavin's melody, cuing Tyler for a chord with a nod to his bass. Dave's pounding out our rhythm on drums and for a minute it's like we're back in Tyler's mom's garage, just playing loud, playing for fun, playing like we're gonna *be* somebody someday.

God, I miss that.

For months, our band's been treading water, a little too high on the success of our first two albums with a major label. But when Gavin took off, maybe that scared us a little. It forced us to get tighter so we wouldn't lose what we've built.

I see a movement from the far end of the loft and the door opens. That tiny girl Stella leads a tall redhead to the couches and I almost miss the transition to the bridge as I follow the redhead's movements.

She bends over a fat, square bag and assembles camera parts. Her long, pale legs end in a pair of dark blue shorts and her flame-red hair falls across her face in wild waves.

I play and watch her, the pieces falling into place. Stella's writing a story on us for her newspaper, *The Indie Voice*, and this is the freelance photographer who will shoot our practice.

She moves with a dancer's grace, her sleeveless white shirt revealing freckled arms and slender hands. She makes me want to keep looking.

No. I *need* to watch this girl, who is the polar opposite of every groupie and fangirl I know.

It's weird. In high school, Tyler and I were always trying to see boobs—he'd nudge me whenever Emma Jackson's bra strap was showing. But now boobs are everywhere. It's not a show if some girl in the front row doesn't take off her top or flash me her tits.

I can't see this girl's tits at all, and it bugs me the same way Emma Jackson's never-to-be-revealed boobs kept me preoccupied in algebra.

I keep playing, but my mind's not on the song. I'm staring—willing her to look up and let that curtain of red hair fall away from her face.

I get nothing.

We switch to a new song and I back Gavin on vocals. I sing the first line of the chorus, and nearly trip over the next lyrics when the redhead finally raises her chin.

She's looking at me. Through me. Her eyes are clear and bright and knowing. This girl is a witch, a sorceress, a fairy princess.

I'm fucked.

***

Dave calls for a break and like a coward, I hit the head. I plunge my hands into the icy tap and splash my face and neck. Since when do I get nervous about a girl? There's nothing overtly sexual about her—no tits on a plate, no dress cut up to *here* and down to *there*.

I shake off the weirdness. It's rare that anyone watches us practice, so maybe that's what's thrown me.

In the living room, Tyler entertains the redhead with a goofy description of his loft. I want to introduce myself but Dave cuts in on Tyler's monologue, his bossy manager mode back in force. I didn't mind when he was our actual manager, but now that we have Chief as our full-time manager, Dave's back-seat driving grates on me.

Dave and the girl apparently make a plan, because suddenly Gavin's ditching his T-shirt, I'm told to leave mine off as well, and Dave's repositioning his drums based on how the light's coming through the warehouse windows.

Thank God there's no posing. Even though I work out hard and I know I look good, I always look kind of angry in pictures. Most people don't notice the scars at first.

We dive into another song and the redhead circles us with her camera. When we break between songs, the only thing she says to me is, "Try not to look at the camera. I want these to feel candid."

She has no clue. I'm not looking at her fucking camera. I'm looking at how her red hair brushes her bare shoulders, how her cheeks are flushed with the heat in Tyler's loft, and how a slim silver bracelet glides down her wrist.

I'm looking at every single detail of *her*.

I'm restless, so I try to get focused back on the music, calling a halt mid-song to work through a chord progression that Gavin has going major, but I think works better in minor.

Dave disagrees, but Tyler backs me up. He always does.

Just when I think we're going to wrap up and I can talk to the redhead, my giggling blonde entourage shows up, followed by Gavin's new girl, Beryl. Teal sits on my lap and winds her arm around my sweat-slicked neck. I feel disgusting after two hours of sweaty practice, so I pinch her ass to get her off me but she just squeals and snuggles closer.

Great. A Klingon.

I stand up just as Stella's leading the redhead out the door before I've had a chance to talk to her. Even before I found out her name.

And just like Emma Jackson's bra strap, I know without a doubt that this girl is going to fuel my frustrated dreams.

CHAPTER 5: VIOLET

I'm nervous about showing Stella my shots of Tattoo Thief.

Maybe hiring me for my first freelance gig is her way of paying me back for letting her stay in my room. We both have Neil to thank for making the connection.

"Tell me what you think, if it matches your story." I fidget with my coffee cup while she stares at my laptop screen. I hope the candid style and natural light catch the mood of her piece for *The Indie Voice.*

"If I hadn't been there when you took this…" Stella's open-mouthed, so I'm pretty sure I hit the mark.

I smile. We're at a cozy restaurant several blocks from my apartment, amid a Sunday brunch crowd full of noise and laughter. "Do you think it will work?"

"Oh, *hell* yes. This is ferociously sexy, especially because it doesn't look like they're trying to be sexy. It looks like you got a sneak peek without them even realizing you were there."

"Awesome. That's what I wanted—something candid that didn't look like another posed rock-god photo."

Stella giggles. "But you've got to admit, those abs—"

"Yeah. I know. Some girls go for abs and some go for butts and legs, but I'm obsessed with shoulders. And biceps." *Yikes. Too much information.* I gulp my coffee and hope my blush isn't too obvious.

"Anyone's biceps in particular?" Stella's brows arch.

"No. Stella, cut it out." I close my eyes to block out the image of the band, of one band member in particular. Jayce, the lead guitarist. All through the photo session, his eyes followed me until I had to ask him to stop looking. It was messing up the candids I was going for.

It was also messing up my concentration. I've never been so completely devoured by someone's eyes, like he was calculating exactly what it would take to own me.

"Sorry." She watches me carefully, and I'm afraid I'm telegraphing my interest in Jayce all over my face. "Violet, seriously, I'm sorry. I didn't think you'd…"

I close my laptop and stuff it in my backpack. "Let's not go there, OK? I'll send that picture and a couple more over to your editor tonight. And I brought your stuff." I hand her a bulky cloth bag with things Neil failed to pack for her from my room.

"Thanks for schlepping that over here." Stella peeks inside the bag. "So how do you know Neil?"

"Friend of a friend. I got a job teaching last September and had to move really quick, and his ex-boyfriend had just split." I don't tell her that my last-minute assignment was also thanks to a few well-placed calls from my father.

"You're a teacher?"

"Was." I bite the inside of my cheek, not wanting to reveal more. Getting fired has left me feeling raw and vulnerable, and I doubt I'll be able to get enough freelance work to cover my meager teacher's salary. My savings might get me through summer. Might.

"What did you teach?"

"I wanted to do art education, but there's not a lot of funding for that, and nothing full-time. So I also taught sex ed."

Stella laughs. "That sounds like a blast. Did you have to show horny eighth graders how to roll a condom over a banana?"

I can't resist giving her my favorite weird detail from last year. "My favorite question was, 'What if you can't find the hole?'"

Stella cracks up and I promise her, "True story, true story."

"Wait. You said you were a teacher? What happened?"

"I got fired." My face blazes with embarrassment, even though she's still laughing about the hole question.

"For what? Explaining how to find the hole?"

No. The school doesn't want someone as filthy as me teaching their children. I swipe away tears.

"Oh, God, Violet. I'm sorry. I didn't mean—I wasn't trying to make fun of you. That sucks. I'm sorry you got fired. You don't have to—"

"Unprofessional conduct," I whisper, praying she won't probe further.

"So, are you going to get a different teaching job or freelance more? Because you're really good."

Stella gives me an encouraging smile, but I snort. Fat chance I'd ever get hired by a school district. The pictures made my teaching certificate worthless.

"I doubt I can get a teaching job again. But I've always been into photography, so I'm giving this a shot. I was really grateful when Neil recommended me to your editor and you took a chance on me."

"The nudes in your room are impressive," Stella says. "Do you sell those?"

"I don't do nudes anymore." No way. Never again. Even though I always took care to make sure the nudes I shot were artful and not pornographic, I never want to be in a studio with a naked subject again. It hits too close to home. "I'm working on a different kind of project now. It's a secret."

***

On Tuesday, I get confirmation from Stella's editor that the pictures I submitted will be accepted for publication. I do a little dance, right there in my apartment.

The texts keep coming, and they vary from sweet pleas for a date to straight-up filthy propositions. I don't respond to any of the handful of numbers texting me. I'm becoming numb to them.

I work up the courage to go online to figure out how to take down my pictures from the *Sexy Bitches* website. There's no straight-forward way to do it, but I learn that what's happened to my photos is called "revenge porn."

I didn't even imagine this had a name.

On Wednesday, I recognize Stella's number on my phone and pick up, expecting more questions about my Tattoo Thief pictures. What I'm not prepared for is a thoroughly drunk Stella slurring into the phone, telling me to come get wasted with her.

It's ten-thirty in the morning.

I'm stuck—there's a new tweet from the graffiti artist I've been following and I want to go track down his latest street art. But I also want to help my new friend, who says she's having a bad day.

By the sound of it, her buddies Jack Daniels and Jim Beam are cheering her up. When I find her at the bar, it's worse than I thought. I drag her to a diner and fill her with carbs and coffee to try to work some of the alcohol out of her system.

Once she's sober enough to walk a straight line, I take her along in search of the artwork. Bingo. We find the piece behind a Dumpster, a little girl bending over a daisy, which is painted like it grows from a real crack in the building's wall. Stenciled words say, "Find your moment."

I carefully document the work before we roll the Dumpster back into position to partially cover it, then we're heading home and I spot *the exact same daisy* in a tattoo shop window.

I'm floored. We go in and when the big, burly guy who's doing tattoos won't talk to me, Stella decides to get a wrist tattoo on the spot. I beg her to wait but she digs in her heels. She's crazy. She's brave—braver than me, anyway.

She's awesome.

And the daisies *are* the same. By the time we leave, I might even have enough of a toehold to convince whoever's doing the graffiti art to talk to me. No promises, the burly guy says. But it's just enough that I see a ray of light.

***

Neil's gone out and I'm settling into a night of photo editing, a gin martini, and some quiet classical music when my phone trills. I feel my gut clench as I grab it. *Please don't let it be a porn lurker.*

Relief floods me. It's Stella again, but her voice is breathy and rushed. "Hi, Violet. I'm sorry to call you so late, but I need another favor."

"Stella." I sigh, but I'm still glad to hear from her. Isolation eats at me; I can't bring myself to contact the teachers I used to call friends, ashamed that I'll have to explain why we're no longer coworkers. And beyond them? Other than my sister, I don't have anyone.

"For the record, I'm not drunk, I don't need pancakes, but I would gladly do anything for you if you could come to Roosevelt Hospital and take some pictures. Like, right now."

The urgency in Stella's voice reaches through the phone and shakes me out of my haze of self-pity and gin. I clear my throat and stand, shoving my feet into sandals. "What's going on?"

Stella explains that Tyler's had a seizure, he's at the hospital, and the media are swarming with speculation. There's a press conference in less than an hour.

"What can I do to help?"

"Get your camera. Come here and take pictures—we need proof that it's not some drug overdose." Stella's voice trembles with emotion and I grab my camera bag and keys, heading for the door. "They'll pay you. I trust you and that's what we need right now more than anything—someone we can trust."

"Tell me the name of the hospital again?"

"You'll do it?" she squeaks.

"Stella, I'm already halfway down my apartment stairs. I'll see you in ten minutes."

I enter the emergency room waiting area and scan the room for Stella, but the first person I recognize is a wall of muscle: thick biceps stretching his faded blue shirt, rumpled shorts and flip-flops. Maybe he's wearing whatever was on his bedroom floor when he got the call.

Bedroom shoots my mind to some R-rated thoughts I toyed with while editing Tattoo Thief's pictures—specifically, Jayce's chiseled, shirtless body. I drop my chin to avoid his gaze.

"You're Violet," he says, and holds out an open palm. "I'm Jayce. You did our band's photo shoot."

His eyes are serious, strained at the edges with worry. When I place my hand in his, he squeezes. The pressure sends a shiver of energy up my arm.

Is it a reassurance? It feels like possession, but it feels safe.

"Hi." I don't trust myself to say more. My face heats, and because I know I'm blushing and I know he can see it, I blush harder. *Kill me now.* Obviously, I don't get out much, or else I wouldn't be embarrassed by this simple gesture.

He drops my hand and clears his throat, as if he's just realized that I'm here on a mission. "Stella's getting changed for the press conference."

I nod and dump my camera gear on a nearby chair, squatting next to it to assemble the lens and fill flash on my camera body. Jayce hovers just at the periphery, watching, and I feel his gaze hot and thick on me the way it felt when I was photographing the band.

He's looking at me as if he could unlock my secrets and lay me bare.

CHAPTER 6: JAYCE

All I see is red.

Red hair in loose curls draped over her shoulders. The red tinge of a blush heating her cheeks and neck.

She's said just one word to me—*hi*—and I'm standing here like an idiot, hands shoved deep in my pockets, waiting for Stella while Violet unpacks her camera in economical, expert movements, the way I handle a knife or a guitar.

I watch her zip her gear bag closed and wind her camera strap around her wrist. It's like I've discovered a new species of girl: where the groupies are bold, she's shy. Where they're tanned and curvy and plucked and polished, she's slim and pale and so fucking perfect it hurts to look at her.

It hurts to touch her. Cool skin, smooth as marble, and when I squeezed her hand it wasn't casual. She lit a fire in the center of my chest, and watching her tightens a vise around my throat so I can barely breathe.

Who is this girl? The way she looks and moves affects me, but I squash my raging hormones down and focus on what the band needs from Violet right now: pictures of Tyler in his hospital room.

Chief says the media will be more appeased by the truth—that Tyler's had a diabetic seizure, not a drug overdose—if we can show them pictures of him resting comfortably in his hospital room.

Violet stands and when our eyes connect, the strength and purpose in them knock me back a step.

Get a grip, dumbass. I channel my best Rico Suave attitude, flash her a panty-melting smile that usually gets me what I want with groupies, and steer her toward Tyler's hospital room.

Stella follows us down the corridor into the belly of the ER. I touch Violet's back to guide her and she flinches at first, but then softens, letting my light touch on her spine turn her left and right until we find Tyler behind a sickly green curtain. He's sleeping.

And then something changes. Like a creature emerging from its camouflage, Violet gathers the energy in the room. She directs Stella wordlessly to Tyler's bedside and motions for her to straighten the sheets covering his chest.

As Violet's camera clicks and the hospital equipment beeps and buzzes, Violet is utterly in control. It paralyzes me. How did this skittish girl suddenly transform? She bends her long, lean frame for a different angle as Stella kisses Tyler's forehead.

Violet's soft yellow shirt rides just high enough to expose a sliver of flesh on her lower back. More smooth skin, white as marble, flecked with delicate freckles.

I snap my jaw shut and shake my head, forcing myself to stop staring at her. But seeing Tyler and Stella together is even more intimate—I didn't realize the depth of their connection until now.

The fire in my chest smolders, a deep want crushing my lungs. No matter how many groupies I've found, fucked, and forgotten, no matter how many times I've gotten off with a girl after an intense night playing with my band, I don't think I've ever found the peace I see on Stella's face when she caresses Tyler's hand.

And suddenly, I want that.

More than a fuck.

More than tits on a platter or a frenzied bang in the back of a limo.

I want *that.* I'm just not sure what the hell *that* is.

Violet startles me with a soft touch on my forearm. The dark blond hair there bristles with goose bumps. *It's the air conditioning.* Her eyes flick toward the corridor back to the waiting room.

I nod, but this time when I follow her, I'm not steering.

***

I introduce Violet to Tattoo Thief's manager, Chief, and she explains how she'll upload the best photos to a site for the media to download. Her soft voice is strong, confident, and Chief points her to a small room where she can work.

"I'm going with you." The words tumble out of my mouth and both Violet and Chief look at me, surprised.

"I can handle this." She dismisses me with a wave of her hand. The fire in her green eyes commands respect. And distance.

I take a step back as she strides toward the room, her camera bag bouncing on her hip. Chief shrugs but I shake my head. No way I'm going to let her out of my sight.

I need to touch her again. Need to talk to her. Need to figure out what kind of magic she has that's messing with my head.

Violet's setting her gear on the table when I push the door ajar. "Violet? Can I help you?"

"I'm OK." She keeps her back to me, pulling out a laptop and a cord, opening the side of her camera and popping out a memory card. Roosevelt Hospital's so-called VIP meeting room is a tiny, windowless office with a couple chairs, a box of tissues, a phone extension, and a round table.

"Please?" I enter the room and close the door behind me. It's like all the air is gone from this space, and I wait, not breathing, for her to kick me out.

Violet looks at me and her eyes soften. "You can watch. If you want to."

Oh, I want to. There's no end to the things I want to do with you in this small room.

I pull a chair around the table and position it behind her legs. She sits, nodding slightly in thanks but she's focused on her computer. I pull another chair for me and bring it close to her—probably too close, but my body's way ahead of my brain—and I lean in so I can see her computer screen.

Images flash in rapid succession as they download. I breathe in the fragrance of her hair—light, slightly sweet. Her eyes are fixed on the screen but I'm studying her shoulders, the curve inside her elbow, the smooth column of her throat.

To be this close and not touch her is torture. I rest my hand on the back of her chair and my thumb grazes her shoulder blade. She shivers but doesn't look up at me.

She doesn't brush me off, either.

"Thank you for coming," I say, then clarify: "to help Tyler." Hell, I'd be happy if she came to give me a root canal.

"It's no problem." She clicks through the images, pausing at the better ones to highlight them.

I'm frustrated, wondering how I can get her to talk to me, even look at me, but Violet is laser-focused on editing her photos.

So I sit in silence with her, listening to her breathe and the tap of keystrokes on her laptop. This quiet moment is more intimate than anything I've had with a woman in ages. I'm frozen—all but my thumb, which keeps making little circles on her shoulder.

The motion-sensor lights go out in the room, leaving our faces illuminated only by the light of her laptop screen.

Neither of us moves.

CHAPTER 7: VIOLET

"That's all of them?" Jayce peers over my shoulder at the photographs now that the download is complete. I feel his hot, sweet breath on my neck and his thumb lightly tracing my shoulder. He's far too close for comfort, and darkness shrinks the room as if we're both beneath the covers in bed.

In bed. I press my knees together and force the thought away, being careful not to move too much and trigger the lights back on. The darkness feels sacred. Safe.

I copy and paste the download link. "When your manager is ready, he can distribute this link and the media will be able to download whatever they like."

I study my laptop's screen, pretending to double-check that all of my pictures are properly uploaded. I'm really just buying time before I have to close my computer and actually face the guy who's making my insides melt like an ice cream cone in a heat wave.

The heavy door muffles the hospital sounds so that I can hear every movement: the swish of fabric, the creak of the industrial-grade chair, the soft tap of Jayce's fingers against the Formica table.

After a long pause, Jayce asks, "So, who else have you photographed?"

"No one you'd know," I answer quickly. Most subjects for my fine-art photography were on my college swim team—they had fantastic bodies and loved showing them off, but none of them were models. "Tattoo Thief was actually my first freelance gig for *The Indie Voice*," I admit, turning toward him.

The lights snap on from my movement and we blink as our eyes adjust. I peek at Jayce's face and his brows rise. "Really? What did you do before?"

I *so* don't want to go there, so I change the subject. "I taught school. What did you do before you were a famous rock star?"

"I cooked." Jayce's eyes crinkle as he smiles. "And before you get some romantic notion of me playing chef, I can assure you, it was a lot less glamorous than that."

He thrusts his hands at me and I gasp and pull back, but then I realize he's showing me something. "See the scars?"

I do. Some are fine white lines, some wider and raised. A few pinkish, shiny patches of skin on his hands and forearms look like burns.

"I like doing stuff with my hands. Playing the guitar, cooking, building stuff. Doesn't matter, as long as my hands are touching something."

I realize just how close Jayce's hands are to my chest, just how slightly they'd need to move to reach out and touch me, and I shudder. I think he realizes the subtext too, because instantly he pulls his hands back and shoves them in his pockets.

The rejection stings.

Jayce shakes his head. "I don't know why I just told you that. It's stupid. I guess I just didn't want you to see all this crazy media circus and think ... well, I don't know what you think."

He stops and his gaze pierces me, his amber eyes flashing, head ducked slightly to keep hold of my gaze.

I take a quick breath and shake my head. "It's not my place to judge. There are plenty of people who will judge you for everything you do, but I'm not about that. I'm just here to take pictures."

Jayce's serious expression morphs back into the genuine smile I saw when he said he'd cooked and he grabs my hand. "Those are the most beautiful words I've heard all day."

***

I watch the press conference from the green room with Jayce, Dave, his girlfriend Kristina, and Gavin's girlfriend Beryl. It's a success, but I hang back as the band wraps up, monitoring my photo site's downloads.

I'm not part of this world, nor do I want to be. Jayce sees me on the fringe of the group and scoots over to me, trying to include me in the victory celebration.

My phone pings with a new text message and I flinch like the text causes physical pain. Jayce's eyes flick to me and then to my phone.

I want you to spread your legs and think of me tonight, sexy Violet.

Jayce reads the text faster than I move to cover it. My face heats and I'm sure my skin is tomato-red with shame.

"Looks like your boyfriend misses you. It's after midnight." Jayce's mouth is a hard line and he puts a few more inches of distance between us. I feel colder without him next to me.

I thought we'd had a moment, but then the text showed up and ruined everything.

The texts always ruin everything. First my job, and now my peace. I need to change my mobile number but since I'm jobless, I'm afraid to spend the money to make the switch.

I shake my head, letting my deep red hair fall in my face to protect me from Jayce's piercing gaze. "I don't have a boyfriend.

Must be a wrong number." I stuff my laptop in the side of my camera bag in preparation to go.

"Bull. The text said Violet."

"It's nothing. I don't know them. It's—a mistake." My voice wavers and I wrap my arms around my stomach. My lying sucks. As if to prove that point, my phone pings with another text and I shield it from Jayce.

Think of me in your room, watching you sleep. Waking you up. Seducing you.

Cold fear slithers down my back and makes me shake so hard I drop the phone.

My address is on the Internet with my photo. If this guy is serious, he knows where I live. He could get inside my building—all it would take is a helpful neighbor. He could get inside my apartment.

Jayce bends down to retrieve my phone from the industrial carpet, and he doesn't even pretend he's not looking at the screen when he hands it back.

His face is stormy.

"Either you tell me what's going on, or I'm going to force the issue."

"It's none of your business," I mumble.

"Fine. Get up." Jayce tugs my elbow and I wobble to standing. He hoists my camera bag and throws the strap over his head, settling it across his broad chest. His jaw is set. "Let's go."

I pull away from him but his firm hand anchors my elbow. "Where?"

"I'm taking you home. Even though you're lying to me, it's after midnight and if you don't know who they're from, those texts were a hell of a lot more threatening than your typical booty call. Unless it was a booty call. Was it?"

Jayce's eyes narrow as he looks at me for confirmation that I truly don't know the sender. I drop my chin and shake my head.

"So we're going home."

Something inside me rears up, defensive against his pushy command. "No." I square my shoulders. At five-nine, I'm only a few inches shorter than Jayce. I swipe at my eyes and blink hard, trying for a stoic mask. "You're not going anywhere with me. I'm fine by myself."

Safe Violet and Smart Violet are at war. Safe Violet knows I could really use an escort home, considering the creepers who could make good on the threatening texts. But Smart Violet knows Jayce is the worst possible escort because being a nobody is all I have left.

If I were a celebrity, my photos would explode like a virus.

Jayce sets his jaw. "Violet, you're not fine. Unless you've got a frenemy playing some kind of sick prank, those texts are worth being worried about." His voice drops an octave. "Believe me, OK? I've got a little experience with this."

Experience? Oh. I guess he's had fans go too far, try to contact him. I don't doubt that if his number got out, girls would blow it up with texts. And probably sexts and photos, too.

I want to hold my ground, but something in the soft way Jayce says those last words, the way his eyes plead with me to let him protect me, are my undoing.

That tips me.

"Fine. But I don't want to be seen leaving the hospital with you."

Jayce's eyes widen and his jaw drops. OK, that might have been harsh. I can't imagine most girls being *against* an association with arguably the hottest member of Tattoo Thief.

Jayce grips my upper arms. "Look, give me a few minutes, OK? I promise nobody will recognize me. Just, promise you won't leave yet, OK?"

His hands are hot and hard, startling me. *He's touching me.* His touch isn't gentle or soft or exploratory. It's insistent, commanding, thrilling.

I can only nod before he releases me and runs out of the room.

CHAPTER 8: VIOLET

I fumble with my keys in the lock of my apartment's street-level entry door and Jayce stands immediately behind me, facing the street and scanning it.

"Thanks for helping me get home, Jayce, but really, I can take it from here." I try to smile but it comes out watery and forced, my brows still pinched with worry.

Jayce holds the door open for me and I cross into the foyer with the mailboxes, giving him a little goodbye wave. But he comes inside and closes the door behind him, jiggling it to make sure it's secure.

"You don't have to—"

"I do." Jayce cuts me off. "I promised to see you home safely. And I'm not going to come onto you—unless you want me to."

He gives me a wolfish grin and he looks brain-meltingly hot in scrubs. Suddenly I want to watch a zillion medical dramas starring Jayce McKittrick, my own personal Dr. McDreamy.

Jayce follows me up the steps to my apartment, his borrowed blue scrubs totally out of place in the dingy corridor. Heck, *he's* out of place here—no way does a rock star belong in my East Village stairwell in the middle of the night.

I confess I considered slipping out of the green room without him, but then I realized he'd trapped me—when he ran out to dig up a disguise, he still had my camera bag slung over his shoulder. I won't go anywhere without that.

Jayce clears his throat. His powerful, broad build makes him feel like he towers over me. "Is your roommate home? Someone who can—"

Another ping from my phone cuts him off and when I look at the readout this time, I scream.

Nice to see you got home safely, Violet, but he's really not your type.

The stairs come up in a whoosh and I fall onto my knees, squeezing my eyes tight. Jayce wrenches the phone out of my hands but I don't have the strength to protest.

I don't have the strength to breathe.

Jayce mutters a curse and I feel his arms circle me. He lifts me up against his chest and climbs the rest of the stairs.

I suck in air in short gasps, my head swimming. This is not supposed to be happening to me. I come from a good family. I've dated two men—*two*—and never once did anything half as kinky as the worst of my text messages.

On the third floor, we stop in front of my door but Jayce doesn't put me down. He reaches a hand from beneath my knees and opens his palm. "Keys," he whispers.

At first I think he's trying to be quiet because of the late hour, but his body is so taught beneath mine I realize it's thinly concealed rage.

Inside, he finally lets my feet touch the floor and I collapse on the couch. He throws both deadbolts and draws the chain.

"Your roommate. Is she here?"

I shake my head, then shrug, confusion trumping everything else. I'm vaguely aware of Jayce stalking through my apartment, opening doors and closets. In the kitchen, I hear cupboard doors open and liquid being poured.

"Drink this." Jayce's voice is close to me again and my eyelids flutter open. The woody, stinging smell of bourbon hits my nose and I recoil. Brown liquor isn't my thing. "Come on, Violet. Just to help you sleep."

I grimace but accept the glass and the bourbon sears my throat, making me cough. Jayce remains beside me for several long minutes as heat builds in my chest and my limbs feel heavier.

Another ping, and Jayce fishes my phone out of his pocket. I crane my neck to read it over his shoulder.

Are you naked and in bed yet, Violet? Send him home and get ready for me.

This. All of this. It's too much. The texts add up to someone obsessed, someone who's watching me.

I hurl a couch pillow across the room and wail, feeling totally exposed to the world. If I were stripped bare and tied to a lamppost in Times Square, I could not feel more naked. More vulnerable.

Again, Jayce's arms come around me and this time I let go of everything. The hurt from my breakup. The fear from getting fired. The devastation of finding the pictures. The hopelessness of having my life infiltrated against my will by an unknown, unseen pursuer.

My tears and snot soak Jayce's sky-blue scrubs and I cry without words, just letting the sobs bubble up in my chest and spill over, like a never-ending fountain of pain.

CHAPTER 9: JAYCE

I can handle crying.

Some girls cry to get their way. Some girls cry because they think they'll change my mind. Some girls cry to win an argument.

But I've never heard crying like this. Violet's fragile body shakes against mine and she cries as if her heart is breaking.

I squeeze my arms more tightly around her as if she'd fly into a million pieces if I didn't hold her together. I want my hold to show her she's safe, or at least stop the earthquake shaking her world.

I've had seven years to get used to fame, crazy fans and a few clingy girlfriends who sent stalkerish texts. But Violet's texts are creepier, and they're specific enough to shatter her sense of security.

I thread my arms under Violet's legs, pull her up from the couch, and carry her toward the bedroom I assume is hers. I don't turn on the lights. After my initial inspection of the apartment, I know her walls are a photo gallery of black and white nudes, and the hulking shape in the corner is a bed covered in a purple comforter that reminds me of her name. Violet.

I bend to place her on her bed and her arms stay locked around my neck so I can't stand up. My pocket pings and I bite back another curse—why didn't I turn her stupid phone off a long time ago? Why didn't she?

I know why. We both need to see where this is going so we'll know what to do next.

I lower myself on the bed beside Violet and her body shudders with the breath-hitching aftershocks of sobs. Her arms are still clasped tightly behind my neck and so I lie on my side, one arm beneath her and my other arm—where, exactly?

If this were any other girl, my hand would know right where to go. Up her shirt and on her tits. Down her hips and around her ass. And it's not like I don't want to do that to Violet. When we were uploading pictures together, each time a strand of hair slipped forward and brushed her collarbone, it made my cock twitch.

But tonight Violet's lying on her bed, broken to pieces, and I don't know how to make it right.

My hand finally chooses a resting spot of its own accord, on her shoulder. That's safe, right? Not creepy? Only my cock seems a little too excited about touching her nearly bare shoulder and I scoot my ass back away from her to be sure she doesn't accidentally brush against me.

What kind of man gets turned on by a broken, bawling girl?

A fucking sick jackass.

But not as sick at the bastard who keeps texting Violet. All she'll say is he's not a boyfriend, but who is he to her? A one-night stand? An ex? The texts didn't really get me riled until the creepy-as-fuck stalker one.

Lie. I hated them the minute I thought she was with someone else.

Violet shudders and a fresh round of tears spill down her cheeks. Her soaked lashes are dark against nearly white skin dusted with freckles. Flame-red hair fans out across her white pillowcase.

Snot and all, this girl is fucking gorgeous.

How did I not see it the first time? Maybe because her boobs are hidden under a plain yellow T-shirt instead of pushed up to her chin like Shelly's. Maybe because she doesn't look like most girls I date.

I have a type. Curvy, bubbly, blonde. Big eyes, big tits, big smile. Easy talk, easy fun, easy hookup. No strings.

That last bit is key.

Violet rolls on her side away from me, leaving me with a face full of hair that smells faintly of flowers and a small, round ass that tapers to a slim waist. Her shoulders still tremble but the keening wail is done. I stroke her shoulder tentatively, and at first she tenses, but then she relaxes under my touch.

I can't leave her like this.

It's almost two in the morning and I'm on a bed, dressed in scrubs, with a snot-covered crying girl who is also fully clothed and scared out of her mind. This is *not* how I do things. I like to keep things light and free from obligations.

But Violet's got some magnetic pull that anchors me here.

When I hear her breathing even out and I'm sure she's asleep, I gradually pull my arm out from beneath her neck. I've got to take a piss.

I finish in the bathroom and go to the kitchen for a glass of water, then check my phone. Six missed calls—four from Shelly, two from Teal—and a dozen texts. I feel like kind of an asshole for standing one of them up (although I'm not sure which one), but Shelly's getting pretty clingy and I need to nip that in the bud.

And I have a good reason for skipping the date. Tyler needed me.

And now Violet does.

I choke on the water I'm drinking as this thought hits me: *I'm not here for me, I'm here for her.* I don't remember the last time I did that for a girl.

I reach into my pocket and pull out Violet's phone to see what the sick fucker texted her last.

Dream of me and all the things I'll do to you when we're finally together.

I slam my palm against Violet's chipped Formica kitchen counter, angry that someone's talking to her like this. Angry at myself—why the hell should I care?

I scroll through her texts and there's more: descriptions of what she looks like, her freckled face and her long, pale limbs. Her neighborhood, the bodega on her street corner and what kind of flowers he'd buy for her.

Some of the texts seem almost romantic. They're about worshipping her body or pampering her, they say she deserves to be happy and he can offer her this. But other texts are more chilling: positions he'd like to see her in, ways he'd bind her hands and feet, how he'd spread her knees and her ass cheeks, how he'd fuck her pussy until she screamed and screamed and screamed.

I'm reading this shit and pain radiates from my jaw where it's clenched so hard I could probably shatter my own teeth. My dick betrays me, though, as I think of the scenarios this freaky texter is writing about, think about how it would be if I were the one doing these things to Violet. If she wanted me to.

I adjust myself and try to clear my brain of this shit. *Think of the smell of the hospital. Think of Tyler's IV drip. Think of Stella's wrecked expression when she showed up to the hospital.*

I breathe deeply. There was something in Stella's expression that was so pure and beautiful when she stood next to Tyler's bed in the hospital. Now I see it clearly: love. She is in love with Tyler.

Jealousy zings up my spine and I stab at Violet's phone to turn it off completely and stop the malicious texts. I feel fucking helpless, stuck in this crappy apartment while Violet sleeps, but it occurs to me there's at least one thing I can do to help her.

I send a quick text and get a ping back in minutes. God, I love New York. You can get anything, anytime, and though I don't have a personal assistant the way Gavin used to, the on-call concierge service I use totally rocks.

One time I even made them fetch me condoms for a one-night stand that kept going and going like the fucking Energizer bunny.

I wait in the living room for the delivery. I'm restless, but instead of television I check the locks on Violet's windows. The bathroom widow lock is broken and I find a dustpan to keep it wedged shut. The rest of the windows, including the one in Violet's roommate's room, are fine. I wish I could set up some more security, though. Two deadbolts and a chain are not nearly enough.

Tomorrow I'll talk to Violet about calling the police about the stalker. I wonder again, *Who he is to Violet?*

My phone pings and I'm relieved it's not one of my girls, but the courier instead. I jog downstairs and sign for the cloth tote bag, then jog back upstairs and set all the locks again. Even the chain. If Violet's roommate wants in, she can fucking pound on the door for all I care.

I stash a few things for breakfast in the fridge and chow down on a slice of pizza that's still pretty warm. The bottom of the bag holds the main thing I wanted: A brand new iPhone.

I grin. It's a stupid, extravagant gift—and I'm not in a habit of giving girls gifts. Girls take it all wrong, get even clingier and start dropping hints about jewelry and shopping sprees.

I don't want a girl like that. I just want a girl who wants to have fun.

I open the iPhone box and its phone number is written on the back of the concierge service's business card. I pull Violet's ancient phone with a scratched screen out of my pocket and kill time transferring her contacts.

I'm still not tired.

Violet hasn't received any more messages but that doesn't mollify me. I transfer all of the numbers associated with creepy texts into my phone, then screen shot the messages and forward them to myself. Maybe I can figure out who's tormenting her?

I'm going to give Violet this new phone, hold onto her old phone, and tell her if she gets an incoming text from someone who's not a total creeper.

It's a great plan.

The sky lightens from black to charcoal gray and I feel the exhaustion of four a.m. I have to get some sleep and at this point it doesn't look like anyone's going to break in. I turn off Violet's old phone and hide it in my pocket again, then go back to her bedroom where she's still curled on her side in a fetal position.

She looks so fragile, her long limbs folded in, her hair dark against porcelain skin in the dim light. She looks like a fucking angel, which is why I'm positive I shouldn't be here right now. I want to curl up next to her and stroke her hair, feel the soft skin of her arm, and inhale the scent of her.

I should be on the couch. Like a gentleman.

Violet was so distraught when I brought her home tonight, she had no boundaries. She just let me hold her and carry her. But I suspect that she's going to be much less pliant in the morning. I pull the purple comforter over her shoulder and she sighs in her sleep.

I should go. I *must* get out of here. Still, I can't resist the pull of her hair—I run my fingers through it, letting the wavy strands sift through my fingers.

Once. Just once.

This could be addictive.

And then I turn and take up a position on the couch.

CHAPTER 10: VIOLET

I cover my head with my pillow to shut out the sun, but when I hear banging at the front door, I jump.

"Violet! What the hell? Let me in!" Neil's familiar cranky voice makes me think his typical all-night escapade didn't end well. I roll off my bed, feeling rumpled in the same shorts and T-shirt I wore when I went to the hospital to help Stella last night.

I emerge from my room in time to see Jayce fill the few inches between the doorjamb and the door, which is open only as much as the chain will allow.

"Who are you?" Jayce growls.

"No, who the fuck are you? This is my apartment. Let me in!" Neil pounds on the door again and yells my name.

"It's OK, Jayce," I say, and my voice is hoarse from crying last night. "That's Neil. He really is my roommate."

Jayce narrows his eyes at Neil, tension radiating off his broad shoulders. He pushes the door closed enough to release the chain.

Neil blows into our apartment in a huff, his tight jeans and too-cool-for-school shirt suggesting he was at a club or a very hip show last night. His hair stands up tall like Harry Styles's and his Adam's apple bobs with annoyance.

Jayce's thick build would make anyone think twice about picking a fight—anyone but Neil. Neil's maybe five-ten in tall shoes with his hair riding high, but he's getting in Jayce's face as if he's king of the world.

"Who'd you drag home last night, Vi?" Neil says in his bitchiest queen voice. "A sexy little bouncer from a club's B-team?"

Jayce takes a step back from Neil and bursts out laughing. "A B-team bouncer! That's awesome." Jayce's grin reveals even, white teeth and dancing eyes and I swoon a little. Even without the scrubs, looks *good.*

And then I realize exactly how good I *don't* look, with my hair like Medusa's going in sixteen directions and my clothes rumpled, tear-stained and rank.

Neil strides to the kitchen. "Did you make breakfast, or does your boy-toy cook, too?"

I follow my nose to discover a skillet full of scrambled eggs and bacon, a couple of extra-large cinnamon rolls and a full carafe of coffee in our coffee maker.

"Yes. I definitely cook," Jayce says behind me. "There's more to me than just a pretty face."

"Don't kid yourself. It's not that pretty." Neil scowls, pours a cup of coffee and swipes a piece of bacon.

"At least I have the body to make up for it." Jayce sasses back. He's taking Neil's abuse and he looks like he loves it.

Neil snorts and stalks out of our kitchen that barely accommodates one. Jayce slips in and pours me a cup of coffee, which I doctor with extra cream while he piles two plates full of food.

I push aside stacks of mail and we sit at a tiny, two-person Ikea table to eat.

I keep my head down and focus on my plate, feeling a flush rise up my chest and neck. I can sense Jayce is watching me, and after what happened last night, I wouldn't be surprised if he was staring at me like I had a third head.

"Violet. Are we going to talk about what happened last night?"

"I'd rather not."

"Why? I mean, I know those texts were scary—"

"That's not it." I cut Jayce off. "It's just too embarrassing. I mean, I totally melted down and you had to see it." My scalp tingles and I let my hair fall forward in a curtain to hide my face.

We eat in silence for a few minutes. I want Jayce to say something, but he doesn't, and it's maddening hearing him crunch bacon and sip coffee like we're a couple.

As if.

Somehow I've got one of the hottest guys in rock music in my living room and I'm eating eggs with him. I take a deep breath and muster something adult, something polite to say.

"Thank you for being here for me."

"Anytime. You were there for Tyler." Jayce's voice is mild and gentle, but it lacks any spark of heat or desire. I realize that I've totally overblown the hot rock star factor in my mind. Sure, I think he's hot. Me and a zillion other girls. But I'm pretty sure his primary emotion where I'm concerned is pity.

I pop the last bite of a cinnamon roll in my mouth. "Thank you for breakfast. How'd you get all this stuff? Did you go out this morning?"

Jayce shakes his head. "I didn't want to leave you. Had it delivered."

"The perks of being a rock star." I try to keep the bitterness out of my voice, but solving a problem that way reeks of privilege.

The silence stretches between us, growing more uncomfortable as I feel his eyes on me. I sip my coffee, desperate to have something to do, plotting my escape so I can shower and change and … why is he still here?

"You didn't have to stay."

"I did." His voice is low, intense.

"I'm a big girl. I can handle it."

"Doesn't mean you should have to handle it alone." Jayce slides a shiny iPhone across the small table to me. "This is for you. A private number."

What the what? "You can't give me your phone," I say stupidly.

"I'm not. This is your phone. A new number, so you won't have to deal with those texts. Take it, Violet."

I know I should be grateful, for this and for everything he's done for me so far, but anger flares instead. *Presumptuous, arrogant jerk.* "Do you think you can just throw money at a problem and it'll go away?"

"It works sometimes, Violet."

My cheeks flame with embarrassment that he thinks I need to be rescued. "Well, it doesn't work for me."

Jayce pushes back from the table and grabs our empty plates, spinning toward the kitchen. Plates clatter and water runs.

I lean on the wall by the sink. "Since when do you think you can just wave your magic rock star wand and *do* this? Fix this? I don't want your pity."

There. It's out there—a four-letter word that stings worse than any filthy epithet. *Pity.*

"Fuck pity. I don't want some nasty stalker sending you messages like the ones from last night. Call it a gift."

I plunge my hand deep into my hair, trying to hold onto my fraying composure. "I don't like your mouth," I hiss, hating the F-bomb as it explodes from his lips.

Jayce gives me a slow look, intimate and searching. His hands drip with water, but he reaches to touch my face. I steel myself. *I will not flinch.*

"Oh, but I love yours," he murmurs, his thumb ghosting across my lower lip. He strokes my cheek as my color rises. I'm frozen under his gaze. "And this blush. I can't help it. Seeing what he wrote makes me a bit ... protective."

I stumble backward out of his grasp. I don't know Jayce from Adam. I was stupid to let him take me home, and to trust him in my apartment while I freaked out and melted down. He could be another stalker, for all I know.

"I don't want to be protected," I say, and the lie slides out of my mouth as I edge back toward my room, wishing Neil would hurry up in the bathroom so I could dive in there and get away from Jayce. "I want to be left alone."

"As you wish, princess," he says, and he winks. He stinking *winks*, like he knows I'll get that line from *The Princess Bride*. Like he knows I can't stay mad at him because he's irresistible.

I can't. He is. But that's not the point.

"You can't just come in here and act like you own me, like you can just *do* things and I'll be OK with that," I say, pointing to the phone, but my argument's already losing steam.

Jayce shakes his head and picks up his keys from a side table. I think he's going to walk out the door—and an apology is on the tip of my tongue—but he spins and walks straight to me, invading my space, backing me up against my apartment wall with a soft thud.

His chest rises and I feel heat radiating off him, less than an inch separating our bodies. There's something so powerful, so masculine about him that my heart beats fast in my chest, and he threads his fingers through the wild tangles of my hair.

"I don't act like I own you," he says, his breath on my cheek, tickling the corner of my mouth.

"You act like you want to control me." I whimper as his hand tightens to a fist in my hair.

"Ah, but control is a different thing entirely. Control can be earned. Power can be given." Jayce's nose brushes my cheek. "You gave me control last night. You *let* me protect you."

I raise my hands to his chest to push him away, to put distance between us, but I falter as I feel his chest rise and fall, feel his heart beat hard inside it. I shake my head. "No."

Jayce's shoulders drop and he allows another inch of air between us, his hands skimming through my hair as he releases me. "No is a word I respect. Always."

I feel his body shift to turn away from me and I'm suddenly bereft without his touch, limp like I could slide down the wall. "But—"

His body is hard against mine in an instant, erasing the air between us. "But I want to have you. And I will." Jayce's mouth twists toward mine and I part my lips, anticipating a kiss. Instead, I feel a sharp sting in my lower lip.

He bit me!

And in one motion, Jayce turns and walks out the door.

CHAPTER 11: JAYCE

My hands twitch as I hold the red embossed business card and tap out ten digits on my phone. As it rings, I take a quick sip of beer and lean into my couch.

Today sucked. My head pounded from lack of sleep at Violet's apartment last night, chased by too much caffeine.

Band practice brought more bickering. Gavin was in his cocky I-can-do-no-wrong mode, with songs coming out of his ass and the rest of us just along for the ride, and since Tyler's in the hospital, Dave and Gavin outvoted me at every turn.

Considering I have more musical training than the rest of the band put together, you'd think I'd get a bit more respect for my ideas when we're working on a song.

But no, the magic's back because Gavin's back.

He's not the only one of us with magic. He might be the front man, but we're a *band*, not a solo act with a bunch of backup musicians.

"Viper Records, how may I direct your call?"

"Darren Bishop, please." I read the smoking man's name from his card.

"Is Mr. Bishop expecting your call?"

No. Yes. I don't know. "Tell him it's Jayce McKittrick."

"Just a moment." I hear better-than-average hold music and guess it must be one of the label's artists. I'm actually getting into the track when I hear Darren's gravelly rasp.

"Jayce. That wasn't so hard, was it?" He chuckles like he's just coaxed me to do a shot of tequila.

"What do you want to talk about?"

"You've got a pretty good idea, I'm sure. I think we should get together, see where you want to take your career next." Darren's voice is confident, like I've already signed with him. *Great. Another cocky bastard in my life.* "How does tomorrow look?"

"Practice at two, that's about it."

"Well, if you come to Viper, your Friday nights will get a lot more interesting, my friend. How about an early lunch?"

I don't know if it's this guy calling me his friend, or the fact that he's talking down to me like I haven't just come off headlining two stadium-grade tours, but his comment makes my skin crawl. Still, I play nice. "I can do that. Name the place."

Darren picks a see-and-be-seen place in Midtown, and I balk.

"Can we go a little bit more low-key?"

"I get it," Darren says. "We'll keep it private for now." He names a windowless pub beneath a better-known restaurant and I agree.

I click off the call and roam my apartment restlessly, finally settling back into the couch.

After the call with smarmy Darren, I'm second-guessing myself. Maybe I was just being irritable at practice, running on too little sleep or distracted by thoughts of a certain redhead.

My phone lit up today with texts from Shelly and another girl I vaguely remember from a month ago, but nothing from Violet. That bugs me. Is she using the phone I gave her?

I walked out of her apartment with her old phone still in my pocket—I didn't want the texts to keep freaking her out. Hell, they freaked *me* out, and after handling aggressive stalker fans, that's saying something.

I curse and switch her old phone back on. There were a couple of random messages this morning from numbers that hadn't appeared before: lewd comments about Violet's body. They got my hackles up, but none carried an overt threat like the texts that proved someone was watching her house last night.

Where the hell is this all coming from? Why is she a target?

I hope she called the cops today.

I hope she barricaded herself inside her apartment.

I hope she thought of me.

Shit.

I slam down the rest of my beer and peek at one new message on Violet's old phone, feeling like a bit of a creeper myself for invading her space. I want to protect her from the stalker shit, but she'd want to know if a friend sent a message, right?

When I touched your skin for the first time today, Violet, it was like silk. Now I want your skin on my tongue and between my teeth.

The text makes me bolt from the couch like a hot poker jabbed me in the ass. How did he get to her?

I fly through my apartment—phone, keys, wallet—and jab the elevator buttons as I stare at this message. *Teeth?* I hate the way the word reminds me of the sexy little nip I gave Violet's lower lip when I left her this morning. Suddenly, it makes my bite … skeevy.

The elevator moves glacially. The town car takes forever. I'm at the door of her apartment building, leaning hard on the intercom as I dial her new phone number.

The intercom crackles first. "Who's this?"

"Violet. It's Jayce. Let me in."

"Are you seriously outside my building? What are you thinking? Someone might *see* you!"

What? I've never known a girl who was embarrassed by me before. Girls I date parade me around like arm candy every chance they get. Before I can splice together the right response, somewhere between offended and apologetic, the door buzzes and I push through into the lobby.

I take the steps to her apartment two at a time and she's standing there, door open a crack but chained.

A frown tugs at her makeup-free face, but it's like my world gets ten times brighter. Her red hair is a halo, backlit from the light in her apartment, and she pushes the door closed a bit to unchain it.

"He touched you. How did he touch you? Where?" I demand, and Violet's brow wrinkles in confusion.

"Who? I've been home most of the day. Alone."

My eyes dart around Violet's apartment but there's no one else here. I fix on a tall bouquet of stargazer lilies and a strange feeling of jealousy weighs heavy on my chest. I squash it down. "Nice flowers."

Violet glances at them. "Thank you. You didn't—" she hesitates, that pretty blush creeping up her chest and neck again. It makes me want to peek down her shirt and find out exactly where the blush begins. "You didn't scare me, you know. When you bit me. I thought it was kind of ... hot."

Her last word is a whisper and it's got *me* hot. I move closer to her and she stands her ground, letting me invade her space. "Good. I wasn't trying to scare you. Just wanted a little taste."

My lips are rapidly closing the distance to hers, my hands aching to touch that soft hair again, when she breathes a few more words. "Then don't apologize."

"I didn't."

"The flowers."

I pull my head back and look at her squarely. "What do you mean, the flowers?"

"You said you were sorry. In the flowers." She turns to them and plucks the card from a little plastic spear at the heart of the bouquet.

I'm sorry for scaring you, Violet.

I shake my head. "No. These aren't from me." The smell of lilies is suddenly cloying, too strong in New York's sticky summer heat. "How did you get these?"

"Delivery. I signed for them this afternoon." Her mouth drops open and I can see the gears working. If they're not from me, they're from her stalker.

"And so you left your apartment, walked downstairs, opened the door—" My voice rises and I take a step back, raking my hand through my own hair instead of hers.

"I buzzed him in," she whispers. "I buzzed him into the lobby and met him on the landing. I signed…"

"Did he *touch* you? When he gave you the flowers, or the paper to sign?"

Violet nods and her eyes widen. She might have just come face-to-face with her stalker, but what's clicking into place for me is that he could have forced her back into her apartment or even taken advantage of her in the lobby.

"So then what happened?" I force my anger to a simmer, leading her to the couch. She looks like she's about to fall over.

"Corey, my upstairs neighbor, came in when I was signing and said he wanted a DVD back that he'd lent Neil last week."

"And so the delivery man left."

Violet nods again. "And then Corey followed me upstairs."

"Into your apartment?" She nods. "And did *he* touch you when you gave him the DVD?" Again, she nods.

I breathe out heavily, resting my head in my hands. It could have been the deliveryman. Corey might have saved Violet from … I don't know what. Or it could have been Corey—he's close enough to know when she comes home. He's close enough to watch her.

"Did you go anywhere else?"

She rewinds her day: she went to a coffee shop around the corner. She stopped at the bodega on her block and bought a few things. As she describes each interaction, I'm building a list of suspects in my head, men who are too close to her, who could have touched her, who could watch Violet, covet her, see her as prey.

"Please tell me you went to the police."

Violet presses her lips together, and for once I'm not distracted by that pretty, full mouth that begs to be bitten. "And tell them what? I'm getting dirty texts? I don't have any proof! You stole my phone!"

I shake my head, unwilling to give it back to her. "I didn't want you to have to see any more texts. I can take it to the police with you. Did you tell your friends about your new number?"

Violet frowns, and I want to kiss that frown off her face more than breathing. I can't, though. The way her shoulders are hunched, her body drawn into itself as if she's bracing to be physically hurt or ill, sets off every alarm bell in my head.

"I sent a few texts, to Neil and Stella and my little sister Katie."

"You have a sister?" Weirdly, this interests me. I don't know why. I never cared whether Shelly or the other girls had families.

"Three of them. Katie's going to be a senior in high school. Brianna's a sophomore and Sam's a freshman. They live upstate." Violet crosses the room to the kitchen, a frustrated huff escaping from her lungs. "Why are you here, Jayce? Are you going to give me back my phone?"

"If you tell me why you're getting these texts."

She crosses her arms. "No."

"Then that's my answer, too. You don't need this kind of shit." I hold up her phone and she strides toward me, lunging for it but I hold it out of reach. "Why won't you tell me what's really going on?"

The gates slam closed on her expression and her hair looks even more fiery when she's mad at me. "It's personal."

"I want to know."

"Do I have to spell it out for you? It's personal, as in, none of your stinking business." She makes another grab for the phone and I wrap my arm around her, hauling her against my chest. Her green eyes are blazing and her cheeks are flushed, but not enough to hide the sweet sprinkle of freckles across her face.

"I want it to be my business," I say, letting my breath fall heavily on her cheek. Her pupils dilate, her body softens against the hardness of my chest, and I admit that I'm not playing fair.

I'll use whatever it takes to get this out of her. I need it to keep her safe.

Violet's old phone chimes, and I read the text over her shoulder, not loosening my grasp on her body.

Get rid of him, Violet, or I will. We're meant to be together.

CHAPTER 12: VIOLET

I struggle against Jayce, my chest constricted by his tight grip around me. I twist to see the text that makes him hiss and hold me tighter, and my lips brush his cheek as I turn.

Jayce's amber eyes turn back to me, piercing me, demanding an answer. I can't tell him why these texts are coming—if I did, I'd have to admit the pictures, the revenge porn site, and what Brady did to me.

What I *let* him do.

I squeeze my eyes shut, remembering that moment in the rented studio space when everything changed. I was behind the camera, shooting Brady for his campaign photos.

I'd unbuttoned my blouse a few inches south of decent because of the hot studio lights, and his eyes were hooded with desire. I laughed and told him to save sexy eyes for the bedroom, that we needed a Mom-and-apple-pie smile.

Brady is a good-looking guy, with a sharp jaw and piercing blue eyes beneath close-cropped black hair. I moved onto the set to smooth his jacket in a new pose and he grabbed me, taking my mouth ferociously.

I put down my camera, let him lay me back on the couch and remove my blouse, my bra, my shorts. I thought we were going to fool around for a bit, but when nothing but a scrap of silk remained between my legs, he grabbed an extension cord and bound my wrists above my head as the lights pounded down on us.

Even as Brady kindled fear, he kindled lust, too. This—to be dominated—was new and wild and wicked. It set fire to my blood and I wanted it.

Until I heard the shutter click. My head shot up in panic, but Brady knew where to touch me to blend desire and fear, terror and want.

"Let me see all of you," he said. It wasn't a request. I felt the cords bite into my wrists, unyielding. "This isn't the good little girl. This isn't Daddy's little puppet."

Brady laughed as he kept clicking—his deep politician's voice smooth. When I met him last summer as he and my father campaigned together, I saw the way he could command power, magnetic and dangerous.

Brady and my father appeared at dozens of town hall events together. Brady's ambition is to be New York's youngest state senator, taking over my father's seat, while my father aims to leave the state senate and become a U.S. congressman.

At campaign events, Brady was the opener, laying out their conservative platform. My father was the closer, tugging at heartstrings with his family values rhetoric. I was the sideshow, there to pick up key demographics—women, teachers and college students.

I knew my speech, "Two great men are fighting for you," backward and forward. While Dad usually intimidated or discouraged the few other men I'd dated, he pushed me together with Brady.

It made a great story. The media ate it up.

Brady clicked and coaxed as I squirmed, finally setting down my camera and popping its memory card into his pocket when tears leaked from my eyes. I knew he liked porn; I just never realized he wanted images of me.

"These are just for me, baby," he said, hushing me with a kiss as he unknotted the cord. "You're so goddamn beautiful, and it's such a long time until I see you again. Thought I'd take a little souvenir until next time."

***

Fingers brush my jaw and I'm slammed back into the present, into the rock-hard chest of another man who doesn't think twice about dominating me physically. I twist and my nipples brush against him, proof that my body is betraying me again.

"Violet. Come back to me." Jayce is still, his sweet breath fanning across my face as he holds me. "I'm not going to hurt you. I just want to know what's driving this. I want to help you stop those texts."

The softness in his voice, the way his arms relax and blend our bodies together with gentleness rather than force, uncoils the knot inside me. I slip my arms around his shoulders, leaning into him for strength, and he hoists me up and carries me back to my room where he sets me gently on my bed.

Oh, God. Where is he taking this?

I bow my head so he can't see the panic on my face and I feel the bed dip under his weight. He sits beside me, sifting his fingers through my hair.

I take a shuddering breath. "You can't."

Jayce's hand makes trails through my curls and he hesitates, but then resumes the gentle stroking. "I'm not someone who likes to be told what they can and can't do. Try me."

Jayce reaches across my lap, threading his fingers through mine. The sweetness and simplicity of this gesture rocks me. I want to make him go away, this man whose fame could explode my Internet secret, and at the same time beg him to stay. I sigh heavily.

"I've tried, Jayce. My name and number got out on the Internet, and that's how the creeps got my number to text me." It's the truth, but not nearly half of it.

Jayce pulls my hand to his mouth. Slowly, deliberately, he locks his eyes on mine and kisses each of my pale knuckles laced between his own. "There's more."

I open and close my mouth, not wanting to give him more. He releases my hand and fishes his phone out of his pocket. "Do I need to Google you to find out myself?"

"No! God, no, don't …" I squirm, desperate for an excuse, but his fingers fly over the screen and he starts scrolling through results. My words tumble out, trying to reach his ears before he finds the *Sexy Bitches* site.

"It was a mistake. I didn't want—I never wanted these pictures to be public. Or to happen. I swear. My boyfriend took them. Ex. Ex-boyfriend. He took my camera and he tied me up and he shot them."

I see Jayce land on the site. The photos load on his screen. Even just a few inches wide, I see myself clearly and cringe at what he must think of me.

"I broke up with him. And this is his revenge."

Jayce's face is hard and angry, his jaw ticking as his shoulders tense. His hand in my hair is tighter, almost painful, but I don't think he even notices. I hold my breath for Jayce's reaction and after a long moment, he drops the phone on the bed beside him and turns to me.

His eyes are on fire and he twists, his hand pulling me back against the bed, his body following until it's hovering over mine. "You never wanted this picture to be taken?" His voice shakes with anger.

"No." I bite my lip, his mouth inches from mine.

"You never wanted to be tied up?" His voice is lower, more gravelly.

"Not like that," I whisper.

"What *do* you want, Violet?" There's an edge of danger in this question, a demand, and his other hand digs into the flesh of my hip.

My heart beats loudly in my ears and I tear my eyes away from his eyes, to his lips, his pulse pounding in his neck, his body so close above me. He could crush me if he'd just let go.

And that's what I want in this moment, to just let go, to let someone else share this secret that's haunting me.

I wrap my arms behind Jayce's head and pull him closer. "You."

More powerful than instinct, more immediate than pain, his mouth is on mine, his lips demanding, his body descending. His hand leaves my hip and moves up my ribcage while the other remains buried in my hair.

I let him in. Let his tongue tease apart the seam of my lips, let his hips settle into mine, let his arousal between my thighs draw out an ache of my own.

I kiss him back with swirling, cacophonous feeling—the need to be protected, the need for comfort, the need for release.

And yes, even if I deny it, the desire to be dominated. Seeing those pictures of me brought equal parts lust and terror boiling to the surface. "Wait. Stop."

Jayce pulls away from me lightning-fast, as if I've bitten him. "What?"

He looks so alarmed that I brush his cheek with my hand to reassure him. "Don't freak out. Just ... just give me a moment, OK?"

"Are you freaked out?" His eyes are serious. Worried.

"No. Are you?"

He sits up and helps me sit up beside him. "Maybe a little. The pictures explain a lot. And the stalker—that's some serious shit, Violet."

I wince at the curse. "I know that's serious stuff, but I can't let Brady ruin my life. That's probably his intent. I can't let him get to me like that."

"So he's enlisted others to do the dirty work for him," Jayce says darkly.

He's right. Brady is cowardly enough to hide behind an anonymous photo upload and an anonymous email to my principal—if that was him. He'd never get his hands dirty with an overt act that the public could see. He wants to win this election too badly, and the primary is less than two months away.

The sun slants through my window and my stomach growls. Jayce cocks his eyebrow and grins. "No dinner?"

"Lost track of time. How about you?"

"Let's go get some."

I balk. Smoldering hot kisses aside, I still don't want to be seen with this guy in public. "Nah, I'd rather just nibble on something here."

Jayce pushes himself off the bed and chuckles. "If you're talking about nibbling something from your frighteningly bare refrigerator, I'd say you're having ketchup with a side of soy sauce for dinner."

My laugh is cut short by the familiar text tone of my old phone.

Tonight, Violet. Ready or not, here I come. Before I'm done with you, you'll be screaming my name.

CHAPTER 13: JAYCE

My eyes bounce around Violet's room until they land on a gym bag. I throw it on the bed and pull open a dresser drawer.

"Pack," I say, plunging my hands into a tangle of frilly things that I'm positive I'd want to peel off her body with my teeth. They go in the bag. Next drawer: shirts. I lift out a stack of them and add them to the bag.

Violet stares, still seated on her bed.

"Can you go get your stuff from the bathroom?" I open another drawer. Shorts and skirts. They go in, and I swipe a pair of sandals and some running shoes from her floor. Socks. Nearly forgot.

"What are you doing? Why are you—?"

"You can't stay here. I won't let you. We'll call Neil and tell him to stay away, too, at least until the police can catch up to this guy." I scan the room and add a hairbrush to the bag.

She's not moving so I roam to the bathroom, grabbing a makeup bag, shampoo and body wash. Out of Violet's earshot, I place a call to my car service and request publicity transport. That means I'm getting a driver who doubles as a bodyguard.

When I return, Violet's at least standing, but her face is set. I'm in for an argument.

"You can't just hide me away."

"I can for now." My voice is rough, a command. I stuff the toiletries into the bag, zip it, and hoist it onto my shoulder.

"Where are we going?" Her face is a mixture of confusion and resistance, but I'm not slowing down.

"Follow me." I'm out of her room and halfway to the door when I see her hesitate. I'll grab this girl and carry her caveman-style if I have to. But Violet bends and picks up her fat camera gear bag instead, nodding once.

I tell her to stay back from the street-level door of her apartment building while I scan the street for the car. There are people out—it's a gorgeous summer night and normally I'd be out, too. I don't see any men walking alone or anyone lurking around the block.

In minutes, a town car with opaque windows pulls up. The linebacker-sized driver emerges wearing a full suit, an earpiece, and a sidearm concealed as a bulge beneath his jacket. He bustles us into the back seat.

As soon as the car starts rolling, I hold out my hand. "Give me your new phone."

"So you can take that away, too? No way." She sets her chin and I want to bite that pink lower lip again, to taste her, sweet like apricots.

"I'm going to text Neil from your phone to let him know the situation."

"I can do it. I'm a big girl," she pouts. But then she taps out a terse message.

We spend the rest of the town car ride in silence, and she follows mutely as I escort her through my apartment's lobby. The doorman, to his credit, hides his surprise. He's never seen me bring a girl home.

It's one of my rules, part of my no-strings-attached mantra. I don't need a one-night-stand showing up here—or worse, a bunch of fans. I'm not about to get my balls busted by my co-op the way Gavin's nearly kicked him out.

But this is different. Special circumstances because of a stalker.

Special circumstances because of Violet.

I lead her inside and wait for the reaction. My place isn't big like Tyler's loft, or opulent like Gavin's. It's the smallest unit in the building, just a one-bedroom, but it has two things going for it: it's got a big terrace with a view of the East River, and it needed a *lot* of work, so I pretty much gutted it before I moved in.

Tyler was a champ. Let me crash at his place for a couple of months while the renovation crew went crazy. I had the kitchen built out the way I like—wide open counters and unobstructed views to the living room and river.

The wood floors, fireplace, and high, pressed-tin ceiling are original, but everything else is new: light, modern, steel and granite.

Violet doesn't comment on my pride and joy, and I deflate a bit. I wanted to wow her, but she's in a trance, probably still quaking from the way I swept her out of her East Village apartment and here to the Upper East Side.

I pull a couple of beers from my fridge, unsure if she'd even like one, and follow her to the terrace.

"It's nice here," she says quietly, and accepts the offered beer with a nod. My ego gets a little lift. Maybe she did notice. We sit and drink in silence as the night air reaches that perfect temperature where it blends with the heat of our skin. Her stomach growls again.

"Don't worry, I can do better than ketchup and soy sauce," I promise. I fire up the gas grill and scoot back to the kitchen, pulling a couple of steaks out of the fridge and some random veggies for a salad. I dry-rub the steaks and carry them back to the terrace.

The steaks sizzle and Violet's soft voice floats behind me. "You can't keep me here forever. You can't keep me safe from—"

"I can try. Until you get this crazy figured out, I don't want you to be a sitting duck, wondering when he's going to come at you next."

"Then what am I doing here? You can't keep me locked up like I'm Rapunzel."

I chuckle and nudge next to her on the couch, intentionally crowding her so I can get another whiff of that hair. I tease a strand through my fingers, then flick it up like a little brush and tickle her cheek with it.

"I promise you, if you let down your hair, you'd have a million princes trying to climb it to get to you."

Violet blushes again, and I love how she's so responsive, how emotion colors or clouds her face at every turn. My cock stirs at the thought of how responsive she could be in bed.

"And what about you? You going to try to climb up my hair?"

"I'd climb just about anything to get to you," I tell her, and alarm bells go off in my brain. What kind of mushy shit am I saying? And—fuck. The steaks. I shove myself off the terrace couch and flip the meat.

Violet's sad eyes are in her lap. "You can't."

What's so wrong with telling her she intoxicates me? Just the slight touch of her sends electricity zinging up my arm. This girl has some kind of magic in her body that I'm not sure she knows exists.

"I can't, or you don't want me to?"

"I can't—I don't. Want you to."

A steel-toed boot to my gut couldn't hurt worse than the words that slip through her lips. I snap my gaping jaw shut and spin around to busy myself with the steaks, furious at myself for putting it out there like that, only to be shot down.

I'm not the guy who makes the first offer.

Tits on a plate. *That's* a first offer.

A phone number. A few willing words. Those are the ante to get in the game.

And somehow my stupid brain forgot that Violet never asked for this, never said she wanted me.

Wait. She said it once. And now she doesn't.

Women are so fucking confusing. So much for keeping it simple, no strings attached. Violet's messing with my head when I'm trying to be a Good Samaritan here. There's truth to that old saw that no good deed goes unpunished.

I plate up the steaks, toss the salad, and we eat, mostly in silence. "I won't touch you, if that's what you're afraid of."

Violet's eyes spark with annoyance. "I'm not afraid of you."

"Never said you were." I struggle to keep my voice mild and even. "Just, I'm not going to touch you. Like you want. Not going to hurt you the way your ex did, or the way your stalker keeps threatening to."

"I never said you were."

Now I'm annoyed. "Good. Then we've got that settled. No touching."

"And nothing public," she adds.

I grimace but agree. She wants me about as much as a bad rash. Buh-bye ego.

When we push back from the terrace table, dinner finished, I show her my room. It's simple—just a platform bed, a trunk and some drawers. No art on the walls, even. I put her gym bag down on the bed. "You're sleeping in here."

Her eyes widen in alarm. "With you?"

And there goes the rest of my ego. What did I say that made her so spectacularly repulsed by me? "Um, no. You're in here, I'm on the couch."

"In here on the bed where you've done it with I don't know how many women? No thanks, I'll take the couch." Violet's bratty side is showing and I grab her arm before she can prance out of the bedroom in a huff.

"Stop it, just stop it." I hiss. "You are sleeping *here*. For the record, you're the first woman to sleep in this bed, though it's definitely not going down the way I'd imagined. You can be pissy about it all you want tonight, but it's not changing anything. We'll go to the cops tomorrow and I'll check you into a hotel until they find this creep. But you are *not* going to sass me about my track record. Are we clear?"

Violet's body goes limp beneath my hand and for a moment I'm afraid I accidentally squeezed her too hard. But her expression says otherwise—eyes wide, lips parted. She looks just like she did the last time I kissed her.

"Are we clear?" I demand again, to snap her out of this weird haze.

"Yes." Her eyes drop to her toes. "Sir."

My cock jerks in response. The sass, then the compliance. Calling me *sir*. What kind of game is she playing? I grab her chin roughly, tilting her head back to see the answer in her eyes. Is she *trying* to fuck with my resolve?

My other hand goes to her hair like a bird to its nest. The smell of it, sweet and floral, like cherry trees in bloom, crowds sane thoughts from my brain. My chest rises like I've just run the NYC marathon. If I were an inch closer, my chest would brush hers and I'd feel the warmth of her breasts through her T-shirt.

I'm way out of bounds, but she's not pushing me away. "Does this count as touching?" I rasp, one hand still buried in her hair, one skimming her jaw and stroking her cheek.

"I'm not sure yet," she whispers. "Try something else."

I take a small step toward her so I can feel the heat of her body across the length of me. My shorts are uncomfortably tight as my hard-on becomes more apparent, and I'm not sure if I want her to know this.

She leans in. She knows.

Her chest moves slightly and I feel her nipples brush against my chest through the fabric of our shirts. I move my hand from her cheek to her mouth, tracing a finger across the seam of her lips, the delicate curve above it, the slight crease in her lower lip that's so ripe, so begging to be bitten.

"How about this?" The question rumbles from my chest.

"Jury's still out," she murmurs as I continue tracing her lip. And then in a swift movement, she takes my finger between her teeth, her green eyes sparkling.

CHAPTER 14: VIOLET

He tastes like steak and salt. My lips close around his index finger and I watch his caramel eyes darken. My teeth keep a subtle pressure around his first knuckle, holding him as I suck.

What am I doing? His erection presses into my belly, hot and hard like the rest of him. Jayce could be my own personal furnace, his blood runs so hot beneath the taught skin that makes me tingle with every touch.

His hand fists tighter in my hair, drawing my head back, exposing my neck to him. If we were in a vampire movie, this is the precise moment when he'd bite.

Our eyes lock together, a battle of wills without words, as I try to decipher what he's saying to me. He promised he wouldn't touch me, then he grabbed me when I wouldn't sleep in his bed. And now we're touching—God, we're doing a whole lot more than touching. With every brush of our bodies the friction sparks more electricity.

I suck hard on his finger, willing him to understand the conflict warring inside me. I want him, but I can't have him. Not on my terms, not ever. The threat of my pictures going public because of my association with him would blow away every shred of my reputation, and most likely my father's as well.

The sad truth is that the best I could ever be to Jayce is some casual, closeted one-night stand. Considering his reputation, that's probably all he wants from me.

And I don't want that. I want more.

I want the kind of depth that lets me trust someone to tie me up without the fear of a camera. I want the kind of person who would protect me first, last, and always, damn his reputation.

Brady wanted me for what I could *do* for his reputation. When I left him, posting my naked pictures was his insurance that I'd never undermine him. They're an ever-present threat to keep me silent about all the things—the ugly things—I learned about him in the ten months we were together.

I release Jayce's finger from my mouth and his chest rises in little pants, visible by the city light that filters through the darkening sky.

Jayce drops his hand from my hair, his expression unreadable. "Go get ready for bed. I'll wash the dishes."

"Yes, sir." I lift my gym bag off the bed and walk to the bathroom, putting an extra sway in my hips, leaving that taunt between us. *Sir.* I know he felt it the first time, but I don't know if he caught its full meaning.

Does he understand me? Does he know what I need?

I scrub my face and let out a frustrated breath. I hardly know what I need. All I know is that one moment, tied up, was one of the most erotic of my life.

And I'm desperate to feel that again.

But Jayce runs hot and cold, one moment controlled, the next, controlling. He's gentle and harsh, sweet and biting. I need to know how to bring out the beast. If it's in him.

I change into sleep shorts and a tank top, no bra, and come back into his bedroom. A bedside light is on low and the windows are open to the night air. This high up, the city's sounds are a reassuring hum.

The water shuts off in the kitchen and Jayce knocks at the door. "Violet? Can I get in the bathroom for a few minutes?"

"Yeah." I shove my bare legs under his duvet cover and pull it up to mask the outline of my breasts beneath my thin tank top. He barely looks my way, just opens his dresser drawer to remove some clothes and shuts the bathroom door firmly behind him.

The shower runs. The minutes tick by. There's no way I can sleep like this. Just as I'm debating going out to the couch to force him to sleep in his own bed, he comes out of the bathroom. He's clad in boxers and I try to mask my startled expression at his unholy hotness.

This. Man. Is. Built. A few drops of water glint off his torso and his hair is wet, dark and sleek against his skull.

A ping sounds from the wadded-up shirt and shorts in Jayce's hands. He fishes in the pockets for my old phone and shakes his head when he sees the text. It's clear he's not sharing it with me.

Jayce shuts off my old phone and drops his dirty clothes in a laundry basket in the corner. He stands at the opposite side of the bed, uncertainty clouding his face. "Can I sit for a minute?"

I nod. *Sit, lie down, curl up, kiss me.* I'd want him to do all of these things, if only I knew it wouldn't end with a broken heart.

"Violet." He breathes heavily and I focus on the Celtic knot tattoo ringing his bicep. "What will it take to get you to trust me?"

"I—I already do," I admit, knowing it's true. I trust him not to hurt me, physically at least. Trust he's protecting me right now. But I don't trust my heart not to fall for Tattoo Thief's most notorious ladies' man.

I'm not that kind of girl.

Jayce raises surprised eyes and turns, rolling on his side toward me. He's on top of the duvet and I'm under the covers, so I'm pretty well protected from any hanky-panky he might have in mind. He rests his head on his arm, the length of his body a couple feet from mine.

"Then what is it? Why do you keep pushing me away? What did I do?"

"It's nothing you did." *It's what you didn't do. What you won't do when this is over.*

"You told me a secret. That's big. Thank you for trusting me with that much." Jayce's hand reaches idly for my hair and I still, feeling his rough fingers skim through a few wavy strands, feeling him smooth them from root to tip, over and over.

"I can't fight it," I confess. "I've never felt so powerless against something. Every time I tried to find a way to get the site to take it down, I hit a brick wall. And today I found more."

His eyes widen. "More pictures?"

"Worse. More sites. That's what I was doing today at my apartment. Research. And even if I can somehow sue and get a takedown for *Sexy Bitches*, now more sites have my pictures posted. They're multiplying and I'm not sure I can ever get all of my pictures off the Internet."

My breath hitches in a little bubble of a sob, but I'm all cried out. I'm past denial, past self-pity, and straight on to resolve. I *will* keep fighting this.

Jayce's hand in my hair makes my scalp tingle, as if he's working my whole body with his fingers. Nobody else touches my hair like this—Brady liked it up in a twist, like a "hot politician's wife," he'd say. As a teacher, I bound it into a low ponytail or braid to keep it out of the art projects.

"So what will it take to get you to *really* trust me, Violet?" His eyes are serious, laced with concern. "What can I give you that's going to prove I'm not a bad guy? That I'm not like *him*?"

I know he means Brady, and maybe that's why we keep doing this weird dance, this power exchange where one minute he's hauling me against him and biting my lip, and the next I'm calling him sir and sucking his finger like it's his ... no.

I have to stop this. The only thing that he could give me that would matter is something as intimate as what I've given him. "A secret."

Jayce nods once, understanding. "Like for like. A secret, because you've given me yours."

"Will you?" My voice is small, but I want this—even a tiny secret, something inconsequential. Something he doesn't share with his groupies.

Jayce's powerful arm comes around me, scooting me, still beneath the covers, until I'm close against him, my head tucked beneath his chin. Even through the duvet, I feel the heat of his body. "I'll make it good, then, and tell you something nobody knows. Not even the band. Can you handle that?"

I nod a little, knowing he can feel my answer through his chin. His other hand keeps stroking my hair, as if I've become his pet.

"There's some interest in me going solo," he starts, and he tells me about the man who confronted him outside a show, the number he dialed today and the lunch planned for tomorrow.

He tells me about how Gavin's absence for two months ripped a hole in the band, and though they're repairing it, he's not sure it can fully be fixed. He tells me about the creative tension, the struggle to get his band mates to accept his instrumentation rather than blindly following Gavin's simple melodies.

When he stops, I'm quiet. It's a big secret. Breathing a word about it to the media could tear up the band, or at least make his life hell. I don't take this trust lightly.

He pulls back to look at me in the dim light, and our eyes meet. I'm not asleep—far from it. I'm entranced by the rich tone of his voice, the way he speaks to the feeling beneath his actions. He might be the first guy who's ever admitted to me what's happening so many layers beneath the surface.

Jayce moves to release me and go back to the couch.

"Wait." I reach for him, my hand settling around his side, fingertips brushing the powerful crease of his spine. "Want to trade me for another?"

"Another secret?"

"Yes." I would trade him secrets all night if he'd just keep talking to me and touching my hair.

"How about a small one this time?" he asks, and I hear the smile in his voice.

"I'll take it."

"My name's not really Jayce. I was born Justin Cameron McKittrick, but I don't think anyone's ever called me that. The day my parents brought me home from the hospital, a Justin Boot salesman came to our door."

"In Pittsburgh?"

"No, I grew up in Colorado. A ranch near Steamboat Springs. We didn't move to Pittsburgh until high school. Anyway, Dad was so tickled about the Justin Boots that he bought a pair, and started calling me Boot. It stuck."

"Boot? As your name?" I choke on a giggle, but imagine it wasn't much fun for a kid to be called something so common. Like getting called Sponge or Plate or something.

"Yep. My dad's name is Justin, too, so most people called me JC. But when I met Tyler, he just called me Jayce."

I *hmm* into Jayce's shoulder, trying on the name Justin for size. Justin—*the just*. The man who'd fight for what's right. Maybe the one who'd fight for me?

"Can I call you Justin?"

"You can call me anything you want, darlin', so long as you call me." He chuckles. "So what's yours? Got another secret to share?"

"I'm stalking someone, too."

CHAPTER 15: JAYCE

Short of changing Violet's name or radically changing her look—and no way can I get behind cutting or dying her gorgeous hair—we've ruined most of the stalker's intel.

She has a new phone number.

A new job.

And a new address, at least for now. Mine.

I feel a hell of a lot better letting Violet chase down the graffiti artist she's been "stalking" for her photo project, knowing that the sicko stalker who's after Violet won't know where to start to come after her.

My place.

I walk to my lunch meeting with Darren Bishop with a wide grin on my face, like I scored big time. It feels like I did. I never laid a finger on Violet last night (unless you count her hair), but we stayed up late trading secrets like junior high school girls.

What the fuck is wrong with me?

I'll tell you what. At some point I skipped right past just caring about getting into her pants, to caring about *her*.

When I first laid eyes on her, I said she was a witch, a sorceress, a fairy princess. I was wrong. She's something far more powerful than that: she's the girl I can't have.

She's not saying why, but I think I get it. Maybe it's my track record with other girls, which the paparazzi take gleeful delight in documenting. And maybe part of it is that we didn't meet under the best of circumstances.

I've been bossing her around, grabbing her, pushing her to do what I thought was right. I never asked for what she needed and wanted from me.

And so now she doesn't want me.

Someone ought to tell that to my dick. It still wants her like *whoa*. I fell asleep with Violet in my arms last night, the comforter creating a damn chastity belt between us where the only parts of her I could actually touch were her arms and her head. I woke up with a raging hard-on and practically limped to the bathroom for a shower and some relief.

I turn down a narrow street as I zigzag through the city toward the out-of-the-way bar where I'm meeting Darren. On my way, I see an unusual graffiti of a man in silhouette, painted like he's hanging onto an actual fire escape ladder. The stencil next to the painted man reads, "Hang on. Help's coming."

I smile. That's the kind of message Violet needs to hear right now. If she'd just let me help her ... I shake my head in frustration and pull out my phone, take a photo and text it to Violet. I start walking again and I've barely gotten a hundred feet when she texts back:

> **Violet:** *This is the artist! The one I've been stalking! Where are you right this minute? Can anyone else see it??*
>
> **Jayce:** *West Village, at Christopher and Hudson.*
>
> **Violet:** *I'm coming with my camera right now. Can you, I don't know, stand guard?*
>
> **Jayce:** *Don't freak out. The painting is safe—it's nearly two stories off the ground.*
>
> **Violet:** *You sure? The people who deface this artist's work are pretty ruthless.*
>
> **Jayce:** *I'm sure. You want me to stay anyway?*

Violet: *Would you?*

I glance at the time—ten minutes 'til noon. If I hang out here, I might be five minutes late to meet Darren, maybe ten.

But Darren wants me; he'll wait for me. Violet says she doesn't want me, but I'm willing to wait for her.

Jayce: *Yes. I'll get a town car to be there before you get down the elevator.*
Violet: *Justin, I owe you a kiss.*

And for that—not because she owes me, not because of a promised kiss, but because she called me Justin—I'm on cloud nine as I stand around and wait for her.

Good to her word, she kisses me. She looks around quickly like she's about to do something wrong, but nobody's watching us. She delivers a chaste peck on my cheek at first, but then she draws back, her eyes settling on my mouth, and she does it. The sweetest kiss, so soft I strain to feel it, to memorize the taste of her mouth on mine.

I have to leave her then and jog to my lunch meeting, but leaving her exposed kills me. Somewhere in the city, her stalker's still out there.

I slide onto a barstool opposite Darren at a raised table. Layers of white paint peel off the brick wall beside us.

"Glad you could make it." Darren's voice is light but he's not the kind of man who is made to wait. His half-empty pint of beer says he was right on time.

"Thanks for inviting me." I pick up the menu. "What's good here?"

"The privacy." He laughs at his own joke. "Don't worry. Decent food here. Get a club sandwich or something."

We order and as soon as the waitress puts a beer in my hand, Darren switches to business. "So what do you think about my offer?"

"I don't think you've made one yet. Have you?" I raise my brow to challenge him.

"You know what I mean. Going solo. You could ditch the dead weight of your band and launch a new career at Viper."

"I'm not ditching Tyler." My dead-set statement falls out of my mouth and tips my hand, showing Darren I've given his proposition more than a little consideration.

"So you want Tyler Walsh, but not Gavin or the drummer?"

"His name is Dave."

"I know his name. He can pound a beat, but he doesn't have the flash and pop that top bands expect from a drummer. I don't know what you guys saw in him."

"His business sense."

I'm torn between defending Dave's musical skills—which I admit aren't virtuoso-level, but anybody who's been gigging on the reg for more than five years like we have is pretty damn solid. The other part of me wants to agree that Dave leaves something to be desired on the musician side of things so Darren'll know I'm discerning like that.

I've taken music lessons since I was four. I took four years of private drum lessons in high school before I decided to focus solely on the guitar, which is about three more years of lessons than Dave ever took.

"But Dave's not your manager anymore," Darren points out, as if we should have cut him loose long ago.

"Still acts like it," I mutter and take a quick gulp of beer to get my mouth to stop flapping. I don't need to alert Darren to all of the petty little annoyances that happen behind the scenes. Especially not if he wants to talk contracts.

"So, no Gavin either. The disappearing act and all. You think he's clean?" Darren's implying that Gavin's two-month hiatus, in which he severed contact with all of us, had more to do with drugs than a need to find himself and finally admit the part he played in the death of his muse.

"I'm sure he's clean," I confirm. "But serious about the music? Not so sure about that. It's like everything he's writing doesn't have room for improvement."

"So, no room for you," Darren sympathizes. "I get it. You're stifled creatively. You want to work with a label that has your back, but isn't gonna wrap you up in a bunch of marketing bullshit and red tape."

I catch myself nodding. "Exactly."

"What's your exit clause look like with Tattoo Thief?"

I mumble something about needing to look into it, but the truth is there's nothing holding me back. I can leave anytime I want, and I'll still get a quarter of royalties for everything we've put out so far.

We don't have future tour dates planned, so there's no exposure on pulling out of that. Gavin's gung-ho about getting *Wilderness* recorded soon and we have most of the songs ready, but another studio musician could sub in for me and no one would be the wiser.

Except me. And my band. They wouldn't be Tattoo Thief anymore.

Or maybe they would?

"So, Tyler. Why do you want to take him along for the ride? I gotta be honest with you: his musical chops are fine, but he's just not solo artist material. His voice can't wail like Gavin's."

"All the more reason to stick with him," I say. "Look, in music it's hard to know who has your back. With Tyler, I know he has mine. Always. And I always have his. Either I go with him, or I don't go at all."

Darren nods. "Fair enough. I'll draw up some terms and courier them to you Monday. When do you think you'll have a chance to look them over?"

I swallow. This is all moving *really* fast. I don't even have an entertainment lawyer outside of the one Chief hired for us, so I'll need to do my research, put down a retainer, schedule time to talk with him or her … the list looks menacing.

Darren must see the strain in my face because he lifts his dwindling second beer in a toast. "Relax, buddy. Not going to rush you. Take as long as you like to think it over, figure out what's gonna fit you best. But just remember: time kills all deals."

CHAPTER 16: VIOLET

Today looks a heck of a lot better than last night.

I've got one thing to do: take my old phone to the police. Jayce grudgingly gave it back to me this morning after I swore I wouldn't look at any more texts. I still hadn't made up my mind whether to make a report when Jayce sent me a photo of this new art.

He doesn't know it, but he's just given me an enormous gift.

"Hang on. Help's coming." The spray-painted words mean everything to me today.

I gaze up at the graffiti, one of the artist's largest pieces to date. How did he reach the fire escape to lay the stencil? Who helped him? The fire escape zigzags up the building past six stories of apartments, so it's anyone's guess.

First order of business: shoot the piece.

I assemble my camera, choosing a mild zoom lens that won't warp the image from my vantage point. Even from across the street, I can see the artist's stylized signature woven into the stencil: VIIIM.

I step into the street to get a better angle and a delivery truck races past me, laying on the horn and nearly taking off my lens with its side-view mirror. Heart in my throat, I jump back onto the side-walk.

That was close.

Stupid, and close.

VIIIM's message could hardly be more perfect. When I was drowning in fear, desperately fighting a monster that vaporized each time I thought I'd found a way to take my pictures down, help came to me.

And not just help. Holy Hotness in the form of a rock star whose hands thrill me with the slightest touch. Jayce. Justin. The more I think of what he's done for me already—protecting me even when I fought against him—the more I see him as Justin. *One who is just.*

I wonder what to make of VIIIM's name. I don't know if it's gang-related, but I do know random graffiti often litters his work as soon as it's discovered. That's why it's so important for me to capture the image before it's lost to vandals.

I've got enough of a photo collection on VIIIM that I could sell a feature to a magazine if they think his work is important enough.

I cross the street to the small lot at the base of the graffitied building, which is surrounded by a chain-link fence. There's a gate, but when I look closer, I realize that the lock isn't clicked closed.

Feeling like a trespasser (which I probably am), I push through the gate and step up to the building to get a closer look.

The bottom of the stencil is at least eight feet off the ground. I open my new phone to look up VIIIM's Twitter feed, my only access to the artist so far.

@VIIIM: West Village People: What kind of music would that band play? #RuinABandName

@VIIIM: Feeling like a giant tonight—my stilt-friends Chris & Hudson hooked me up for some vertical mayhem.

@VIIIM: The difference between a flower and a weed, and between art and vandalism, is your point of view.

@VIIIM: Who are you calling 8,000? I'm a person, not a Roman numeral.

I see how the clues add up—the vertical mayhem is here in the West Village, at the corner of Christopher and Hudson.

VIIIM's last tweet makes me chuckle. When I started following him, I wondered if his name might be Roman numerals or maybe a date. VIII is eight, M is one thousand. But eight thousand isn't written VIIIM, it's just VIII with a line over it. So, no dice.

And yes, I had to Google that.

As I wrap up the last of my shots, my spine prickles with a sense that someone's watching me. I turn, but it's nothing. A woman pushing a baby carriage. A uniformed delivery guy hauling boxes with a hand truck. A curvy, tattooed girl with pink hair and headphones at a bus stop.

I watch the delivery guy closely, but I don't think it's the same guy who came with my flowers. Then I lock on another guy idling up the street. With his shaggy brown hair and slouch, he looks eerily similar to the man who works the newsstand at the bodega near my apartment—which is on the opposite side of Manhattan.

The unease of being watched hovers over me like a cloud and I beat a hasty exit to the chain-link gate. I hustle down the sidewalk toward the subway without even packing my camera back in my gear bag. The girl at the bus stop gives me a long, slow look but I don't care if she thinks I'm a tourist.

I cross town on the subway to the police precinct, fill out paperwork and wait. And wait. When a detective finally meets with me and scrolls through the stalker's texts, our conversation earns me little more than frowns and a few scrawls in his notebook.

I tell him about the flowers.

"So this delivery guy didn't threaten you? Didn't touch you?"

I think of the moment when his hand brushed mine as he handed me the vase and shudder. "No—not really." I think of the million little interactions—the barista at the coffee shop around the corner from my apartment, the clerk at the bodega, and my neighbor. It could have been any of them or none of them.

"Do you think he was the one who's been sending the messages?"

I point to the text that says he touched my skin. "I don't *know*. All I know is someone's too close."

"I can trace the number. But if it's a burner-phone, there's not much we can do to track him."

"Can't you find a credit card he used to buy the phone? Or the location where the texts originated?" I rack my brain for ideas, mostly fueled by cop show reruns. "Can't you do anything?"

The detective's mouth forms a hard line. "These texts are aggressive, but there's no incident to follow, Ms. Chase."

I hear the subtext. *It's not a priority.* "You mean he has to hurt me before you can do anything?" My voice rises.

"We'll do what we can. But you've got to accept your responsibility in this, too. Get your pictures off the Internet. Change your number."

I tell him I *have* changed my number. Even moved out of my apartment, but the texts on my old phone—and there were three new ones today—keep coming.

Where have you gone, my sweet Violet? Are you waiting for me? Wanting me as much as I want you?

I try to describe the delivery guy but it's worthless, like telling an airline your lost luggage is a black rolling bag. There are thousands of thirtyish white men, medium build, just under six feet tall. I don't know his hair color because he was wearing a baseball cap.

"Would you recognize him if you saw him again?" the detective asks.

"No," I confess. The delivery guy seemed inconsequential and I was so surprised by the flowers that I barely looked at him.

We go through the same routine with the other guys I spoke to yesterday. I describe Corey, the clerk, and the barista. "Did you interact with any other men yesterday?"

I hesitate, thinking of Jayce. "No." I'm already afraid my police report will get noticed by a reporter; I don't need Jayce McKittrick's name anywhere near mine to expose my secret completely.

The detective closes his notebook. "Go home and get some rest. Stay safe lock your doors, check before you let anyone in. This should be a matter of course for a young woman like you."

I hate the condescending tone in his voice, as if I live a life that beckons danger. From my careful existence in my parents' house to my conservative college lifestyle, I've been the model of safety.

Now the only place I feel safe is with Jayce. Strong shoulders, watchful eyes, commanding presence that takes action. I leave the precinct and pull out my phone to text him, but his number's not in it.

Oh. It's my old phone. Before I switch it off, I see a red badge indicating that I have voicemail.

I take a deep breath. Considering how many creeps have my number, this could be ugly.

"This message is for Violet Chase. You stopped by Righteous Ink a few days ago and asked about one of our freelance artists. Come by the store or return my call."

My heart speeds up and my body points me toward that East Village shop where Stella got her crazy, spur-of-the-moment tattoo.

The antiseptic in the air is more intense than I remember it, the store just as quiet. I don't see the burly, tattooed man I talked to last time, just a girl behind the counter, bent over a sketchpad.

She straightens when I see her, and there's something oddly familiar about her pink-streaked hair and arms laden with tattoos. A black, scoop neck T-shirt stretches across her ample chest and a piercing above her lip sparkles.

"You're here for a tattoo?" The girl gives me a once-over, my pale limbs not bearing a single tattoo. Her voice is low and Kathleen Turner sexy.

"Um, not really," I say. The girl, who is about my age, goes back to sketching. "But I got a call from this shop. I wanted to meet one of your freelance artists."

I take a couple of steps closer to the counter and she closes her sketchbook before I can see what she's working on. Her blue eyes, dark at the edges, meet mine. "Which one?"

"That's the thing. I don't really know his name. He did this design"—I skip over to the window to point to a stylized daisy, like the one I found with Stella on graffiti around the corner—"and I was hoping to meet him."

"Why?" Now the girl looks put out.

"Because … because I admire his work. Because I think he does other stuff, bigger canvases, and I want to know about it."

"*He's* not here." Her scowl deepens. "And the artist doesn't do canvases."

I shove my hand in my hair, tangling in a few curls, trying to keep my composure. "I know. That's not what I meant. I think he does much bigger stuff. Like walls."

I wait and watch for recognition in her face. Her lip twitches but she says nothing.

"I think his name is VIIIM," I say, pronouncing it *Vim.*

She laughs at this. "Vim. Right. Where do you get that?"

I pull out my camera, desperate to keep her engaged. I click through a few frames that I shot earlier, the silhouetted man hanging from a fire escape ladder. I touch a button and zoom into the corner of the digital image.

"See that? V-I-I-I-M. It's on all of his work."

The girl looks surprised. "How much of this work have you seen?"

I smile. "A ton. I have twenty-seven works captured from around New York and Paris, not counting that daisy in the window," I say.

"Paris?"

"I took a trip to Europe because VIIIM's Twitter feed said he was going. I found six paintings there, although only four were intact." My face falls with the memory of being too late to capture two of them. "Vandals got there before me on a couple."

"Vandals? You don't think what Vim is doing is vandalism?"

"It's art!" I say, before I can stop my rush of enthusiasm. "I've been tracking him since last fall, trying to figure out why he leaves these perfect little paintings around the city for people to discover."

"What are you doing with these photos?"

I let out a breath and the cloud returns. "I'm a freelance photographer—well, actually, I was a junior high art teacher, until I got fired—and this is all I have left. This project, and a few assignments from my roommate's newspaper. I'm hoping to sell the project as a photo feature to a magazine."

The girl's eyes harden. "Sell it?"

"Well, yeah. It's amazing art, and I want more of the world to see it than the few folks who do before taggers ruin it." I pause, searching her face for an answer. "What do you know about this guy?"

CHAPTER 17: JAYCE

"Let's take ten," Dave says, and I can't drop my guitar fast enough. I escape to the kitchen for a beer and to simply get away from the bad energy swirling in our practice space.

Every fucking thing is a battle today. Gavin's endlessly contradicting himself, indecisive over the shape of his songs. *His* songs, as if we have no ownership in them at all. As if the rest of us don't write them, too.

Tyler's quiet, his tongue still healing, and a black cloud follows him in the form of a media firestorm after his diabetic seizure and the claims of some slut who *wishes* he were her baby daddy.

I told him then and I'd tell him again now: he's too good for that gold-digger. But now's not the time for told-ya-sos.

Dave's being a bossy little bitch, but I can't call him out on it because Chief's right here, and our current manager seems content to let our ex-manager call the shots.

"I need to know if you'll be ready by next Friday," Chief says to Tyler. "I booked studio time for us in LA and I need to know now if you'll be able to lay it down."

"Mah fingahs wook fine," Tyler says, wiggling his digits. "An tung wuh heal."

It can't happen fast enough. I need Tyler's tongue to heal just so he can back me up in these stupid arguments, not to mention nailing the recording session Chief's proposed.

We've got a bunch of songs, a promised album, and our label chomping at the bit to capitalize on the press Tattoo Thief's gotten with Gavin's return. Oh, yes, it always comes back to Gavin Slater.

"I know it's not ideal recording over the weekend, but it's the best setup we can get with this kind of timeline. I've got a charter flight and the rooms booked." Chief nods to Dave. "You going to have Kristina wrangle the girls?"

"Yep. Beryl's coming, Gavin?"

"Assuming she can get away from work, absolutely." Gavin's never had a nine-to-five job in his life, so it's pretty funny to see him tamed by his *girlfriend's* schedule.

"Tyler?"

"Stella's in." Tyler lisps her name but I see a smile stretch his face just talking about her. I never thought I'd want to see him fall like this, but the way he worships Stella makes me rethink everything I told him about keeping it casual.

He really loves her.

Damn.

"Jayce? You bringing a friend?" I don't like the sneer in Dave's voice, the taunt that's always simmering below the surface. It's no secret that he's the settled-down one, the guy who's managed to hang onto a girlfriend longer than we've hung on to our place at the top of the charts. But he doesn't have to rub it in.

"Maybe," I answer vaguely. "Chief, can you get me a suite, just in case?"

"A suite? Who are you bringing? A whole cheerleading team?" Dave snickers.

"Sure can." Chief taps notes into his iPad. "Just let me know the name or names before we fly for the passenger manifest, OK?"

I nod, but a chill of panic rests in my stomach. What will Violet do if I take off to LA? Will she try to go back to her own apartment? What if the stalker catches up to her? No matter how much you try to shake your past, in this digital world, someone or something's bound to catch up to you.

Break's over. We go back to practice, honing the seventh song in our album set. This one makes me sweat—it's full of tricky transitions and intricate timing, demanding the way a great song needs to be.

A darker sky, a deeper sea
A midnight hour, she comes to me
I drink her in, her taste, her touch
Intoxication
Sweet elation
I'm closer to heaven when she holds me here
Close to broken when she disappears

It's the kind of song where things can come apart. You miss a beat, miss a transition cue, and you're drowning in an ocean of notes with nothing to grab hold of.

In this run-through, we stick together—barely. Chief's head is bent over his tablet and I can't tell if he's ignoring us or listening intently.

I want to yell at him to yell at *us,* to tell Gavin and Dave to pull their heads out of their asses, buckle down and fix what needs fixing. Even tell Tyler he's falling behind Dave, that he needs to reconnect with the rhythm.

My brain's muddled from the late night with Violet, whispering secrets and then stroking her hair. I feel like I left part of me back in my apartment with her, my thoughts still reaching for hers.

We run the song again a dozen times and get tighter, make it work the way it's supposed to, but there's still something missing. Gavin finally calls it a day and we wrap up just as Stella arrives at Tyler's loft.

I'm packing my guitar in its case when Stella approaches me. "You look like shit."

"Hi to you too, Stella." I swat at her but she doesn't flinch. After helping her cope with Tyler's hospitalization and the shitstorm that came down, we're pals.

"So what gives? No workout tonight?" Stella crosses her arms and nods to the weight bench.

None of us are in the mood to pump. The tension is too thick, the looming deadline of our next album suddenly too real.

"I'll just hit the gym at my apartment," I say, and give Tyler and Stella a wave so I don't have to watch them suck the faces off each other. Gently. Tyler's still got a busted tongue.

I blow out of Tyler's place and my fingers itch to dial Violet. No answer. I hope she's taking a bubble bath or some girly shit to get her head straight after the stalker-weirdness.

But my apartment is too quiet when I get home, and from what I can tell, she hasn't been at my place since morning.

No way is she still at the police station. Even with taking pictures of that graffiti, I can't imagine it took her this long.

I try her phone again. Again, no answer, so I send a text.

Jayce: *Hi. Just checking to see how things went today, if you're doing OK. Where are you?*

I wait, but there's no text back, or even an indication that my message has been delivered. I'm stymied and restless, and I pace the apartment. Violet's clothes are all neatly packed away in her gym bag.

I hate that. It tells me she can just pick up and leave at any moment, and I don't want her to. I pull open a dresser drawer and scoop up my shirts, relocating them to a lower drawer. There. Now there's space for her if she stays a little longer.

What the hell am I doing? When did I put my no-strings mantra on ice and start playing house?

I call again. Maybe her ringer's off? Maybe—shit, I hate this the minute I think it—she found a hotel or a friend's place to crash tonight? But then, wouldn't her bag be gone, too?

I have to have an answer, or I'm going to tear up the city to find this girl.

CHAPTER 18: VIOLET

I leave the tattoo shop with more questions than answers.

The girl from Righteous Ink wouldn't tell me much. Just that the artist works on appointment, and only under certain circumstances. She wouldn't tell me what those are. It seems like a funny way to run a business.

Even if I can't get VIIIM to reveal more about himself, I want to talk to him so I can build the photo captions before I submit the profile to a magazine. What inspires him? What does he call his pieces? And how did he manage to paint the one on the fire escape?

I gave the tattoo shop clerk my new phone number, but she looked doubtful when I asked if she thought he'd call me.

In a funk, I wander from Righteous Ink to the coffee shop not far from my apartment. It's comforting and familiar, with the sound of chatter and smells of rich coffee and baked goods. The barista, a tattooed guy with shaggy brown hair and a good smile, winks at me.

I smile back, but I shiver. He's looking at me too closely. He was here at the shop yesterday, too, before I got the flowers. His long fingers brushed my hand when he gave me my coffee, the same way he does today.

My fingers tremble as I balance the latte bowl on its saucer.

I take a seat by the window, tuck my camera bag under the table, and sip my coffee. As long as the stalker is out there somewhere, am I going to be afraid of my own shadow?

The scrape of a chair snaps me out of my daze. A man slips into the seat across from me and he looks a little familiar, but I can't place him.

"Hi." He smiles, his hazel eyes laser-focused on me.

"Do I know you?"

"Not yet, but I'd like to know you." The smooth, rich tone of his voice is music.

My pulse pounds as he leans toward me, and I pull back. "I think you've got the wrong girl."

"Do I? I don't think so. I've been watching you."

Watching me? A thousand spiders skitter across my skin. "Go away." I push back my chair, feeling adrenaline pump through my veins.

The man's smile fades and his brows knit. "Wait. You haven't even given me a chance."

"I don't have to." My voice is breathy with panic. "I said, *go away.*"

He holds up his hands in surrender. "All right, I'll go. All I wanted was to get to know you better. You're beautiful."

For a moment, his sad eyes make me think my instincts are wrong. Maybe this guy is just in the wrong place at the wrong time? Maybe he's just trying to be nice? "Sorry. I just have a lot on my mind right now. It's not a good time."

"That's OK, Violet. I can wait."

My eyes snap wide. "What did you call me?"

"Violet. That's your name, right?" He smiles and his slightly crooked eyeteeth look menacing, like they could rip my flesh.

I stand, backing away from the table in horror. "How did you...?"

He stands too, and steps toward me, grasping my hand. "Every time you come here, I can't take my eyes off your pretty red hair."

When I fuck you, I'm gonna pull that pretty red hair of yours until you scream.

The text echoes from my memory. *Pretty red hair.* I wrench my hand from his grip and run—out the door, down the street, running blind until I realize my feet are carrying me home.

But not even my home is safe, and as I approach the street-level door to my building I'm strangled by one thought: I left my bag behind.

My camera. My wallet. My phone.

Panic squeezes my lungs. I could have left the Hope Diamond at the coffee shop and there's no way I'd go back. I have nothing but the keys in my pocket, not even a few crumpled dollars to get myself on the subway to Jayce's apartment.

I drag in ragged breaths and punch my key in the lock. My eyes bounce over my shoulder to see if someone followed me.

There are men everywhere—standing outside the bodega, smoking on a stoop across the street, leaning against an alley wall, walking on the sidewalk.

And every single one of them can see that I'm home. Alone.

CHAPTER 19: JAYCE

The East Village is buzzing with activity, everyone gearing up for the kind of summer night that makes you want to stay out forever. The kind that makes you feel immortal.

I scan the street and try to memorize faces: a guy reading a newspaper on the stoop across the street. A guy repainting an iron railing. A guy selling magazines at the bodega. A guy hauling trash to an alley Dumpster.

I lean on Violet's intercom and there's no answer. Good, sort of. I can't imagine that she'd come back to her place. I try more buttons on the intercom panel and one of the residents, C. Greer in 4D, answers.

"Hello?"

The voice sounds about my age, so I take a stab in the dark, hoping C. Greer is the neighbor Violet told me about. "Corey?"

"Yeah? Who's this?"

"It's Jayce, one of Violet's friends." My voice is casual, but my heart's beating hard in my chest. "Can you let me in?"

"Sure, man, no problem."

I push through the buzzing door and frown at the shit security. At least at my place, there's a doorman.

I climb the stairs to Violet's apartment and knock, softly at first, then harder. My skin feels too tight, too hot, as if I'm working up a case of claustrophobia. No answer.

I take another flight of stairs to 4D and knock. A muscular guy about my height answers it. His brows crease so I paint a smile on my face to put him at ease. "Hey, how's it going?"

"Do I know you?"

"No, but I've heard about you. From Violet, your neighbor?"

His smirk sickens me. "The hot redhead? Nice piece of ass."

"Yeah." I take a step closer to the door and for a moment, I don't think he'll let me in, but then he moves aside and nods. "Thought we might want to work something out about her."

"Hey, I've been trying to work something out with her for months." His laugh is low and slimy, and I want to punch the leer off his face. "She's got a boyfriend, some slick guy in a suit from upstate. Says she doesn't want any on the side."

"No boyfriend anymore." I curl my fist and then force my hand to relax. "You've tried to get with her?"

"'Bout a dozen times."

"You got her number?" I need to know if he's one of the fuckwits who's been texting Violet.

"Dude, she lives downstairs. I don't need her number."

"You want it?"

He crosses his arms over his chest. "Why do you care?"

I paint a harmless smile on my face and make some shit up. "Well, I've got a girlfriend, and now that Violet's single, my girl's fucking jealous, you know? So since I heard Violet talking about you, I thought maybe if you two were going out, my girl would lay off."

Corey nods with me, grinning, like we're both saying *chicks are stupid.*

"Violet's shy. So you got to call her." I put out my hand. "Give me your phone. I'll put in her number."

Corey hands it over and I put *my* number in, not Violet's. No way I want this jackass calling her. "Hey—I was wondering, what was the movie Neil borrowed from you?"

"Bent on Annihilation. Good shit."

"Can I check it out?"

Corey turns to the entertainment system in his living room that's littered with DVD cases. He paws through the stack, buying me just enough time to switch over to his text messages and verify that he hasn't texted Violet.

When Corey hands me the DVD, I hand back his phone and pretend to read the movie blurb on the back of the case. "Looks good."

"You can borrow it if you want."

"Nah, you'll be doing me a favor if you just keep an eye out for Violet. Be a gentleman and shit. Keep that up for a few weeks and I'll bet when you call she'll be all over you."

Keep that up for a few weeks and I'll figure out who's messing with her. And I'll mess him the fuck up.

I mentally cross Corey off my list of suspects and descend the stairs, but pause again at Violet's door when I hear a small noise behind it.

I knock, and then as disgusting images of the stalker tear through my brain I pound on the door harder and yell, "Violet? It's Jayce! I have to know you're OK!"

I listen, and another tiny sound encourages me to wait. I press my ear to the door and hear a muffled footfall, a sniffle, and then the chain sliding back, the deadbolts clicking open.

Violet's face is red and blotchy, her eyes puffy and tearful. Her hair is tangled and limp, her T-shirt rumpled.

Another sniff and then a sob. She falls in my arms and I react without thinking, catching her and wrapping her into me. "Shh, honey, oh, Violet, it's OK. You're OK."

That might be the biggest lie I've ever told. Violet's body is limp as I hold her, refastening the chain and locks behind me, carrying her back to her bedroom. This is starting to become a trend, and I'm afraid to hear what spurred this new horror.

I do the one thing I know makes her feel good, the one thing that feels right to me. I curl my body around hers and stroke her hair.

"He found me," she finally whispers.

I pull back to see her face, and maybe I'm looking for physical signs of damage.

"I went to a coffee shop near here, a place I go pretty often. He sat down at my table."

"Did he talk to you? Did he hurt you?"

She shakes her head at the second question. "He said he's been watching me. He told me I was beautiful, and that he wanted to get to know me. He knew my *name*, Jayce."

Violet buries her face against my chest and I feel the hot stain of tears on my shirt. I keep petting her hair, inhaling its cherry-blossom scent, comforting her the only way I know how.

"I got up and ran," she says, "but everything—my camera gear, my wallet, and the phone you gave me—they're all gone. I left them. All I had were the keys in my pocket."

This sets off a fresh wave of tears and I crush her against me.

"What did he look like? Was he the delivery guy? Or the barista or the clerk?"

"I don't *know!* I was so surprised when he sat down. When he grabbed my hand, all I could see was him touching me."

I wait for her breathing to even. "Listen to me, Violet. That stuff? It's nothing. We can replace it, buy a new phone, and order you new cards. We can fix that."

But it kills me that I can't fix the real problem: she's not safe. The fact that she was so close to him, that he could have *done something* to hurt her, shakes me to my bones.

I can't let that happen. Seeing her broken like this, shaken to her foundation, frightens me more than the prospect of what he could have done.

"Come here, Violet. Let's go home."

I lace my fingers through hers and try to pull her up, but she resists. Her lips purse and she shakes her head.

"No. This is where I live. Go home, Justin."

CHAPTER 20: VIOLET

I can't let him keep rescuing me. I can't hand him the keys to my life and expect that he'll just take care of this. I force breath into my lungs to quell the sobs, rub the tears from my puffy eyes, and sit up on the bed, scooting a few inches away from Jayce.

He reels as if I've slapped him. "Go home?"

"Yes." I turn away from him, barely hanging on to my resolve. I'm a big girl. I created this mess by trusting the wrong person. I don't want it to spiral into an even bigger mess by trusting the wrong person again.

Jayce isn't someone who sticks and stays. Worse, he comes with a truckload of baggage he'll never shake—the curse of the media microscope.

I saw the feeding frenzy firsthand at the hospital, when they cut down Tyler with nasty speculation about a drug overdose.

Jayce reaches for my hand but I slip it away. His jaw twitches and I see a dozen emotions slide across his face—anger, frustration, maybe even want.

"You don't have a phone," he says.

"I'll figure it out." I'm not sure how yet, but I will. Neil can help.

"You have lousy security."

I let out an exasperated sigh. "You can't be the one to protect me." Time to put on my big girl panties and deal with this.

"What if … what if I want to?" Jayce's words hang between us, the most raw admission I've seen. Want. His caramel eyes are warm and pleading.

"And what happens when you don't? When you get tired of me? You can't make me your Rapunzel."

I force myself to stand and cross my arms over my chest, gathering the courage to say something I know will cut him deep.

"Thanks for coming by. As you can see, I'm OK, just a little shaken up about losing my camera gear. But I think it's best if you don't come back. I don't want a reporter following you here and blowing up my life because of you."

Jayce's jaw tightens, his eyes going dark and angry. It kills me to say it this plainly, but I think that might be the only way he'll really understand it. He has to know this isn't a game.

I'm not *playing* hard to get. I *am* hard to get.

Considering the threat of the photos, I'm pretty much impossible.

"Don't do this. Come back to my place for another night and then we can sort all of this out tomorrow. Can you give me one night, Violet?"

Jayce is pleading, and it's so tempting, like a hot cup of tea on a cold morning. I want him to feed me, cuddle me, weave his fingers through my hair and whisper secrets until dawn.

But I know better than that. The police haven't promised to do much to battle my stalker, and Jayce can't do more.

And a tiger doesn't change his stripes—I'd never heard of Justin Cameron McKittrick before my freelance assignment with *The Indie Voice,* but now that I've Googled him, I know he's a player.

And I don't want to be played.

I stride to the front door, trying to look confident about my decision even while my heart is stabbed with disappointment and loss. I pull back the chain and place my hand on the doorknob, ready to see him out.

"One night?"

I realize I still haven't answered him. "No. I know how to quit when I'm ahead." I pull open the door and turn away so he won't see the indecision and pain on my face. One night—chaste, sweet, wrapped up in a blanket burrito while we traded confidences instead of kisses. While he stroked my hair.

I hear him breathing, hear his steps carry him out of my apartment and into the hall.

I close the deadbolts behind him and listen for footfalls, which pause for a long moment and then finally descend the stairs. I hear the faint sound of the apartment lobby door opening and closing to let him out to the sidewalk, and I grimace, hoping nobody spotted him.

I open my laptop and pour a glass of wine in preparation for a long research session ahead. *This is the day,* I resolve, *that I'll figure out how to make the stalker stop.*

***

I was wrong. Friday wasn't the day. Saturday wasn't good, either. I get nowhere on the revenge porn sites. I trade emails with my little sister Katie, borrow cash from Neil, and buy a bus ticket. I'm going to fix what's broken, starting with a new driver's license.

The four-hour bus ride to Ithaca gives me plenty of time to think. For the millionth time, I'm kicking myself for shutting Jayce out of my life. Despite the fact that he's a well-documented playboy, he never once treated me like I was disposable. He acted like he really cared.

But maybe that's just an act, how he scores his women.

I'm also kicking myself for running away from the guy in the café and leaving my camera gear bag. With nothing but a backpack full of clothes and a laptop on the bus seat beside me, I feel naked without it.

I tried using Neil's phone to contact the coffee shop about my bag on Saturday, but of course it never turned up in lost and found. There's a couple thousand dollars' worth of equipment inside, a twenty-first birthday gift from my parents. I'm lucky I didn't have my laptop inside; I never packed it to take to Jayce's house.

Jayce. I forced him from my mind yesterday. Canceled my credit cards and ordered new ones. Trolled Craigslist to see if my camera gear was being sold. Called the police and left messages, begging the detective to tell me he'd made progress.

All dead ends.

The bus pulls into the Ithaca station and I call Katie from a pay phone. She picks me up in the beat-up Honda she just bought with her own money saved from years of babysitting.

"You made me leave the church social," she pouts.

"Pie?" My mouth waters. The after-church potluck is a pie-making throwdown among the church ladies. For my dad, it's a chance to round up more votes.

Katie grins and reaches behind my seat for a paper plate laden with a slice of strawberry pie and gobs of whipped cream. Even before I thank her for snagging me a piece, I stab the point with the plastic fork and swallow, in ecstasy.

"Mrs. Ernst, right?"

"She's amazing," Katie agrees. "I think she puts crack in the filling."

The bright red gelatin quivers, stuffed with the last of the season's fresh berries. Katie drives us home and I wolf down the pie.

I follow her upstairs to our old room, which she now has to herself because she's oldest. Brianna and Samantha share. Twin beds still line the walls like when we were little.

Katie sweeps most of her closet off the bed that's supposed to be mine and starts hanging her clothes up in the closet. I drop my bag and lie back on the pillow, remembering the way we used to talk at night.

The way I talked to Jayce. My cheeks heat, remembering the smell of him fresh from the shower, his spicy body wash, and damp, dark hair that curled slightly on his forehead.

"Spill it, sister," Katie orders, her back to me as she hangs up a short dress that I'm positive isn't Dad-approved.

"I told you in the email. I lost my purse. Had to come back here to get my birth certificate so I can go to the DMV tomorrow and get a new license."

"What's the rest of it?" Katie hears the evasive answer better than my parents would.

"I, ah, I'm not teaching next year. At my school. They let me go."

"What?" Katie spins around and instantly she's perched on the bed beside me, concern shining in her eyes. "You were really excited about next year!"

I scrunch my face, confessing that much is true. I can't tell her about the pictures, so I just say that my principal rearranged teaching assignments. She doesn't look convinced.

Our old chocolate Lab's gruff barking alerts me that the rest of my family's home from church.

"Bree and Sam are going to be so surprised to see you! I didn't even tell Mom and Dad you were coming. Mom's making ham for dinner, and I'm supposed to make rolls. You want to help me start the dough?" This is Katie trying to take my mind off the loss of my job, and I'm grateful for the distraction.

I follow her downstairs, eager to hug my little sisters, but my heart plummets. Standing in the foyer talking to my father is a tall, dark-haired suit. He turns and his piercing blue eyes crucify me.

Brady.

CHAPTER 21: JAYCE

I don't care that she kicked me out.

I don't care that I can't reach her.

Right now, all I care about is finding that bastard and beating him to a strawberry pulp.

My four crappy leads are down to three after talking to Corey.

One, the flower delivery guy. Two, a barista from a coffee shop near her place. Three, a clerk from a bodega. Because I don't have anything that really describes them, I start with what I *do* know—the stalker's phone number.

I put all of the numbers and texts that I snagged from Violet's old phone into my computer to figure out which ones matter. The most threatening texts that show the stalker is watching her are blocked numbers, but I want to believe that the stalker might have sent her other messages from another phone.

Maybe he hoped she'd reply?

From a few dozen phone numbers, I can tell who's texting Violet most. I move them to the top of my list.

I look at what each text says. Some are limp-dick come-ons and some are specific—too specific—about exactly what they want to do to Violet. I move those to the top of the pile.

Three numbers stand out. I try reverse lookup for the numbers. There's a personal trainer in Wilmington, North Carolina and a real estate agent in Taos, New Mexico. The last number has a New York prefix and is for something called "EKH Enterprises."

I make the call. "Hi. I got a call from this number. I'm wondering if this is a business line?"

"Yes, we are business." The older woman's heavily accented voice is Asian, I think.

"Where are you located?" I pause. "Your address?"

"Six and A."

"You're in the East Village, right? East Sixth and A Street?" My pulse pounds. That's on the corner near Violet's apartment. What's the name of your business?"

"Easy Market," the woman says. "What you need?"

"I'll come by and get it."

"We closed."

I look at the time and it's ten after eleven. Have I seriously been at this for three hours? The hunch in my shoulders and grit in my eyes confirms it.

"OK, I'll come by tomorrow. Thanks." I hang up, sure this woman's not sending the texts, but maybe an employee? A relative?

I snoop a bit more online and peg two coffee shops within a couple of blocks of Violet's. I wish I'd asked her which one she lost her bag at, but at least I remember the name of the florist from the card in her bouquet. I look it up, and it's on the Lower East Side.

Violet might shut me out, but I'll be damned if she's shutting me down. Tomorrow, it'll be my turn to find *him*. Just like he texted Violet: ready or not, here I come.

***

Pictures of Violet haunt my dreams.

Not memories of the redheaded girl who whispered secrets in this bed. Not the sweet, even wholesome girl who defies every type I thought I had.

No, it's the pictures of her—bound and wanting, stripped of clothes and raw with emotion on that *Sexy Bitches* site—that wake me before dawn, drenched in sweat and tangled in my sheets.

I've had no rest, no real sleep, just the image of Violet writhing on a couch, her arms pinned above her head by an electrical cord, fear and desire flushing her cheeks until her freckles nearly disappear.

I give in and grab my tablet. Self-loathing washes over me as I find her photos on the website and look.

And look. And look. I imagine it's me she's bending to, not this unseen photographer. I imagine I'm the one tying her up, dominating her body as her spirit rises to match mine with lust and intensity.

I thought I could flush the photos from my mind by looking, like a vaccine to inoculate me from their power, but looking only makes it worse. The fire in my chest burns hotter.

I study her curves—the outline of her pale breasts and berry-pink nipples, the crest of her hip and taper of her thigh. The way the cord bites into the skin of her forearms. I imagine the same skin between my teeth, tormented by nips and bites, soothed by strokes from my tongue.

My cock throbs as I stare at the pictures, hating myself for invading her privacy like this. It's different looking when I'm home alone, rather than soothing her with my touch and trying not to stare at the site on my phone.

Fuck it. I zoom in. Her navel dips and curves slightly at the top. Her sheer panties reveal the outline of her cleft, her thighs parted and beckoning.

She told me it's called revenge porn, and I don't know which word makes me feel more disgusting—the fact that I'm looking at porn of a girl I want *and actually know,* or the fact that this photo, or at least its public disclosure, is intended for revenge.

I can't wrap my head around why anyone would want revenge against her. She's too sweet, too fragile. I flip to the next picture and my teeth clench. Her eyes are closed in this one, her red hair cascading over white shoulders flecked with more freckles.

I fist my cock and tug. My finger flicks the tablet to see the third picture, with Violet's green eyes burning hot, her lips parted. The lines of her ribs are visible, as if her chest is rising with rapid hot breaths, panting.

I'm panting. My balls draw up tight, ready for the release that I know will come in a few more strokes. I close my eyes against this invasion of Violet, but her image is still there in my mind, burned into the back of my eyelids. It morphs from the bound girl in the photo to the girl I know. I see her face turn to me in bed, softened with sleep, and she says my real name. *Justin.*

Her lips form the word in my mind, lips that could be parted and fixed around my cock the way she teased my finger. Her tongue brushed the rough pad of my finger, and I imagine what it could do to the head of my cock.

I explode.

Prickly heat creeps up my shoulders as my hand finishes what her photographs started. The white stream slicks my belly as my body pulses with heat and hunger.

Fuck. *This is not right.* I'm just as bad as her stalker, using her pictures without her permission for my own pleasure. I toss the tablet on a pillow and get up to shower the sticky mess away.

She doesn't want me. I'm an idiot, jacking off to a girl who doesn't even fucking want me. When she told me to go home—practically threw me out of her apartment—I didn't believe it at first.

She pushed me away when I could have given her anything—a safe place to stay, a new phone, even new camera equipment. She has nothing but a barely-there roommate. No security. No phone. And the stalker's still out there.

I know I sound like a million guys when I say I don't understand women. But even if it means a shitload more trouble, I *want* to understand Violet.

I step out of the shower, wrap a towel around my waist and start coffee. I hate myself for leaving her alone and want to hate her for pushing me away. But two things she said to me forced me out of her place.

One: Rapunzel.

I don't know why we got going about that stupid fairy tale, but she said I can't protect her forever. Like she's so sure I'll eventually lose interest and cut her loose.

I drag a razor over my face and watch myself carefully in the mirror. *I'm not that guy.* Am I? My track record says otherwise. Of course I eventually lose interest in the groupies. No strings means I never have to have "the talk" when I do.

But they're nothing compared to Violet. The tall girl who moves as gracefully as a deer, who isn't made-up and blow-dried and wrapped in a push-up bra. Not that I mind those. It's just that Violet has a subtlety and grace that speaks to me, louder than all of the fake lashes and platform heels that follow our band at every show.

I rinse my face, brush back my still-damp hair with a few strokes and scowl at my shirtless reflection. I'm working on defining my shoulders more when I lift, but even pumping doesn't bring me the peace I felt when I held Violet.

Two: Reporters.

The other reason Violet shut me out is the media. She said a reporter might see me and ruin her life, and I get it. The gossip rags were halfway to ruining Tyler's reputation when Gavin and Stella turned the tables on the groupie who was telling lies about Tyler.

It could be far worse for Violet. If the paparazzi connect us publicly and learn her name, it's only a matter of time before they Google Violet Chase and find out more.

Shit. I need to know how much more is out there.

I need to find this bastard before he finds her.

CHAPTER 22: VIOLET

A sharp, predatory smile stretches across Brady's face and he opens his arms. I lean back on the stairway wall, six steps from the bottom, and cling to the banister for support.

My father smiles up at me, a gleaming smile, a politician's smile, but unlike Brady's, his eyes hold true warmth. "Violet, sweetheart! I didn't know you were coming home!"

Katie swoops past me down the stairs with the save. "She wanted it to be a surprise. Let's see what Mom needs in the kitchen, Daddy, and give Vi and Brady a minute."

My father's eyes flick from me to Brady, aware of our breakup last month but with no inkling of what's happened since. As far as he knows, it was a mutual parting at the end of my school year, and then I flew off to Europe to take pictures. I haven't been home since.

Dad nods and follows Katie, leaving me to face Brady alone.

I force my rubbery legs to descend the last few steps but stay wide of Brady's reach until he finally drops his hands.

"How. Could. You." My voice is shaking with rage, pain and fear, but I hope all he hears is the rage.

"No need to be dramatic, babe," he chides me. "We're all adults here."

"We're not anything."

"Of course. We parted ways amicably. Our relationship had run its course. We're still very good friends." He parrots this as if it's a press release.

"Don't feed me that garbage. Friends don't—" I can't bring myself to even whisper the atrocity he committed. "The pictures. You did it."

"That's ridiculous." Brady shrugs, confirming his guilt simply by knowing what I'm talking about. "I'd never date someone who'd put herself in such a morally compromising position."

"*You* put me in that position," I hiss. "You took advantage of me!"

"Or perhaps I left you when I realized that you didn't share my traditional values," he says lightly, as if he's asking for cream, no sugar, with his tea.

It's a threat, and it cuts deep. There's so much I know about him—his kinks, his little pornographic obsessions—that he never hid well when we were dating. I think he wanted me to know, to test me, to see what I'd be willing to tolerate.

He rocks back on his spotless dress shoes. "Have you ever noticed, Vi, that a news story really isn't a story without a picture?"

I shake my head, my stomach churning as I sense where he's going with this.

"Call it insurance." The hiss in the last word slithers over my body. "I'd like to believe you have the good sense to keep private things private. And if you don't, well, pictures play better than words."

Brady arches his brow and the message is clear: I might have stories, but he has evidence.

I grasp the newel post at the base of the stairs as it sinks in. If I threaten his moral high ground, he'll cut me off at the knees with a scandal. Instead of just being seen by lechers trolling porn sites, my pictures could be splashed across papers and regular websites, nipples carefully blurred.

"But my *job*. Why?" I square my shoulders and face Brady, my wrinkled shorts from the long bus ride in stark contrast to his suit and monogrammed shirt. Even in sandals, I'm nearly eye level with him.

His lip curls and I see those white teeth again. "I thought you should see what a well-placed message can do. To you or to someone you love."

The subtext points directly to my father. It's one thing for a potential U.S. congressman to have a wild child, yet another for him to routinely hold her up as a model of family values and righteous upbringing, a product of public school, church youth groups, and a stable heterosexual marriage.

"Get out," I growl. "Get out of my parents' house *now.*"

Brady tuts. "That's not playing nice, babe."

Katie blows through the door from the kitchen back into the foyer. "Bad time?" She looks from me to Brady and back at me, and some psychic sister thing actually *works* between us. "Brady, are you being mean to Violet after she came all the way to visit us?"

"Of course not, Katie." Brady's voice is smooth and rich, the oily hiss gone. "What makes you say that?"

"Well, Violet looks like she wants to puke all over you. And you're her ex-boyfriend. And you two have been whispering out here so I can't hear a thing from the kitchen." Katie frowns at him and then crosses to the front door, opening it. "I want to hang out with my sister, and I'm pretty sure she doesn't want to hang out with you. Go home and bug Dad at his office tomorrow."

Brady opens his mouth to protest and then snaps it shut. "It's good that we had this talk, Violet." He edges toward the door, an expression like he's caught a whiff of sewer. "I'm glad we have an understanding."

"See ya, loser!" Katie calls as Brady crosses our front walk to his car. She slams the door and I smother her with a hug.

"You were magnificent," I tell her, giggling at first. But my wound-up crazy feelings start spiraling, bubbling up like a geyser, and the giggles turn to gasps, then sobs. When the waterworks come on, Katie grabs my arm and propels me upstairs to our room.

"Shit. What did I say?"

I give her a sharp look for cursing.

"Sue me. He's a jerk. You broke up with him—way too late, if you ask me—but he still acts like he can come around here anytime, like he's one of *us.*"

I nod. When we were dating, and particularly when we were in public, Brady *did* act like one of our family. Now I wonder how much of that was for show or simply to curry favor with my father.

"Also, he's being super-creepy. He's way too nice, telling me he likes my hair and stuff. It's gross. I *so* don't want your sloppy seconds."

Katie makes a face like Brady is a used Kleenex and laughter conquers my tears.

CHAPTER 23: JAYCE

I sip a cup of coffee and watch the Easy Market's opening routine across the street. So far this morning there's been a steady stream of traffic through its doors.

Behind the counter, I spot the graying, Asian woman whom I think I talked to last night. A younger Asian man is stocking shelves, and a white guy's out front setting up boxes of fruit, racks of magazines and buckets of flowers.

I cross the street and confront him. "Hey, you got a minute?"

"What do you want?" The thirty-something man squints at me, his slender face pinched and grouchy. I think he needs my coffee more than I do.

"Curious if you've seen this girl before." I show him my phone, where a zoomed-in version of one of Violet's revenge porn images shows just her face and her blazing hair. I cropped her naked body out of the picture.

Recognition flickers on his face but he drops his gaze, picks up another bucket of flowers and shakes his head. "Nope."

"You sure? Because she lives around here." I point diagonally across the street. "I'm pretty sure you'd notice a hot chick like that. Unless you don't like girls."

He takes my bait and straightens. "You saying I don't like girls? Of *course* I notice her."

"You recognize her."

"I—" he realizes I've caught his lie. "What are you, a cop?"

I decide against impersonating a public safety officer. For now. "No, just a friend of hers. You see her around, don't you?"

"Yeah, she's in here couple times a week. Nice girl, polite. Hot, if you're a leg man."

"Are you?"

"I'm a boob man." He gestures to a magazine rack. "You want some of the second-shelf stuff?" I realize he's pointing me to the porn.

"No. But I think you've seen that girl." I use my height to get in his face. "Online."

He curses and goes back to arranging the flower buckets. Stargazer lilies catch my eye.

"You sent her a message, didn't you?" He still won't look at me. "Look, I saw the number for this store on her phone. I know you sent her a text."

"You know nothing."

"I know stalking is a crime."

"Stalking?" he cackles. "I don't have time for that shit. I was just paying her a compliment. I didn't think she'd be a porno girl."

"That's the thing. She isn't." My jaw ticks and my shoulders are tense, ready to spring on him the minute he admits it. I'm begging this man to tell me more, something that I could channel into fist-pounding rage.

"You've got nothing on me. I sent her some texts. So what? She's the one spreading her legs. I'm just kickin' back and enjoyin' it."

I kick the flower bucket in front of him, spraying water and lilies across the sidewalk. He lets loose a string of filth and I take off, angry at myself for letting him get to me like that.

When I slow down a few blocks later, cold sweat prickles my back. I'm a fucking moron. If he *is* the stalker—and I still don't know the truth—will he retaliate against Violet?

I march back to my condo and make more coffee. Violet's apparently unplugged my brain because I'm acting like a Neanderthal instead of using what I've got.

A handful of platinum cards. Access to pretty much anything. Influence in the right places. A concierge service, car service, doorman. Everything at my beck and call.

Except her.

What does the stalker have? Nothing but his anonymity, and I intend to strip him of it using every resource in my fucking arsenal.

I take my laptop and coffee to the terrace. By the time I've finished my second cup, I'm six pages deep in Google's search hits, and I know a hell of a lot more about Violet Chase.

The first part is easy. She's a fantastic photographer, and her online portfolio is stunning. I see a mix of photojournalism-style street scenes, a few formal portraits, and a boatload of black and white nudes like the ones in her bedroom. They're sexy as hell but not pornographic, more about form and texture, curves and skin and muscle and shadow, strength and sinuous motion.

Her website doesn't tell me much more except that she earned a bachelor's degree in fine art with a teaching certification. Her name pops up on a Brooklyn junior high school's website about a student art show, listing her as the teacher sponsoring the exhibit.

I also find her name in a political article about school funding, but it doesn't list Violet Chase as a teacher. She's the eldest daughter of Bradford Chase, a conservative state senator who's now running for congress.

"My father has been a tremendous supporter of public education standards and funding, and he's seen the effects of good and bad decisions firsthand with all of us girls," she told the reporter.

Several more search hits reveal that Violet spent a ton of time campaigning for her father and another guy, Brady Keller, last summer. I find a video clip of her speaking at a town hall meeting and I hear the slight nervous tremble in her voice. The blood rushes south in my body and my shorts tighten.

Even her *voice* affects me. Shit.

I switch to an image search and see her photography and pictures of her at a couple of campaign stops with her father. Brady Keller is there, grasping her arm, a gesture of ownership.

My teeth clench as I read the caption. They're a couple. And this guy's angling for more than just Bradford Chase's daughter—he wants his seat in the state senate. I hate him on sight, his neatly trimmed dark hair and tailored suit, his gleaming smile full of teeth.

Is this the ex who exposed her? The one who took her pictures and posted them online? I seethe as I scroll through more political pictures, Violet and Brady together, Violet and her father.

Then I find *her*—the photos of Violet, bound and posted on the revenge porn site.

It's worse than Violet realizes, because they're spreading further. I copy and paste ten URLs for different sites where these pictures appear.

She might not be Rapunzel, and I'm no prince, but a visceral need to protect her, to vanquish these demons and guard her honor, overwhelms me. I jerk my phone from my pocket, search for a number, and dial.

"Leverda, Maloney and Probus," a chipper voice answers. "How may I direct your call?"

"Gus Carson, please." I clear my throat against the rising bile and force my eyes away from Violet's pictures again. "Tell him it's Jayce McKittrick."

"Is he expecting your call?" The receptionist asks.

"No, but he's going to want to take this." It's just after nine in the morning and if my old college friend doesn't pick up, I'm going to harass the shit out of him until he does.

"Jayce? Dude, haven't talked to you in ages! What are you up to?" Gus's smile travels through the phone.

He's a big black guy, a couple years older than me. We lifted together in college, locked in an unspoken contest for who'd outlast the other in the weight room, even when the rest of his football team had packed it in for the day.

"Not on tour right now, so I'm in the city. Just rehearsals and shit. You still lifting?" Gus was a kickass football player, and he was smart. He knew he'd never be big enough to turn pro, so he milked his scholarship for all it was worth and got a law degree. He also got a sweet job in New York, the only black associate among more than a hundred white guys.

With his size and attitude, I doubt they intimidate him.

"Here and there. Crazy hours, you know, but I'll bet it's the same for you." Gus pauses for a moment. "I guess this isn't a social call?"

I take a deep breath. "Yeah. It's a tough one. I've got this— friend—and she's got some pictures up online. Needs to get them taken down. You do that stuff, right?"

"That's my division. Cyberlaw. The senior partners act like it's not a thing, but our team's got a ton of work. You want to have your *friend* come talk to me?"

I hear the taunt in that word but don't rise to his bait. "That's going to be tough. She's…" I struggle with the right way to describe what's happening with Violet, and the fact that she doesn't even want to see me. "She's pretty embarrassed. But I think if we could show her how to get her pictures deleted, she'd want it."

"I can't issue takedown demands without her backing it up," Gus says. "But if you want to hire us for, say, research, we can at least get started and figure out what needs to happen."

"Let's do it."

"What's her name?"

"Violet Chase." I give him a few more details about her and email him the links to the sites I've found. It kills me that another guy's going to be looking at her body, but I trust Gus.

"She your girl?" Gus has always had a sixth sense about what's left unsaid. It makes him a killer lawyer and a damn annoying friend.

"Not yet."

Gus's rich laugh bursts from the phone. "Look at you. Wanting someone you can't have. That's a first, huh?"

"Fuck off."

"I'll take that as a yes."

I bite back another curse and focus on the other legal issue nagging me. "I also need a referral. Someone in entertainment law who can go over a contract with me. And I don't need to tell you this needs to be quiet."

"I can make an introduction. We've got a guy upstairs I respect. Quiet but wicked smart."

I tell Gus that I'll messenger over the contract I got from Viper Records for review, and a retainer deposit to cover both cases. Gus pencils in tomorrow afternoon for a meeting with Violet.

Now I just have to get her to come with me.

CHAPTER 24: VIOLET

My family is smotheringly nice, especially since my breakup with Brady, Dad's wannabe Number One Son.

They *ooh* and *aah* over my Europe pictures on my laptop, and Katie squeals when she sees a VIIIM graffiti I found in Paris. At dinner, Mom tells us about teaching art to senior citizens, Sam declares she's become a vegetarian after doing dissections in biology, and Brianna gloats about making it onto the varsity volleyball team.

It's so normal.

Like a black cloud isn't hanging over me.

We make it through ham and green beans and rolls and salad, through tea and cake (A two-dessert day! Winning!), and through perennial arguments about schedules and chores without mentioning Brady once.

I do dishes side-by-side with Sam and get a lecture about the revolting ingredients in chicken nuggets. As I climb the stairs back to my old room, I think I've dodged a bullet.

My father clears his throat from his office under the stairs. "Violet?"

I pause. I can't pretend I didn't hear him. "Coming."

I descend the stairs and pause in the doorway.

"Pull the door shut," my father says, his eyes still fixed on a file in front of him. "We need to talk."

Even though I'm twenty-three, I feel like I'm sixteen and facing a firing squad for breaking curfew or pulling a C in chemistry. I sit in the wooden chair facing his desk. He's ensconced in a tufted leather monstrosity that my sisters and I call The Chair of Doom.

When Dad sits in The Chair of Doom, you shut up and listen.

You take orders.

You don't talk back.

After a long moment of silence, he closes the file and looks up, his wide-set green eyes identical to mine. I can see the strain of juggling a family, a legislative calendar, fund-raising, and a campaign in the fine lines around his eyes.

"So what are your plans for the summer?"

It's a question I didn't expect, and I fumble for an answer. "More photography, I guess. I'm working on that photo project about VIIIM, and I got the new shots in Paris, so I think I have enough to try to publish. I'm just trying to get an interview with the artist."

My father tents his fingers on his desk. "None of this work is … lewd, is it?"

I scrunch my face. It wouldn't matter if it was. "No, Dad. It's nice stuff. Most of it's happy. Like a picture of a girl finding a flower in a sidewalk crack. The words were, 'Find your moment.'"

"But it's vandalism, Violet. Are you sure you want to hold up something like that and call it *art?*"

"It *is* art."

"But it's your name. Our name. If you publish photos, you're pretty much endorsing an illegal activity."

I huff. "Dad. I'm not saying it's OK to deal drugs or shoot people. But I *am* saying this is art, and it deserves attention. And linking my name to that is worth it."

"I just want you to consider the fact that you're linking our name to everything you do." Dad filters through a pile of papers at the far side of his desk and I go cold, imagining how *our* name could be linked to my pictures online.

"You know I hate to pry, Violet, but can't you just work this thing out with Brady?"

I snort a laugh. He *loves* to pry. "What?"

"I was hoping now that school is out, you'd campaign with us. Do the events like you did last summer."

"I don't think that's a good idea." It's the most terrible, horrible idea.

"Violet, it's a great idea. You're a perfect bridge between the two of us, and you're picking up the demographics where we struggle the most—women, young people, and teachers."

"I don't ... I don't want to campaign anymore."

My dad's face is etched with disbelief as if I've told him I'm not a fan of breathing. "But you were so good at it last summer! People just loved you."

"And I was terrified the whole time. And now it'll be awkward, having to be around Brady the whole time."

"Not if you don't break up. Not if your little trip to Europe was just that—a little trip. Give him another chance, Vi. For me. You can dump him after the first Tuesday in November for all I care, but right now, we need this storyline."

Storyline? I shake my head, almost too angry to speak. "And what about what I need? I'm not dating him just because it's politically expedient. Brady's a jerk, Dad. He was a jerk to me and he's being a jerk now, and he doesn't deserve someone like you sponsoring him, just so he can go jerk the Fifty-Eighth District around."

Dad glares at me. "You can get away with saying that in this office, Violet. But nowhere else, you understand me? Nowhere."

"I get it. No telling tales out of school." My voice is sullen. I've devolved into that sulky sixteen-year-old who hates getting lectured and hates being told what to do.

"Then we understand each other." Dad's voice switches from pushy parent to smooth politician so fast it baffles me. "As a compromise, I won't press you about making things right with Brady if you can commit to four town halls." He slides the paper he'd been looking for across his desk.

Each campaign stop is neatly labeled with my presumptive appearance. *Every stinking one* has some connection to a school or education.

"I can't." My voice wavers. "I can't do it."

"You're my secret weapon, Violet." Now my father's voice is pleading, conciliatory. "You can speak from experience about how we need to transform education, and how funding has trickled down to the classroom level. I need you in on this."

"I told you I can't."

"You will."

"If it were just a matter of wills, Dad, you'd win. You always win. You will it, and it happens." I stand, sick to death of The Chair of Doom and my dad's demands, and my voice rises. "But there's nothing you can do about the fact that I'm not a teacher anymore, so I *can't* be your special guest speaker. I can't be your squeaky clean marionette and you can't pull the strings."

"You quit your job?" My father is rarely surprised, but this did the trick. "How could you do that without even consulting me first?"

"What? Like I didn't check the poll numbers before I broke up with Brady?" I turn on my sarcasm full blast. "I hope it doesn't mess up your campaign too much. You'll have to write a new speech for a different daughter."

I turn to storm out of the office, but my dad's too-calm voice halts me.

"I'll get you a new job."

"No." I say, still facing the door to go.

"I could give your old principal a call, see what your options are."

"No!" I yelp. God help me if Principal Dash told my father the real reason for my firing. "I'm an adult. I don't want you pulling strings again. I have to do this myself."

***

Dad's gone to the office and my mother's out at her volunteer thing by the time I get up the next morning. Katie drives me to the DMV and then the bank to withdraw enough cash until my new debit card comes.

Some of that cash goes immediately to buying a new phone, and at the store Katie talks me into an argyle phone case. At least I can keep the number from the new phone Jayce gave me—the stalker doesn't have that.

Our last stop is a local favorite burger bar, and I suck down half of a malted vanilla shake before Katie begins her interrogation.

"Who's the guy?"

"What?"

"The guy you keep thinking about. Don't say there isn't one, because I know that look. Same as when you started dating Brady. Same as when you went out with that guy Craig."

"Greg," I correct her. But I can't deny she's onto me. What kept me tossing and turning last night wasn't my argument with my father—it was the look on Jayce's face when I forced him out of my apartment.

He only wanted to help me. Despite his man-whore reputation, that counts for something. It counts a lot.

"So spill," Katie says. "What's really going on, why you came home?"

I take a massive bite of burger and chew thoroughly to give myself time to invent a couple of good answers. But Katie's sharp. She'll see through them.

"His name is Justin." That's not a lie.

"And?"

"And he's a … musician. I met him through Neil." All true, but maybe not quite. He's a *rock star* and I met him because Neil hooked me up with a freelance gig to *take pictures of his famous band.*

"So what's wrong with him?" She steals one of my fries and dredges it in ketchup. "Too flaky? I mean, I don't really see you with a musician."

"He's not flaky," I answer quickly. "He's … solid. Like, reliable. Protective."

Katie snorts. "Are we talking about a boyfriend or a bike helmet? He sounds boring."

"Not the littlest bit." Jayce might be protective, but there's that thin edge of danger that hangs with him too, a sense that he could snap if he was pushed too far.

Maybe I pushed him too far. I pushed him away because I couldn't bear to let him rescue me one more time. I didn't want him to see me weak, to feel obligated to protect me when what I really want is for him to want me.

Katie eyes me thoughtfully. "Bring him home with you next time, K?"

I shake my head. "I think I screwed it up. I told him to go away and leave me alone."

"Sounds like third grade." Katie waves her hand. "Justin's not going to listen to that. If he wants you, he won't care what you told him. Only that you changed your mind."

But Katie is wrong. She drops me at the bus stop in the afternoon, and I dial his number three times during the bus ride home.

He doesn't pick up once.

CHAPTER 25: JAYCE

I stomp up the old warehouse stairs to Tyler's loft in a thunderous mood, daring just one person to put their toe out of line, one guy to come at me.

After I got off the phone with Gus, I spent a good slice of my day trying to find Violet. No luck—she didn't answer when I buzzed her apartment, none of her neighbors answered either, and I didn't see her in any stores or coffee shops while I walked around the East Village.

But I found the coffee shop where she lost her camera bag, just a few blocks from her apartment. I showed the barista her photo and he recognized her.

I pressed him for details about what happened when a man approached Violet.

"She freaked out and left, and the guy did too," the barista told me.

"Did he go after her?"

"No, he was too slow. She slammed out of here like a bat outta hell, but he kind of just wandered out." The barista shrugged.

"So did he take her bag? The square gray gear bag she was carrying?"

"The one on the floor? No, man. Some other guy picked that up. I tried to stop him, you know, save it in lost and found for her, but he jammed out of here before I could even get around the counter."

I grilled the barista about what each guy looked like. Both were white and thirty-ish, but the guy at the table had a paunch, while the guy who took her bag was slender, with longer brown hair.

It's not enough. And now I'm questioning whether the stalker approached her in the coffee shop, or if the stalker was the guy who stole her camera bag. And how did either of these guys manage to touch Violet a few days ago?

After the coffee shop, I even looked up Violet's roommate, Neil. She told me he was her connection to *The Indie Voice*, where she got her first freelance gig to shoot Tattoo Thief, so I went to the paper's office.

Neil told me she hasn't been home since Sunday, but he wouldn't say where she is. Said he doesn't know, but I don't believe him. I raised my voice, got in his face, but he just scowled and reminded me I was drawing attention.

Something Violet doesn't want at all.

I push open Tyler's loft door and hear dishes clanking in the kitchen. He's cleaning up, and I'm the first one here for practice. Maybe he can get my head straight, suck some of the poison out of my mood.

I grab a bottle of water from the fridge and perch on a barstool without greeting him.

Tyler wipes his hands on a dishtowel. "Who peed in your beer?" He pulls an exaggerated pouty face and I can't not laugh. Dammit.

"It's been a rough day. Walked all over the fucking East Village and I can't find Violet."

His eyebrows peak with interest. "I heard they have some newfangled thing called a telephone." Tyler's words are still a little thick since his tongue is healing, but I understand him well enough.

I shake my head. "She lost her phone. And either she's not answering her door, or she's really not there. Her roommate won't tell me. Asshole."

"So what are you going to do about it? Because squeezing that water bottle until it explodes is not going to make either of us happy."

I glance down at my white knuckles and force myself to relax my grip. I screw off the top and gulp down half of it, wishing it were something stronger. "I don't know. I've got to find her. She's got this freaky stalker, and I think I found a way to help, but I need to talk to her."

"So, Shelly and Teal are out?"

"Long gone."

"And Violet's in?"

I shake my head in frustration. "Not by a long shot. Fuck. I walked her home from the hospital after she came to take pictures of you there, and she got under my skin."

"Hate to break it to you, but she got under your skin *way* before the hospital. That day she came to practice with Stella and took pictures of us, you couldn't take your eyes off her." He pauses and cocks his head. "She's different, isn't she?"

I finish off the water before answering. "What do you mean?"

"Like, she's not your usual. Groupie. Easy. More tits than brains."

I'm not sure whether to be offended. "You saying she's not hot?"

"Hell, no. She's got legs for miles. But she doesn't seem like—"

"I got it, Ty." I cut him off. "She's not another bimbo. Check. Which means she's probably too damn smart to go out with me."

"That's not what I meant."

"Fuck you."

Tyler whirls around and grabs my shirt, using the three or four inches in height he's got on me to really get in my face. "Take it back. You got woman problems. I get it. But don't take it out on me."

My adrenaline spikes and I want to hit somebody, but not Tyler. Not my best friend, the one who's saved my ass as many times as I've saved his. "Fine." I add, quieter, "Sorry."

Tyler drops my shirt and steps back. "Look. Took me forever to get shit sorted out with Stella. But once it works, it's worth it. You gotta get a grip and figure out how to *be the man*. Not the frickin' Tattoo Thief playboy. Not the one dripping in groupies. You figure that shit out, and you'll actually have a shot with this girl."

I take a breath, feeling my adrenaline wane. "Promise?"

"No guarantees. The difference is that groupies come to you, so they're easy. But now you're going to Violet. It'll be hard. You've got to win her. Show her you're worth it."

I shake my head and pick up my guitar. "I have no idea how."

"Start by not being an asshole." Tyler laughs and crosses the loft to our practice space. "Want to see something I've been fooling around with?" He straps on his bass guitar and plucks a fast chord progression that actually sounds awesome.

I immediately feel the beat and a melody bursts into my brain. I listen to a few more bars, then add my own from my guitar, playing against his chords and listening for his changes. I love how Tyler gives me space to move around in a song, as if his notes are the scaffolding and I can build anything I want off of them.

We jam until the song plays itself out.

"Damn, that was hot." I grin at him. "Since when are you writing songs?"

Tyler dismisses the question with a wave. "I'm not writing songs. Just chords, maybe a little melody here and there. I don't have the words, usually, though I did a song for Stella that I'm hoping she'll be into. Gonna show it to her tonight."

I have him play it for me and it's damn good. It takes my mind off Violet and refocuses me on the most important thing in my life—music.

I glance at the door but the rest of the band still isn't here. They're late, and I'll give Dave shit about that since he's usually the drill sergeant who bitches when any of us show up late.

"I want to tell you something, but I don't want the other guys to know. Not yet." I watch Tyler carefully and the seriousness in my tone makes him sit on a stool near me.

He nods for me to continue, a promise to keep my confidence.

"I got approached by a guy from Viper Records. Darren Bishop. Says he's interested in helping me explore a solo career."

"You told him to go take a fucking long walk off a short pier, right?" Tyler asks, but my expression arrests him. "Right?"

I shake my head. "I told him I'd talk."

"So then tell him to fuck off when you talk to him."

"I already talked to him, Tyler."

"What? We're a *band*, Jayce, and in case you haven't noticed, we're one of the top bands in the whole country right now. You walking would torpedo all of that, kill our next album."

"And what did Gavin's disappearing act do? It didn't exactly help, Ty." His brow is creased, so I push on. "And Dave's all over me like a bad rash, giving me shit for being two minutes late and then not even showing up on time today."

Tyler glances at the clock on the wall and the guys are twenty minutes behind. "We can work that stuff out. I put this band together and I don't want you to take it apart."

"But what's more important? The band or the music?"

"The band," Tyler says, his mouth set.

"And I say it's the music. I want to play with you. Hell, that jam we just did was the best part of my day so far. But I'm not going to keep playing with my friends if we can't make the right music. Gavin acts like he can do no wrong with his songs, but I don't want to play backup for fucking Gavin Slater for the rest of my life."

Timing is everything, especially if you're in a band. So it should be no surprise that *this* is the moment Gavin makes his appearance in Tyler's loft for practice.

***

My comment hangs in the air like a filthy cloud all through practice, though no one acknowledges it. Tyler covers for me, of course, but Gavin's eyes shoot daggers.

Dave's all business, not apologizing for being late, but turning up the pressure as we run through the set, demanding we get sharper and cleaner so we'll be ready to hit LA on Friday.

It's coming too soon. I blow out of practice the minute we put down our instruments, skipping weights again even though the other guys are lifting. I have to find Violet.

I walk to her place to skip the cross-town rush hour traffic and focus on what I know.

I have the name of the school where she last taught—but she was fired, and I doubt they'd tell me anything. Her father's in politics, and I could track his office phone number down, but then what do I say?

"Hello, sir. You don't know me, but I've been jacking off to your daughter's naked pictures on the Internet. Do you know how I could contact her?"

Not fucking likely.

My best shot is probably still her apartment, as much as it kills me to know that her stalker could be hanging around. I round a corner on Avenue A and catch a glimpse of flame-red hair on a tall girl with a backpack.

No. It couldn't be. I start jogging, then break into a run. She's a block and a half ahead of me, and she turns the corner on East

Fifth. I'm sprinting, afraid she'll reach her apartment before I reach her.

I turn the corner and see her plunge her key in the lock. It's definitely Violet. My heart's racing with need and relief and some other emotion that freaks me out.

Violet pushes open the door and slips inside.

"Wait! Violet! Wait!" My legs carry me the last half-block to the glass-front door. I see her inside climbing the stairs, so I slam my hand on the glass.

She flinches, then slowly turns, a haunted look marring her face.

"I need you," I pant, "I need you to talk to me!" *Fuck it. I just need you.* "Please," I say loudly enough to carry through the glass. "Let me in. Give me a minute."

I take my Yankees cap off and wipe the sweat from my face, but this movement looks like it scares her even more than my hand on the glass. She yanks the door open.

"Don't do that! Someone will see you," she hisses, and lets me inside. "Don't you get that you can't just show up here? What if someone sees you?"

I think she means a photographer, not the stalker, but the main thing is, I'm in. I'm standing in the lobby of her apartment, my heart slamming against my ribs, not because of running but because I've finally found her.

"I'm sorry," I start, recalling Tyler's sage advice: *don't be an ass-hole.* "I have to talk to you."

CHAPTER 26: VIOLET

I hold up a finger. "Wait. Don't say anything yet." I start up the stairs to my apartment, glancing back when Jayce doesn't immediately follow. The eye contact seems to shock him into motion. My heart beats hard with everything I need to say to him.

I unlock my apartment and listen for Neil. Not home, as usual. I hear Jayce close and lock the door behind me, his breath heavy from running.

"I'll be back in a sec," I say, and race to the bathroom. I don't really need to pee, but I need a moment to gather my wits now that he's here. In my apartment, even after I sent him away.

I practiced the speech for the last four hours on the bus ride home, but it's all garbled in my brain. All I can do is wash my hands, run a brush through my wild hair that's gone even curlier with the humidity, and hope.

Hope I haven't ruined this.

Hope he'll understand.

When I emerge, he's still standing in my living room, rooted to a spot by the front door. I take a few steps toward him, and his face is unreadable.

"I went home for a few days," I start. "Had to get my birth certificate to get a new driver's license."

Jayce takes a step toward me and I stand my ground, but he doesn't reach for me, and doesn't come close enough to touch.

"I have to handle this myself. I can't expect you to be the one to rescue me or protect me. It's too much."

"I told you, I wanted to."

I hear the past tense and my hope fades. I shake my head. "I'll figure it out. I found an organization that deals with revenge porn. The woman who created it was a victim herself. I sent her an email."

"An email," he repeats.

"Yes. And I got a new phone, and cash to last me until my new debit and credit cards come. I'm fine, really."

"So you don't need me." His tone is flat and cold, and I sense he's already retreating to the door.

"Why did you come here, Justin?"

His real name makes his eyes spark. "I came for you."

"For me, or because of the stalker?"

"Fuck the stalker. For you."

"I don't like you cursing."

His mouth opens and closes in surprise, like I've just told him I don't like sex. "Sorry. I mean, *forget* the stalker."

I smile to acknowledge his effort. He looks shy, more unsure of himself now. "But that's not why I had to see you. I mean, it's a little part of it, I might have found a way to help, but mostly, I just wanted to talk to you. To be with you."

It's clumsy, but it's real. A thrill rushes through me like I've just been picked at a junior high snowball dance.

"I want—" the words I'd practiced on the bus ride scramble in my brain, and I can't talk to him about needing to be something more than a fling, or needing him to accept my dark urges that I don't even really understand. He's already seen my pictures, but he doesn't know what's behind them.

He doesn't know what I really wanted. What I'd asked Brady to give me. And if I tell him, I'm afraid it will send him running the other way in disgust.

"Tell me."

I shake my head. I can't get the words past my lips.

Jayce takes another step toward me, now close enough that he reaches for my jaw and strokes my cheek with his thumb. "I want to know all about what you want, Violet." His voice is low, vibrating from his chest. "So if you won't tell me that, let's start with something simple. Do you trust me?"

I nod.

"Do you want me?"

"Yes," I whisper.

Jayce drops his hand from my cheek and steps back. "Give me your shirt."

I watch him to be sure of his meaning, then cross my arms and lift the hem of my shirt up over my stomach, my eyes locked on his until I pull the shirt over my head. I hand it to him.

His eyes sweep my neck, my freckled chest, my peach lace bra, and my stomach.

"Your bra." It's a quiet command, and my blood heats. I feel a flush of color rise from my décolletage to my cheeks, and my breasts are taut when I release them from the lace and wire.

I place the bra in his waiting hand.

"Sandals. Shorts." His voice is gravelly and I watch his pupils dilate as I flick open the button at my waist, draw down the zipper and let the navy cotton slide down my hips. I hand them to him as well.

With the exception of some tiny panties that don't even cover my whole butt, I'm totally exposed to him. *This is not normal,* my inner voice chides me. *This strip-on-command isn't what normal couples do.*

I force the thought aside. I'm not terrified. I'm thrilled.

Maybe because this time, I'm going willingly. This time, I've handed over control and I'm not afraid of how he'll use it. Or if he'll use it against me.

Jayce drops my clothes on a chair and comes close but doesn't touch me. I feel the heat radiating off his body as he moves to my shoulder, the smell of his sweat like salt and leather. He breathes on my shoulder and instantly my nipples tighten, then his lips move down my arm, still an inch from my skin, and I feel his hot breath all the way to my fingertips.

"I love how you smell," he whispers, and continues moving around me. My body sparks with contradictions—frozen in place but on fire inside, wanting him to grab me, yet savoring how he restrains himself.

I feel his warmth across my back, near my bottom, by my shoulder. He does another slow survey of my skin with his lips just an inch away, across my collarbone, down the valley between my breasts, stopping just above the lacy top of my panties.

His breath fans across my lower belly and the flesh between my thighs throbs with need. I'm afraid he can see the moisture spreading in my panties, smell my sex heating with just the touch of his breath to my skin.

Suddenly, he straightens. His hand reaches for my hair but it freezes before he touches me.

"You don't have to do this." His face is pinched, like a deep muscle's painful twinge.

"I want to."

"You don't have to do anything I ask. You can say no. You can walk away right now." Jayce's eyes are pleading with me. *Is he asking me to walk away?*

"I won't." I drop my eyes, embarrassed but needing to say the next words. "Unless you tell me to."

A rough hand fists in my hair and Jayce drags my eyes back to him. "What do you want? Tell me what you want, Violet."

"You."

"Not good enough. That's a cop out. Tell me what you want from me. What makes your blood sing? Tell me what you dreamed about last night, because I sure as hell dreamed about you."

Jayce captures my mouth with a rough kiss, a punishing force that steals my breath and most of my words. I know he just told me to do something, but ... he dreamed of me?

"I can't."

"Can't, or won't? This is not a question. This is a command. Tell me what you dreamed about last night. Or—"

"Or what?" I whisper, current shooting up my spine with the hint of a threat. Will he force me away if I can't describe the twisted madness of my dream? How he bent me to his will and I loved him for it?

"Or show me."

There. The challenge is down.

Jayce's hands are still tightly woven through my hair and I reach up and release them. He's watching me intently, and I guide his hand to brush the tip of my nipple.

Our breaths hiss at the same time.

I drop to my knees in front of the bulge in his shorts. My fingers work the button open and his erection springs forward inside his boxers.

I tug his shorts down over lean hips, stretch the waistband of his boxers to expose his hard shaft. My lips part, eager to taste him, and I look up to see dark eyes watching me.

I take him in. Taste his salt and sweetness, feel the velvet of his skin glide past my teeth and over my tongue. I stroke him with my mouth, a building pressure as I pull him deeper into me, my hands sliding up the back of his hard thighs, inside his shorts, to the base of his rear.

"Violet." My name is his plea for more, and I tug harder with my mouth, graze my teeth across the head of his shaft and then down the length of him until I feel the pressure at the back of my throat.

I run my hands across his rear, the soft hair on his legs tickling my inner wrists. I suck him and explore his creases and folds, his sac that draws tight beneath the base of his penis, the soft skin and deep musk that bewitches me.

"Violet. You have to stop. I'm close." He's warning me, but I pull him closer, suck him deeper until I'm barely breathing, lost in the rhythm of his body as it thrusts toward me.

My fingers curl at the seam behind his sac, pressing into him as I cup his balls to say: *Let go. Fill me.*

He gasps as a hot stream hits my throat, his spasms out of rhythm but more primal, more intense. I swallow and swallow and swallow, my eyes watering as I hold him in my mouth until I know that his climax is finished and he's emptied himself completely.

Only then do I let him go. I draw my body back up his as he pulls off his shirt, kicks off the shorts where they fell around his ankles, and pulls me close.

Skin to skin. Heart to heart. Mine's hammering a beat of exhilaration at what I've just done to him. His face is full of wonder, the tension that clouded it when he arrived at my apartment gone.

This time, when he kisses me, it's soft. Careful. His hands glide up and down my back in sweeping strokes, then find their way back to my hair.

"That's what you dreamed about?" he asks.

"There's more," I confess, a smile tugging at my lips.

"I'm dying to hear all about it."

CHAPTER 27: JAYCE

"Bedroom. Now."

I follow her lithe, nearly naked body with an ass I want to sink my teeth into to the back of her apartment. She pushes open her bedroom door and freezes. I nearly run into her.

I scan the room. Nothing seems out of place and her bed is neatly made.

She turns to me, a look of panic and horror on her face. I pull her to my chest and her skin is clammy, her breath coming in sharp, desperate pants.

"Tell me what's wrong. Please, Violet." *God, what did I do? Did I fuck this up already?*

I came over here with every intention of just getting her to talk to Gus tomorrow, or just getting her to talk to me, and somehow it turned into her naked and kneeling. I'm either a total asshole or the luckiest bastard anywhere.

I hold her tighter, my thick arms squeezing her frail shoulders.

"My—my bag." She points to a square, gray camera bag on the floor, like the one I thought she left at the café after the run-in with the stalker. "It's here."

I want to believe it simply turned up at the café's lost and found. "He brought it back?" We both know I don't mean Neil.

Violet nods against my chest.

"Get dressed. You're not safe here."

She opens her mouth to protest but shock wins. I push open her closet, scan the thin space beneath her bed, and check Neil's room and the bathroom to be sure this guy isn't lying in wait.

There's nothing.

I throw my clothes back on in the living room, dial the car service, and go back to Violet's room, where she's sitting on her bed, still undressed and staring at the camera bag. I pick it up as if it's infected, holding the strap away from my body, and I worry that there might be more surprises lurking inside.

"Can you pack some more clothes?" I ask gently. "Maybe for a week or so? I don't want you to have to come back here unless ... we're clear."

Mute, she dresses and then grabs a small stack of clothes. She carries them to the living room, stuffing them in the backpack she had when she arrived at her apartment.

There's no tears, and that freaks me out worse than when she'd been crying. In the car, I open my palm. "Give me your phone."

She obeys.

I dial Neil.

"Violet? You home? Your bouncer guy showed up at work and was a total jackass."

"Jackass speaking, Neil."

"Why are you calling me from Violet's phone? Where is she?"

"She's right next to me, but she's pretty shaken up. I need you to tell me if you found her camera bag."

"The big gray one? She said she lost it at the café."

I let out a breath to ease the tension in my voice. "That's not the question, Neil. I need to know if you found it, or if someone brought it back to you, and if you put it in her room."

"Haven't seen it, sorry." His dismissal gets my hackles up.

"So the fact that it turned up in her room has nothing to do with you?"

"You mean, she forgot she'd brought it home?"

I struggle to keep my voice even. "No, I mean *somebody* put it in her room. And if it wasn't you ..."

The weight of my meaning sinks in. Finally. "Holy shit."

"Exactly. So I'm taking Violet to my place for a while, at least until the cops catch up to this jack—uh, jackhole, and I'm not sure it's a good idea for you to be there, either."

"Great." Neil's put-out tone makes me want to throttle him through the phone. "Thanks for the words of concern, bouncer boy. I'll be fine."

I hang up before I spew a slew of words that would make Violet cringe and hand back her phone. She stares at it like it's a foreign object, like she doesn't quite know what to do with it.

I guide her up to my apartment in a daze, holding her backpack and camera bag, my hand never leaving her body—her back, her elbow, her shoulder. I need the touch to tell her she'll be OK. We'll be OK.

I shove aside the dirty thoughts that set my brain on fire less than an hour ago. I need to snap Violet out of this catatonia.

I try food. I pull some berries and cheese out of my fridge, but she shakes her head. My stomach rumbles so I plate up the food anyway.

I try drink. Violet shakes her head when I offer her wine, a cup of tea, a glass of water. She's hanging on to the edge of my kitchen counter and I close the distance between us, really get in her face. "Tell me what you *will* drink, then."

The command works, and she whispers, "Gin."

"Martini?"

"Muddy."

I nod and fix the cocktail with extra olive juice, then grab a beer for myself.

I carry the food and drinks to the terrace, the sun recently set but warmth still lingers in the velvety air. I have to go back to the kitchen to retrieve Violet and guide her outside.

"This will get better," I promise. "They'll catch the guy who's doing this to you, and then you'll have your life back to normal."

Violet accepts her drink and sips. "I thought I could fix this myself."

The fragility in her voice wrecks me. I twirl a strand of her red hair around my finger, loving its softness, like a silk cord wrapped around naked skin.

No.

Fuck, no.

How can I even go there, think that, when the pictures of her tied up are *exactly* the thing that got us here? I flash to her wrists bound with the electrical cord, the pictures that fueled my day-dreams and wrecked my nights, and self-loathing hits me.

I can't do that to her. I want to—God, if I was thinking with my dick like usual, I'd be begging her to submit, let me bind her and pleasure her until she loses her mind. But now, after the stalker and whoever took those pictures stole every good and sexy thing from that situation, I can't.

I can't tie her up.

Control her.

Fuck her the way I want to.

And I'm back to the way it's always been for me, because none of that kinky shit's gonna fly when you're into a casual hookup. Not with my profile. Not with the no-strings-attached groupies. All of my dark fantasies of attaching more than just strings to their wrists go out the window when I imagine what they'd tell the gossip rags.

Fuck that. I'll take my vanilla one-night stands over getting dragged through the mud for being some sick fuck who wants to cause pain.

I'm not. I just like being in control. Absolutely.

I unwind my finger from Violet's hair and put the plate between us. I get her to accept a few berries but I eat most of it.

The food gone, I bring up the thing I've been avoiding all night, especially since she's been so adamant about fixing this herself. "Violet? I want to ask you a favor."

Her green eyes study me, her face luminous in the twilight.

"I have a friend. He's an attorney here in New York, specializes in cyberlaw, and I think he might be able to help you get your pictures taken down."

She bites her lip, squeezing the flesh that I'll bet tastes of berries. My dick stirs in my shorts and I drop my arm to cover it. Down, boy.

"So, anyway, I asked him to look into it, and he'd like to meet with you tomorrow." I finish in a rush, needing to get it all out before I chicken out. "I can go with you, if you want, if you'll go, I mean."

She drops her eyes to study her hands in her lap and shakes her head. "I can't afford a lawyer."

"Doesn't matter. He's not charging you."

"But he's charging *you*, isn't he?" Her green eyes are back to meet mine, and there's no way I could lie and make her believe it.

"Yeah. But it's fine. It's something I want to do. For you."

She shakes her head again. "I can't let you do that. I'll—I'll *owe* you, then. I can't have that kind of debt."

"I'm not going to make you pay it back!"

"That's not what I meant. I mean, I'll owe you a favor. Like, then you can ask me to do what you want. And I won't be able to say no." A tear crests over her lashes and drips down her face, and my tongue waters to taste it, to kiss it away.

But I get what she's really saying. She's afraid that if I pay for this, I'll be able to control her in other ways. Suddenly, the naked pictures of her, afraid and unwilling beneath her haze of desire, make absolute sense to me.

"This is about control, isn't it?" I push the plate and our drinks aside, and pull Violet closer to me on my terrace couch. I press her hand against my chest so she can feel my beating heart. "You're afraid that if you let me do this for you, then I'll control you."

She nods.

And this is the moment of truth for me. I can lie and promise her I don't want to control her, that some random attorney's fees are just pocket change for me, no big deal. But that's not the whole truth. And with Violet so raw and open to me, I have to tell her. Everything.

"Violet. It doesn't matter what you decide about the lawyer, or whether you'll let him, or me, help you through this. No matter what it costs, you owe me *nothing*. There's no scorecard, and no obligation. But I can't tell you I don't want things from you. I want them deeply, desperately. Violet, I *want* to control you."

CHAPTER 28: VIOLET

I tug my hands from Jayce's chest and flee the terrace for the only refuge I know—the bathroom. I perch on the closed toilet lid and let tears make hot trails down my face.

I feel like such a crybaby. Such a wimp that I can't find a way to just deal with this, delete the pictures, somehow punish Brady and get the stalker to leave me alone, once and for all.

But none of them play by the rules. Not Brady. Not the stalker. Not whatever slippery devil runs the revenge porn website. After living my life playing by the rules, it doesn't seem fair that I can't use the rules to make things right.

Despair makes the prospect of handing this whole mess off to someone else so tempting. That's what Jayce is offering, really—a hired gun who can wave a magic legal wand, make the pictures disappear, and prevent more creeps from coming out of the woodwork and after me.

And maybe, if I'm really lucky, I can put this mess behind me before it explodes into the public eye and takes me, my father and Jayce down with it. I'm lucky I've barely been with Jayce anywhere except for our apartments. That's probably the only safe way to even see him.

And I don't want to stop.

I wipe my eyes and squelch that thought. I'm getting carried away by feelings for a guy who's everything I don't want. A playboy.

A celebrity. A controlling, pushy man who makes my insides liquid and my panties incinerate with just his breath on my skin.

He wants to control me.

I can't even believe he just said that. It was always unspoken with Brady—he controlled me with little comments, tiny gestures and veiled threats that together had a powerful effect. I dressed how he wanted and wore my hair the way he liked it. At events, I hung on his arm, my eyes always riveted on his face when cameras were around. Just as he instructed.

So what's possessed me to even *think* about what Jayce says with something other than revulsion? Just as I finally had the courage to break up with one controlling boyfriend and take the trip to Europe that I'd always dreamed of, the one I put off at Brady's demand, now I have another guy wanting to push me around.

I stand up and pace in frustration. The scary part is, being controlled by Jayce doesn't sound so bad. He's Justin. *The just.* He's already powerful, already comfortable in his own skin, not some wannabe politician who gets his kicks from being obeyed.

Mostly, I tell myself, he's not Brady.

I hear tapping at the bathroom door before I've made up my mind whether I'm freaked out, turned on, revolted, or ready.

The tapping persists. "Violet? Are you OK in there? I—I didn't mean to scare you."

I go to the door and open it, immediately regretting my flight to the bathroom when I see Jayce's eyes pinched with worry. It ages him a decade, even though he's only a couple years older than me.

"You didn't scare me. I just needed some space. To think." I open the door wider, as if to prove that this is really simple, that I'm not hiding anything.

"You can have all the space you need," he says, and takes a step away from the doorframe. "I'll be on the terrace if you want to talk … about what I said." His head is bowed and my heart goes out to him in this moment of assumed defeat.

I need him to know, at least, that I'm OK.

"Justin." I catch him with his real name, and he turns back to me. "I don't need *that* much space."

He matches my small smile and it spreads until I see his twinkling caramel eyes. I beckon him closer and his hands move to my hips, a loose hold that centers us, our chests a few inches apart.

"Just give me some time to think about what you're really asking, OK? Because I know this isn't just about going to see your friend tomorrow."

"You mean you'll go?"

"I'll go. I'm all out of options, and because you want to help me, I'll let you. But for the rest—" I pause and I can't force out the word *control* yet "—just give me some time."

"All you need." He smiles again and strokes my cheek, then drops his hand when a yawn seizes me and contorts my face. "Sleep. You need it."

"No, I'm good."

"Liar. Brush your teeth. Get changed. I'll meet you in bed."

My eyebrows jump faster than I can control my startled expression.

"Not like that. I'm just going to help you relax."

***

Jayce sits on the opposite side of the bed in boxers and a T-shirt, a low light at the bedside casting shadows across his face that sharpen his strong jaw and square chin. His eyes are unreadable in shadow, but I cross to the bed in my sleep shorts and tank top as a flutter builds in my chest.

"Lie down on your stomach," he says, and again, I obey his command. I realized halfway through brushing my teeth that he didn't ask me to do it—he *told* me, without a please, without the option to say no.

It's a little thing, but it's control.

I lie on my stomach, my arms forming a pillow under my head. Jayce immediately stands and begins arranging my body, his warm hands moving my arms down to my sides, tipping my head into a pillow and brushing my hair back, moving my ankles to adjust my legs, and bolstering my feet with another pillow.

His hand tugs at the hem of my tank top. "I'm giving you a massage, so I'm taking this off."

Again with the command. I lift my chest to give him access as he pulls the material over my head. I feel warmth as his breath brushes the naked skin of my back, then I hear a wet sound and rubbing. His palms touch my shoulder blades with lotion, his wide hands stroking across my back and up my spine.

"Unnnh." So much for coherent conversation. I let my body unwind under Jayce's magic hands. Minutes tick by and he coats my back with lotion, working my muscles until they're hot and supple, as if I've been doing yoga for the last hour.

I peek open an eyelid and find my face even with his boxer-clad crotch. Evidence that he's enjoying this massage every bit as much as I am tents the material, but he doesn't move to satisfy the urge. His hands work my neck, shoulders, arms, and lower back and I close my eyes again, blissed out.

I feel the mattress dip beneath me as Jayce positions himself lower to work my legs. The air shifts—it's heavier, more sultry, and I lift my hips when I feel the tug on my sleep shorts. Jayce pulls them down my legs and I hear his breath hitch. I don't think he realized they were the last scrap of clothing on my body.

"Oh, Violet," he breathes, and his hands cruise up and down my calves and the back of my thighs. It's a little bit weird to know he's staring at my bare ass, but his hands keep up the long, sweeping strokes even as they move up my legs and work my glutes. From my lower back to my rear and the back of my thighs, he moves against me, the energy from his touch sending swirls of excitement through me.

I force my body to be still. I clench at my core, praying he can't see my arousal as obviously as I see his. His hands pull together, thumbs skimming lightly down my butt and I thrill to his touch. His hands sweep down to my thighs and then back up, each time closer to my center.

He's tormenting me, and I moan with undisguised pleasure. The strokes become more insistent, less massage-like and more intimate as the seconds tick by. One thumb slides right down my center—crack, hole, cleft, God, what words do I even have to describe where he's touching?—and it pauses at my entrance, wet and wanting.

I roll, desperate to see his face, wanting to feel him above me, to let his fingers explore me more. His hands freeze as our eyes meet and I give him permission. "More. I love the way you touch me."

Light fingers stroke the hair on my mound, graze my thighs and then move back between my legs, feathering over my folds. He's kneeling on the bed beside me, his expression inscrutable as I feel a stroke up my stomach, between my breasts and around them, and then one hand cups my breast as his thumb brushes my nipple.

A bolt of energy shoots straight down my legs, inflaming the flesh between them. The room smells of lotion and sex as shadows dance across his face, the roughness of his fingertips teasing energy to swirl through my body like a gathering storm.

Jayce chuckles. "I love how responsive you are." As if to prove his point, he brushes my other nipple and my body jerks in response.

When his fingers dive lower, deeper between my legs, I see his jaw clench and his eyes darken. He finds the bud with his finger, pinching and rolling it, his eyes fixed on mine as he creates little quakes, fissures in my self-control.

I twist and writhe under his hand, his fingers plunging and spreading moisture across me. He moves faster and I'm coming apart, lower lip aching where my teeth bite down against the scream building inside me. Flick, twist, swirl. Plunge, twitch, withdraw.

Release. It floods me with sensation and the scream escapes. I'm flying, tethered only to his finger and that tiny bundle of nerves that's a red button on a nuclear reactor. Meltdown.

I pant and twist, in overdrive as I peak and ride the high that drags all the air from my lungs, all the energy from my limbs, all the emotion from my heart. There is no dam strong enough to hold back this torrent, and no control left in me.

Except his. His deliberate movements that *know* me, that light my skin and my soul on fire.

His hand gentles to softer strokes, longer and more languid caresses. I'm spent and I just lie there, looking up at him in wonder.

"I need your skin," I say. I pull at his T-shirt and he strips it off, his hardened chest glowing in the dim light of the room. "All of it," I beg. He stands, pushing his boxers down lean hips, and his erection springs free.

I'm still paralyzed from my climax and I don't reach for him, but he climbs back into the bed next to me, his arm sliding beneath my neck as he wraps me against his hot skin.

He buries his face in my hair, inhaling, then he releases me enough that our faces are a few inches apart.

"You were never more beautiful than just now," he says, his voice raw. "When you came apart in my hands. When you gave me control."

CHAPTER 29: JAYCE

Her skin is like satin—cool and smooth, begging to be touched. I pull Violet against me again so she won't have to answer my stupid-as-hell comment.

Why couldn't I just tell her she's beautiful?

That she's sexy?

That she makes me crazy with lust?

I suppose she could guess that from the way my cock's digging into her hip, but she doesn't reach for it.

Shit. I'm doing this all wrong.

Less than an hour ago, she was running away from me because I admitted I wanted to control her. And now I've just screwed the pooch with another comment about control. If that doesn't make her run far and fast, I don't know what will.

I listen to her breathing and I'm grateful she doesn't answer me. My grand plan—to get her nice and relaxed so she'll be able to sleep after this new freaky stalker thing—went out the window as soon as I laid eyes on her bare skin, her bare ass, and those legs that just don't quit.

My hands, just like my dick, evidently have a mind of their own.

Violet curls into me, tiny sounds of contentment humming from her chest as the minutes tick by and I stroke her back. When her breathing evens, I loosen my grip enough to kill the light by the bed.

We're in darkness, with only the city light filtering through my window. It's a safe little cocoon—my apartment, my room, my bed—far enough from the stalker and the media and all the bullshit with my band and the Viper Records deal that I can finally think.

I think I'm an idiot.

I feel Violet's breathing deepen with sleep and I glide my hand up the back of her neck to thread in the thick strands of her hair, to pull through them and comb out a few tangles, to fan the puddle of bloodred across my pillow.

I dip my chin and inhale her scent, cherry blossoms and sunshine. I still smell her on my fingers, too, sweet and alkaline, like milk and honey.

Skin to skin, Violet is everything, a whole world of scent and sensation, her softness blending into my hardness and we just fit. She feels right. I'm not pressed against rock-hard fake boobs, accidentally stabbed with fake nails, smeared with lipstick or smothered with hairspray.

Groupies come with a lot of cosmetics, I've learned. But Violet, she just comes naturally.

God. I am so fucked.

Before I sleep, I make three resolutions.

One, I'm going to make those pictures go away. I know what they do to me, and I hate the thought of some other guy jacking off to her, even if Violet wakes up and tells me she doesn't want me. I don't care what I have to pay Gus to make it happen, I want them gone.

Two, I'm going to get the sonofabitch who's after her. If the cops don't make it happen first, I'm going to nail his balls to the wall to be sure he never comes at Violet again.

Three is the hardest. I'm not going to lose control again. She deserves better than this, better than me coming at her with my hands or my dick just because I'm horny and tormented by pictures of her. Until she tells me she wants me, and on what terms, I'm not going to keep pushing her.

Because I know I could break her. *I could get what I want. It's there for the taking.* I could wrap the feelings I see plainly on her face together with little manipulations, little steps that tip the balance of power.

I could win her, but it would break her.

And I want Violet whole. Or nothing.

***

Dawn knocks the cobwebs loose in my brain and it takes me a minute to understand why I'm sweating. The redheaded furnace in my arms is the answer.

Her skin is normally cool to my touch. But last night as we slept, our legs tangled together and my arms wrapped her tight against my chest. The heat between us roared to life.

I peel back the damp sheet and pull it up, letting it fall back against our bodies and sweep cool air over us. Violet murmurs something and then her dark lashes flutter, butterfly wings opening to reveal bright emerald eyes.

I press my lips to her forehead and gently disentangle us. "You can sleep. I'm grabbing a shower."

I roll and walk to the bathroom, hoping she doesn't see my cock bobbing as I go. Shower's gonna be cold.

When I finish, she's sitting up in bed, the white sheet barely tucked under her arms to cover her breasts. Her phone's in her hand and she's grinning like she just won the lottery.

"It's the graffiti artist," she squeaks. "I got a text last night from the girl at the tattoo shop, Willa. She said the artist is willing to meet me today at Righteous Ink."

I smile and go to my dresser for clothes, not really getting what she's saying but happy she's happy.

"I'm going to text Stella. Get her to come with me, so she can write the captions for my photo essay." Violet taps out a message on her phone and I slide open a drawer, expecting shirts, but finding nothing.

Violet's drawer.

I don't over-think it, just grab her bag and start emptying her stuff into the drawer: shirts, shorts, and a mound of lacy things that undo the work of the cold shower.

"What are you doing?"

"Unpacking for you." I keep my tone neutral, my back to Violet as I dress.

I turn and she's staring at me.

"You gave me a drawer?"

"I'll give you whatever you need." I hold her eyes for a beat and understanding flashes in them.

Dammit. I've been awake thirty minutes and already I'm pushing her, pecking away at the question that hangs between us.

What will she give me? Control?

"Coffee." I flee the bedroom and busy myself in the kitchen, not only coffee but omelets and toast and the rest of the berries. By the time Violet emerges from the bedroom, showered and dressed casually as always, I'm turning a fluffy half-moon of egg onto a plate.

"This looks a lot better than just coffee," Violet says, and I hand her a fork to dig in. She waits for me to finish the other omelet, though, and only when I'm seated beside her at the kitchen bar does she take the first bite.

"You cooked," she says. "Seriously."

I nod. "It gets pretty serious when that's how you make rent. I cooked until we were gigging on the reg, touring regional shows and making more than just a scrape off the door. It took four years, but eventually we didn't have to have side jobs anymore."

Violet nods, looking around my kitchen as if for the first time. Knives and measuring cups line a magnetic rack on the back wall. Hanging pots with their bottoms blackened by use all point to another endeavor that speaks to what I need.

Control. It's in the fire, ingredients, and chemistry of cooking. In music, it's in the precision of pitch and timing. Even on the weight bench, it's not just about adding another dime, another ten pounds to the rack. It's about having the control for the precise lift that's balanced through the stroke.

I let her enjoy a few bites in silence, then clear my throat. "So, today. We're supposed to meet Gus at noon. Practice is at two, and I'd like you to come with me." I struggle to keep the command out of my words. "If you're OK with that. Please."

"Where do we meet Gus? I'm meeting Stella for coffee and then we'll go to Righteous Ink when it opens at ten."

I give her directions to his office and clear our plates. I've got my own meeting with the other attorney to go over the proposed Viper contract this morning.

Violet moves to pick up her camera bag.

"Stop." The command is out before I soften it with a *please,* but caution prickles along my spine and I move between her and the bag. I was too messed up with hormones racing through my system last night to even think to inspect it, but the fact is, *he* had it.

The stalker.

I zip open the bag. Lying on top is a cream envelope, her name scrawled on top. I grab a tissue and stuff the envelope in a zip-top bag, then slip that into my messenger bag.

"We'll go to the police with this. But I don't want you to have to carry it around today."

Violet shakes her head, not letting me boss her around any longer. "My letter, my problem." She takes the letter from me, and I want to beg her not to open it to some fresh new horror.

She takes my tissue and removes it from the bag. Takes a knife from the kitchen and slices the envelope open. Takes care not to touch the paper as she pries a note from inside it.

I hover over her shoulder to read.

I'm watching you, Violet, and waiting.
You left your bag and I returned it.
Do you see now how I can take care of you?
Do you see how I love you?
It's only a matter of time before you realize how much you can love me.
That time is coming.

Violet folds the note and returns it and the envelope to the plastic bag with shaking fingers. She won't meet my gaze.

I'm angry she ignored me and angry at the stalker's words, but I channel my fury into focus. I work my way through the rest of the bag but there are no further surprises—only her camera gear, lens-cleaning papers, memory cards and a few pens. Her wallet and the cell phone I gave her are in a side pocket.

I hand her the bag and my hand brushes hers, a jolt of electricity affecting both of us. I soften my stance, move closer, and she bends to me, her mouth turned up, eyes open and expectant.

"Be safe today," I tell her, and take her face between my hands. I plant a soft kiss on her forehead, the only place that doesn't lead to her mouth and absolute temptation.

When I release her, there's confusion in her eyes. "I will," she promises. "See you at noon?"

I nod and she's out the door.

CHAPTER 30: VIOLET

"If you had asked me two weeks ago if dating Jayce was a good idea, I'd say no." Stella frowns into her frothy latte. "I still say no, but it's kind of weird and awesome of him to let you stay with him while your apartment's being fumigated."

It was the best lie I could come up with. I make a mental note to tell Neil so he'll cover for me if he talks to Stella. I hate lying to her, but I can't tell her about the stalker and the pictures. It was hard enough admitting I was recently fired from my teaching job.

"I know he's a good friend," Stella says. "He was awesome to me when Tyler had his diabetic seizure; he even stuck up for me when the rest of the band blamed me."

Jayce's playboy reputation is well-deserved, Stella adds, but that doesn't mean I should write him off.

I take a sip of my caramel latte, and weigh the evidence. "I can't get over the mixed signals. Like, last night he's all hot and bothered, and this morning he kissed me on the forehead like I'm his little cousin."

Stella shrugs. "Maybe for once in his life he wants to take it slow?"

I remember how he moved against my skin. He didn't push me to do the deed, but he wasn't chaste, either. "Do you think he's still … dating other people?"

"You mean the shallow end of the gene pool?" Stella snorts. "Doubt it. I'm not saying he's going to get religion and quit being a man-whore, but from what Tyler's told me, none of Jayce's girls have been hanging around since the night we were at the hospital."

I tuck the timing of that into the back of my brain and check my phone again. "The shop's open. Let's go."

Willa's behind the counter at Righteous Ink again, drawing in her sketchbook.

She closes it as we approach. I study her face, guessing she can't be much older than me. She's curvy, about halfway between my five-ten and Stella's five-two, with short, pink-streaked hair and delicate tattoos woven up the length of her arms.

She looks a lot cooler than either of us. "You brought a friend?" Willa frowns.

"And coffee." I set the peace offering down on the counter, to-go cups for Willa and VIIIM, and drop a handful of creamers and sugar packets beside it.

Willa nods to Stella as she doctors her coffee. "So you are?"

"Stella Ramsey. I used to be a reporter for *The Indie Voice* but now I'm kind of between gigs. Violet asked me to come along to interview VIIIM and write captions or maybe a feature to go with the photo profile."

Willa's eyes narrow. "I saw you on TV."

Stella ducks her head, an admission. "Yeah. Nothing like defending your boyfriend on national television."

Willa snorts. "I hope he's worth it."

"He is."

I'm edgy from the challenge in Willa's voice and Stella's steely reaction, and the fact that VIIIM isn't here yet, so I change the subject. "Willa, did you know Stella had a tattoo done here a few weeks ago? One of your coworkers, a big guy with a lot of tattoos."

"That describes pretty much everyone I work with," Willa says.

Stella rolls her wrist to reveal delicate, tattered angel's wings paired with a Latin phrase, *Alis volat propriis.* It means "she flies with her own wings."

Willa's eyes flash with recognition. "That's Thomas's work. He's really good. He's done most of these for me." She rolls up her sleeve to reveal several lifelike bees sucking honey from flowers. "I designed them, but he did the ink. He has a nice touch with shading."

Stella's still admiring her own tattoo so I clear my throat, eager to get going on the interview with VIIIM, "So, when do you think the artist will be joining us, Willa?"

"I'm here."

"You?" My mouth drops open stupidly. "You're VIIIM?"

"No, I'm Willa. You just don't know how to read my signature." Willa cracks a grin at my surprise.

"You're the one who does the street art?" I'm floored, absolutely stunned, as if I'm finally putting a face to a famous voice. In the last year, as I've collected more than two dozen images of this artist's work, I've nurtured a vision of who he must be in my mind: a hard-edged guy with paint-streaked fingers and a rap sheet.

Seeing Willa as this elusive artist rocks my world and challenges every assumption. If you blink past the pink hair and tattoos, she could be just like me and Stella. One of us.

"Wow. You're really—young." Stella blurts, and I'm thankful she puts that awkward question out there right away.

"I've been on my own for eight years," Willa counters.

"But you're—"

"Twenty-three. Life isn't always a yellow brick road." Willa's statement is defensive, but it connects with Stella and she softens.

"You're right." Stella dips her hand in her bag for her notebook and uncaps a pen. "Look, I'm sorry we started out weird. Obviously, we didn't expect you'd be so ... accomplished. Can I get a do-over?"

Stella offers Willa a sincere smile and I'm thankful for my friend's ability to do the talking and tease information out of her in the interview. I listen to them banter as Stella starts with the easy questions. That's why I brought her with me, because if it were just me here, I'd still be stuck on the question, *"You're* VIIIM?"

And that brings me back to something Willa said. When they pause, I ask, "Willa, you said we didn't know how to read your signature. What do you mean by that?"

She flips open her drawing pad and uses a fat, brush-tip marker to hastily scrawl V-I-I-I-M across the page. The graffiti script is full of movement, the letters distorted and stylized. She pushes the pad toward me. "Tell me what you see."

"VIIIM," I say.

Willa nods, then rotates the pad a hundred and eighty degrees. "Now what do you see?"

My fingers trace the letters, now in reverse order. M is now a W. The first I is without a serif, but the next two I's have just enough of a serif extending from them that they could be L's. And the letter I'd always read as V, when inverted, looks like an A. The dot in the middle of the V, which I thought was decoration, now reads as a crossbar for an A.

Stella lets out a low whistle.

"You can't sign your name the regular way if you're doing street art," Willa says. "Too easy for the cops. But I didn't want a fake tag, either, so I just flipped my name upside-down and messed with the letters a bit."

"I thought you were a mad genius when Violet showed me your art," Stella says. "Now I *really* like you."

Willa blushes with pleasure at the compliment.

I pull my camera out of my bag, trying not to think of the stalker touching it, as Stella dives in with more questions for Willa. She knows when to shut up and listen, too. At this rate she'll be able to write a huge article.

I snap a few test-frames as they talk, Willa's animated face over her sketch pad with the large VIIIM/WILLA scrawled across it. I check my light balance in the digital display and Willa's head snaps up.

"I never said you could take pictures of *me.*"

"Sorry. I just thought, since you agreed to talk to me—"

"You thought *nothing.* I only agreed to introduce you to the artist. Which I did. Here I am. And I'm talking to you, so you won't assume something stupid like I'm a man. But I never gave you permission to take a picture of me and make it public!"

I'm reeling from the force of Willa's fury, and Stella steps in to try to calm her down. "We don't have to use that picture. Hey, Violet wasn't trying to screw with you. I promise." Stella reaches for Willa's hand but Willa withdraws as if she's been stung.

I hold out my camera to Willa. "I'm sorry. Erase them if you have to. I really just want to do a photo profile on your art. If you don't want to be pictured, I can live with that."

Willa accepts my camera and starts pushing buttons on the digital display. "It's not that I don't want to. I *can't.*"

Before I can ask her what that means, she turns the digital display around to face me, her face scrunched in an *ick.* "Is that your boyfriend?"

I take the camera from her and the naked body of a man fills my display screen. His head is just out of the photo and one hand extends toward the camera, triggering the shutter for this selfie. The other hand grasps his erect penis.

"Is this the new selfie?" Stella cracks, catching an eyeful from beside my shoulder. "I thought it was the Duck Face."

I'm speechless, terrorized beyond words. Not only am I seeing my stalker in this picture, I know exactly where he is. Behind him, there's a too-familiar shade of purple.

My duvet. My room.

CHAPTER 31: JAYCE

I spot her flame-red hair before Violet sees me in the building lobby of Leverda, Maloney and Probus. Even though it's only been a few hours, I grin because I'm happy to see her again.

The last time I looked forward to seeing a girl this much was … never.

Apparently, the feeling is not mutual. Violet forces up the corners of her mouth in a tight smile and goes through the motions in security. We're the only two people in the elevator car.

"How'd the interview go?"

"Fine."

"Did you meet the artist?"

"Yeah."

And then there's silence for forty floors.

I introduce us to the receptionist, who takes us to a conference room to meet Gus. Gus explains he intends to help Violet get her pictures off sites by sending takedown letters on her behalf and threatening further legal action.

"I've got some good news and bad news from my research so far."

Violet takes a sip of water and nods, her eyes red.

"The good news is that most of the sites with your photo are operated from the US, so it's a lot easier to track down the site owners and make legal demands that actually have teeth," Gus tells her, and I feel a weight lift from my chest. Maybe Violet's nightmare could finally be over.

"The bad news," Gus continues, "is that there are a lot more sites than we thought. Jayce sent me ten."

Violet turns to me and her brows lift, unaware that I'd found more sites than the one she'd shown me.

"I found forty-two more," Gus adds.

And just like that, all of the air in the room is gone.

"How can there be so many?" I demand.

"The site that originally posted your pictures probably shared them with several more, and then those shared with others, and so on," Gus says. "Some of the revenge porn sites are even operated by the same people, or guys who know each other. They're betting that you won't go after one of them because there are so many others that there's no point. It's just like the pirate sites where you can download music. Proliferation is insurance for these guys. They spread out the risk of getting caught."

"I want every damn one of them gone," I hiss. "All of them. No matter how long it takes." I tell Gus about the letter we found in her camera bag today.

Gus pushes papers across the desk for Violet to sign. "This gives us the power to act on your behalf to demand the sites remove your photo."

But Violet's staring at her lap, shaking her head. "It won't help," she whispers.

I disagree. "What? I don't want some random creeps looking at you—"

"No. It doesn't matter. The creeps already found me. The stalker ..." She digs into her camera bag. "Look."

Images of a guy jacking off light up her camera display. My mouth turns in disgust and I point it to Gus to let him in the loop.

"That's my room. My stalker," Violet confesses. I hate the way she says the word "my," as if he's already got his hooks in her.

"Jayce told me a little about him," Gus says. "You need to go to the police with this and the letter. It's evidence."

***

I take Violet to the police and it kills me to leave her there and head to band practice. I program my car service number into her phone and make her promise to take it over to Tyler's the minute she's done.

I try to shake off the hopelessness Violet projected in the meeting with Gus and focus on what we can control—he'll send at least a dozen takedown letters today. Violet already has one filthy guy after her. I don't want her pictures online a minute longer, for fear she could attract more.

Gavin and Dave are already at Tyler's and we practice with little small talk. Kristina and Chief lounge on the couches. Things are tense in a few songs where we're still ironing out the kinks, but Chief doesn't comment—he dives straight into plans for LA when we wrap.

"I've got our bookings, a new producer lined up who I think you're going to like, and we've got a publicity op for Saturday night if you're up to it," Chief says, rattling off notes from his iPad. Details of a birthday party for an A-list starlet make Saturday night sound like a blowout—and a royal pain in the ass.

"We don't have to go to that, right?" Tyler asks. I know what he's thinking. He'd rather spend the night cuddled up with Stella than fighting off the Hollywood freak show of silicon-enhanced groupies. That was *my* scene.

"Either we all go, or none of us do," Dave counters. "We've been seen apart too much, particularly with Gavin's solo on *Late Night*. We need to present a united front."

I exchange glances with Tyler. The rest of the band doesn't know about Viper Records' offer, and I haven't decided whether to act on it, but Dave's always had a sixth sense about strategy and keeping up appearances.

"Then we're going," Gavin says. "We can't make this trip all work and no play. Let's lay down our best stuff Saturday, blow off steam at the party Saturday night, and then regroup Sunday for the do-overs."

"Can you organize dresses for the girls?" Chief asks Kristina.

"It's really short notice, but I've got a couple of designers I can call." Kristina frowns and taps a couple of notes into her phone. "Can't we just wear something we've got?"

"No." Chief is adamant. "This is the full deal—we're probably going to get press pickup on this in conjunction with recording *Wilderness*, and while studio time isn't sexy, this better be. Appearances count."

"Be sure you have something for Violet." Five pairs of eyes turn to me.

"She's going?" Kristina asks, like she's saying, *Are you really going to wear that?*

Tyler gives me air cover by distracting the guys while I beckon Kristina to the kitchen for a quiet sidebar. I grab a beer and offer her one, but she shakes her head.

"Seriously? Bringing a girl's only going to cramp your style, Jayce." Kristina gives me a flirty pat on the arm like she endorses this, even though ninety percent of the time she complains about the girls I date behind their backs. To their faces, she's always syrupy sweet.

"It's not a problem. Violet's important to me."

"Like, girlfriend-important?" I hear the challenge.

"That's not even the point. When I say she's important, she is, OK?" I can't keep the rising frustration out of my voice.

"Chill, Jayce. It's not like you've got to marry her."

The M-word makes me choke on my beer. "Don't mess with me."

Kristina laughs. "I totally just did. And I got to you. I win."

I set down my beer on the kitchen counter—hard—and get in her face. "Listen to me. There's something going on here. Something you don't even know about, but when I say it's important to me for Violet to come, you're just going to have to deal with that. She *has* to come with me."

Kristina crosses her arms. "Then tell me. What's so important that you're going to force another girl on us? How long did Shelly last? Two weeks? And how about Amelia? Amanda? What was her name?"

"Anastasia," I shake my head to bring the memory into focus. "I think. That's not the point. The point is Violet needs me. And I want to be there for her, even if it means taking her to LA."

"Tell me why." Kristina's chin is set and now I know I've stepped in it. I dangled some random piece of information out there and she's like a dog on a bone; she won't quit until she's pried it out of me.

Fuck.

I consider lying, but maybe the truth will make her gentler with Violet. I swear her to secrecy and she nods, eyes wide.

"Violet's got a stalker. He's doing all sorts of creepy shit, sending her messages and watching her. He broke into her place when she wasn't home, so I've got her staying with me. And I don't want to leave her in the city by herself."

Kristina's eyebrows soar. "And how exactly did a nobody like Violet get a stalker?"

I pinch the bridge of my nose, knowing she'll rip me a new asshole if I lie and she finds out. "You promise you won't tell anyone?"

"I just did. And haven't I always been the model of discretion?" There's a taunt in her voice, but I take her at her word. She's been Dave's girlfriend so long that she's got dirt on all of us.

"There are pictures of Violet online. Naked pictures, tied up and shit. She never meant for them to get out—some ex took them and posted them for revenge."

Kristina's expression softens with pity. "And you believe that?"

"Why wouldn't I?"

The pity's not for Violet—it's for me. "Jayce, what turnip truck did you just fall off of? She told *you* that she didn't want them public, but between having kinky pictures taken in the first place and then dating you—that girl's a starfucker just begging for attention."

My hands move before my brain engages and I grab the sleeve of her shirt. If she were a dude, I'd punch her in the face for what she's saying about Violet.

"You will not. Fucking. Tell. A. Soul." I seethe. "Are we clear?"

"Crystal." Kristina's voice is ice and steel and she shakes my hand off her shirt. "I'll get a nice little dress for your good little girl. Wouldn't want to disappoint, would we?"

"Shut the fuck up, Kristina." I walk away from her, long strides to the bathroom to get away and cool off. I hate that I just spilled Violet's secret to the one person I shouldn't even trust with my dry cleaning.

"So, Chief." I hear Kristina's voice just before I close the bathroom door. "Looks like we've got a full flight to LA."

CHAPTER 32: VIOLET

When the town car drops me at Tyler's loft, I'm not sure if I should knock on the door with the big *Do Not Block* sign or call for Jayce to let me in.

"Violet?" Stella walks up the sidewalk, eyes darting around for lingering press, but we're the only ones on the street except for a delivery guy halfway up the block. "Good timing. Practice is probably over." She unlocks the door for us and hustles inside.

We climb the stairs and I spin a lie about how some perv messed with my camera while it was in the coffee shop's lost and found. In truth, the police took the letter and my memory card into evidence and dusted the camera for prints. I still don't have any promises beyond "we'll look into it."

"That's just scary," she says and opens the door to the loft. Gavin, Tyler, Dave, Chief and Kristina are sitting on couches in an animated conversation.

"Speak of the devil," Kristina says and looks at me.

What the what? I've barely said two words to this girl and she's calling me the *devil?*

"Play nice," Tyler warns. Stella wraps her arm around his shoulder, nuzzling him with a kiss. Their tenderness warms me.

"Oh, I will," Kristina says, but her face says otherwise. "I'm getting us all ready for the party Saturday night. Stella, you know the drill."

Stella sees my trepidation and reaches a hand out, gesturing to me to sit on the couch beside her. "It is kind of fun, Violet," she says. "Kristina has some designer hookups and we get to play dress-up."

No, no, no. That does *not* sound like fun. That sounds like something public. Something potentially embarrassing. "Thanks, but I'll pass."

"Doesn't look like you have a choice, girlfriend." Kristina makes *girlfriend* sound like a dirty word. "You're on the hook to go, says Jayce, or else he's going to have to dig up some other groupie for his arm candy."

"Stop it, Kristina." Gavin narrows his eyes. "I picked Beryl. Tyler picked Stella. If Jayce wants Violet to come, that's his prerogative. You can't get all snippy."

"I'm not being snippy. I'm *cooperating*." She draws out the last word like a kindergarten lesson.

Chief clears his throat. "Fine. Then we're set to go. Wheels up at 9 a.m. Friday."

"Too freaking early," Gavin says.

"It's an extra five grand if you want to leave at noon," Chief counters. "But I got you reservations in a private room at The Ridge for seven."

"We'll be there," Tyler says. He winks at Stella. "You don't want to miss that."

"I feel like I'm missing something," I whisper to Stella.

"Jayce signed you up for our trip to LA," Kristina says.

I shake my head. "Oh, no. I can't go on a trip right now." A million excuses swirl in my brain but they all stink.

I don't have a job, so I can't blame it on not being able to take time off. I don't have much money, but it doesn't sound like I'm expected to pay. And the real reason—that I can't afford to be in Jayce's orbit because I'm afraid of publicity—is something I can't explain without telling the truth about other things.

Only Jayce knows. I can't even bring myself to tell Stella.

"We're recording and there's a party Saturday," Chief explains. "You'll be Jayce's date."

"That's nice to be invited, but I'm not really big on parties." That's the truth. After attending dozens of functions in the shadow of Brady or my father, I prefer to avoid them. I feel like a trained pony, trotted out for show.

Chief frowns so I try to be conciliatory. "Maybe some other time?"

"Don't hold your breath, honey," Kristina says. "You might not even make it until Saturday."

Jayce emerges from the bathroom and his eyes are thunderous. "Violet. Let's go. Now."

I stand up automatically, following his pointed finger to the door. I give Stella a small wave as Jayce bends and whispers something to Kristina and Chief. From the shocked look on their faces, it must have been vicious.

***

"When were you going to tell me about this trip to LA?" The silence stretched between us in the car ride back to his place, but now that we're inside his apartment, I can't avoid speaking to him any longer.

Jayce plunges his hand into his hair and then scrubs his face. "It's a fu— a flipping mess. I'm sorry, Violet. I wanted to ask you, not have you hear the plans from Kristina."

"But you made plans."

"I did. I don't want to leave you alone while that guy is still out there."

I stand awkwardly in the space between his kitchen and living room.

He comes to me, placing a tentative hand on my shoulder. "I don't want anything to happen to you. I—I care about you."

Those last four words thaw the ice that's coursed through my system since the minute I saw the pictures of my stalker on my camera. Jayce cares, without the layers of judgment anyone else would heap on me for being so colossally stupid to let those pictures happen in the first place.

It makes me want to hug him, and so I do.

At first, I feel his body stiffen. But as I pull him close and smell the mixture of sweat and warm skin and laundry soap that lingers on him, he softens and his hands rest on the small of my back.

Jayce tips his head down until his forehead touches mine. His dark lashes fan across his cheeks, eyes closed, and I listen to him breathing for a few long moments. "Please come with me. I don't think I can even concentrate on recording if I'm afraid of what you could be going through back here in New York. Please."

The plea is gentle, but its pull is strong. I *want* to give in, want to please him, but I'm terrified of what comes after. What if my brush with someone famous means that fame rubs off onto me?

"I'm afraid of what might happen."

"With us? I promise you, I won't even touch you if you don't want me to," Jayce's eyes are wide with sincerity.

"It's not that. It's—what if the paparazzi catch on to me? What if they find out my name?"

"We'll be careful. We're not even booked under my real name at the hotel."

I'm suddenly shy. "Would we be sharing a room?"

"Yes, but it's a suite. You'll have your own bedroom. I won't come near you unless—" He trails off and now he looks shy.

"Unless what?"

"Unless you ask. I know this thing with us, it's not ... normal. I promise to give you all the time and space you need until you decide what you want from me. Even if you don't want anything."

I close my eyes, feeling the weight of his meaning. "OK."

Jayce loosens his hold on me and steps back. "You don't want anything from me?"

"No."

I see resignation in his eyes and I grab his hand when he turns away. "I mean, no, as in, no, that's not it. I do want ... something with you. I'm just figuring it out. And I meant OK, I'll go."

"To LA?"

"Yes. If you really want me there."

His arms are around me in a heartbeat. "Oh, Violet," he breathes into my hair. "I definitely want you."

Those words echo in my head above everything—the sounds of him making dinner, his talk of the Viper Records contract and the next steps to get an independent agent to review it, the clink of our wine glasses and the sounds of the city that filter up to his apartment terrace.

It's all so domestic. So normal, as if the elephant in the room, the question of where this is all going for us, doesn't hang over us. I suspect he's trying to prove that he *is* normal, or can be, anyway. Isn't this what normal couples do? Make dinner and eat together?

We sink into the couch on his terrace, finishing our wine. When I put my glass down, he pulls me under his arm so my ear is against his chest. His heartbeat is strong and I feel his fingers sift through my hair.

This is safe. Well-fed and relaxed from the wine, I let myself melt against his hard chest and feel my scalp tingle under the pressure of his fingers, the smooth strokes that weave through waves of hair and send energy through the roots and down my spine.

"Jayce, I think I'm ready."

His eyes are on me immediately, but he's silent.

"You know, for us to try. The control." The last word sounds like a gargle.

"You're not ready."

"I am."

"I can see it in your eyes. There's still fear there. I don't want to control you if you're afraid of me. Even the smallest amount."

He's right, there's fear. But I'm not afraid of him. I trust him to protect me and treat me with care. But I don't trust that it will last, and I'm afraid that once I've given in to his wish to control me, I'll lose my novelty.

He'll move on.

"Please, Jayce. I want..." the words die in my throat. How can I tell him that what I want more than to be dominated is the simple reassurance that I'm not like the others? That we'll last.

"Violet. Listen to me. There's nothing I want more than for you to say you're ready, but you can't just say it, or say you'll try, when I see you still have doubts. You have to *know* it. I don't want to take advantage of you."

Jayce moves a few inches away from me and I stretch to get that closeness back. My body pleads with his.

I watch his expressions, intense and indecipherable, and then he has a decision.

"I won't say yes yet," he continues, "but I can't tell you no. So tonight, we'll find a way between those. You want to try that?"

I nod.

My head drops lower and I stretch out on the couch, my feet up and my head in his lap. I roll to my back as he continues to stroke my hair, watching expressions cross his face like clouds across the sky.

I close my eyes and focus on breathing, the heat between us, the current humming like power lines on a summer night.

"Don't move." He lifts my head from his lap and places it gently on the couch cushion as he stands. "I'll be back in a minute."

I hear him walk inside, the refrigerator door open and close, and dishes clank on the counter.

"Eyes closed?" I hear him at the door to the terrace.

"Yes." My senses are on alert, wondering what he's up to.

"Open your mouth."

My eyes flutter open at this request and Jayce holds a plate above me but I can't see what's on it.

"Closed." He says sternly. I obey. "And just to make sure you keep them closed, lift your arms."

I lift my arms and feel him tug at my shirt, pulling it up over my stomach. My body quivers in anticipation, feeling warmth pool deep in my belly. Jayce lifts the fabric up higher and I angle my shoulders to let him pull it off, but he stops when the neck of my T-shirt reaches my nose, trapping my arms above my head and effectively blindfolding me with the material still covering my eyes.

"That should hold you," he chuckles.

I whimper, feeling the night air caress my exposed stomach. The lacy cups of my bra don't offer much protection.

"Now, open your mouth."

I do, and a bumpy, fragrant object brushes my lower lip. I bite into a burst of juicy sweetness. Strawberry.

"This one's easy. We'll play a little guessing game. You get it right, you get another."

I chew and swallow the berry. "And if I get it wrong?"

"Then I get one."

It sounds simple, but I know there's more to the game. I guess correctly on the tangy grape and subtly gritty pear, but then he places a piece of cheese on my tongue. It's sharp and salty.

"Parmesan?"

"Aged cheddar. And now one for me." I feel a cool slice of something placed on my stomach, just above my navel, and then Jayce's breath just above me. His hot mouth covers the slice, his teeth grazing my skin. "Delicious. Pear."

I squirm and press my knees together, feeling warmth gather between my thighs as I remain imprisoned by my T-shirt and my own will.

I'm letting this happen. *Wanting* this to happen.

"Another?"

"Yes." My voice is barely a whisper as hormones zing through my system, tasting the depth of dark chocolate, bitter and sweet, as it melts on my tongue. Another flavor, pebbled texture but exceptionally sweet, follows it.

"I—I don't know."

"Fig." Jayce tells me. He trails a piece of fruit down my chin and neck, finally letting it rest between my breasts. "My turn."

Jayce's tongue follows the path of the fruit, hot and moist, until it curls and flicks the fruit into his mouth. His tongue returns to the place where the fruit rested and he traces the lace edge at the top of my breast, then dips inside the cup to brush my nipple. "So sweet."

I shudder, a soft moan escapes me.

"More?"

I nod and open my lips for another taste, but this time I taste Jayce's lips as he holds a morsel of chocolate between his teeth. I close my lips over this gift, but then reach my lips for more of him.

Jayce deepens the kiss and the flavor of chocolate and fruit and his tongue in my mouth sparks a hunger. I kiss him like my whole body is starving for his touch, feel his cool fingers trace my ribcage, his thumbs brush over my bra and then sweep inside it to pluck my nipples into firm buds.

I pant with want, begging him to take this further, and he pulls my shirt the rest of the way over my head, so our eyes finally meet. Freed from their prison, my arms reach immediately around his neck and I pull him closer into a deep kiss.

Jayce wedges his hands beneath my shoulders and knees, pulls me up from the couch and carries me to his room.

"I couldn't help myself," he confesses as he lays me out on his bed. I let him undress me down to my underwear, tuck me in bed, and watch as he removes everything but his boxers. He slides under cool sheets next to me and holds me close. "I just wanted a taste, but you are too sweet. I need more."

CHAPTER 33: JAYCE

"Take a nap, or a shower, or whatever. I don't care what you do, just give me an hour and then we'll figure out dinner." I dump Violet's gym bag on her bed in the hotel suite and back out of the room as fast as possible.

I hear a weak "OK" as I shut the door and instantly I feel guilty. I don't need to snap at her. It's not her fault that the flight to LA was a nightmare.

On one side: Gavin, Chief, Dave and Kristina.

On the other: Me, Violet, Tyler and Stella.

I feel like a human shield who took fire from both sides. The girls were in some covert little war, pitching snide comments at each other.

Among the band, it was more overt. We tried to do a meeting on the flight and none of us could agree on anything, even stuff as simple as the order we'll record songs tomorrow.

"I don't care how you change up the song!" Chief finally shouted at us all when the playlist argument devolved into a bitch-fest about one song that's not guaranteed to be part of our album. "We're going into the studio tomorrow and recording *something*, even if I have to grab you by your balls and drag you in there."

It's going to be a fucking disaster. I wish I could time-travel back about five years to when we'd just spend our Friday nights playing and drinking on the house. We'd take some girls home or stay up all night jamming, and we'd sleep off the hangover the next morning. No talk of hitting a studio stupid early.

But Chief's got a punishing schedule for us now that the album rollout is planned. We're going to get it done, come hell or high water.

It's going to be hell, I guarantee you.

I drag my suitcase to my bedroom on the opposite side of the suite and strip for the longest, hottest shower possible. My skin blisters under the prickly water pressure until my muscles finally release the tension I realize I've been carrying the last seven hours we've been in transit.

Carrying. That's a pretty good word for all the baggage and bullshit that goes with our band now. I get that it's the price of fame, but the cost is staggeringly high. Sometimes I wonder how much of our effort and attention is really on our music. I'd bet craft doesn't even get into the double-digits, percentage-wise.

The water's never going to run cold in this hotel, so finally I give up and flip the handle. I'm scrubbing my hair dry with a towel when I walk back into my bedroom naked.

A little squeak alerts me I'm not alone. I pull the towel off my head and Violet's on my bed, up by the pillows on top of the covers. Her face is crimson and her eyes are on her lap.

"I'm sorry! I didn't think you'd come out of the bathroom so … so … naked."

I tuck the towel around my waist and chuckle, enjoying the pretty pink flush that colors her cheeks and her neck. I unzip my suitcase. She's had my dick in her mouth, so it's not like I'm showing her something she hasn't seen before.

I watch her as I drop my towel and pull on boxers and then shorts, but she keeps her eyes down. "Why are you here, Violet?"

"I wanted to talk."

"So talk." I fight to keep the irritation out of my voice. She was pretty much the only person on the plane who didn't piss me off.

Well, Gavin's girlfriend was fine, too. Even when feisty little Stella kept pushing Kristina's buttons, daring her to say another rude thing, Beryl stayed out of it.

"Who's side are you on?" Kristina demanded.

"I'm Switzerland," Beryl said, turning back to her e-reader. "You're not going to make me choose between my boyfriend and my best friend. I choose both. Always."

I snuck a glance at Violet then and she sat apart from all of us, curled up on a skinny leather airplane couch, watchful. Now she's in the same position on my bed, a defensive posture that suggests she doesn't quite trust her surroundings.

"I heard Kristina and Stella fighting over something about dresses and going out. You promised we could stay in tonight." Her eyes plead with me.

"We will. We've got room service, and a zillion channels, and I can have them send up playing cards if that's what you want to do." I walk around the edge of the bed and sit near Violet's bare feet. Her slender arms are wrapped around her knees.

"So they're all going out and you've got to stay here and babysit me?" Violet's chin juts out. "I'm sorry I asked. You can go. I'll stay here. I'm fine."

"No, that's not what I meant at all. I don't know what everyone else is up to tonight, but considering all the togetherness on the flight"—I wrinkle my nose and Violet smiles a little, catching my meaning—"I figured it would be better if we all just did our own thing."

"So what's the deal with the dresses and going out, then?"

Guilt washes over me. I signed her up for something she didn't want to do, and now I'm too chickenshit to come out and *tell* her what's expected tomorrow. At what point did I think this was a good idea? Like she wouldn't notice that it's a photo op?

"There's a thing tomorrow," I explain. "Some actress's birthday party. Kiki Kennedy?"

Violet's lips part with surprise. "I know who that is. She's in the next superhero movie."

"Right. And it makes our label very happy when we show up to things, even though they don't have much to do with our music." I reach for Violet's hand, maybe to anchor her here for a moment longer. "The band's expected to make an appearance."

We're supposed to look good and turn on the charm, and the girls are expected to be the best kind of arm candy—what guys *want* and girls *want to be*. I don't tell Violet this, but she puts the pieces together lightning-fast.

"And you want me to *go?*" she asks in horror, as if I've asked her to cover her body in spiders. "I thought Kristina was talking about a normal party. If I go anywhere near a publicity mess, my life is *over*."

I stutter out excuses, but Violet pulls her hand out of my grasp and practically leaps off the bed like I've stung her.

"Is that the real reason you brought me here? To be your groupie?" Her lip curls in disgust and I open my mouth, but she holds up a hand to silence me. "Don't. Don't make it worse than it already is. Don't talk to me."

Violet slams my bedroom door and then her own, and I don't hear another peep from her through the long, painfully quiet night.

***

"Nobody fucked up their voice last night, did they?"

Chief stares us all down and we shake our heads, schoolboys brought in for interrogation by the principal. I sip tea and Gavin chugs water. We're bringing our A game.

Tyler, always our comic relief, sticks out his tongue. "All better!"

Chief introduces us to Ravi, a little Indian dude with Coke-bottle glasses who couldn't be much over thirty. I catch Gavin and

Dave exchanging looks—this guy is totally new to us, and it looks like our label just signed us up with a producer who's more sound tech than creative director.

He's in for a wild ride. Gavin or Dave will chew him up and spit him out.

We start with an easy song, "Can't Fall for You," in the sense that it's something everyone can agree on. The lyrics have been solid for a couple of weeks now and I'm happy with the instrumentals. The song hits a sweet spot for Gavin's voice, and when the rest of us fill on the chorus, it's a ballad with real sing-along punch:

I know better than to fall
Know my heart and build a wall
Been through the forest and been misled
Been down that dark path to your bed
And I can't fall
Can't fall for you
Again, this time, no matter how you beg me
No matter how my heart bleeds for you to take me
Back again

We rocket through that recording, four takes in under an hour. Ravi's quiet coaching boosts the tempo, brings my guitar forward in the bridge, but nothing throws us.

Until the next song. "This Girl's Gone," is a powder keg in just about every way, and I'm struggling to keep my cool as Gavin gets bossy with Ravi, Dave bitches at Tyler over some timing thing, and I feel like we're still not getting the chord progression right on the end of the first verse. An hour ticks by without even one take to show for it and my stomach grumbles for lunch, still another hour away.

"Let's take ten." Ravi's out of the booth and into the studio, his voice cool and smooth.

"We don't have time to take ten. Lunch is in an hour, and we've got to get this track down," Gavin counters.

Ravi straightens up to his full height—maybe five-five—and looks Gavin dead in the eye. "I said. Take. Ten."

Ravi's voice isn't even one decibel louder, and his expression doesn't change. But just like that, the balance of power shifts in the room. We know who's in charge, and it sure as hell isn't Gavin.

I slouch on the stool behind me and idly pluck at my guitar, trying to figure out "This Girl's Gone" without the rest of my band.

Ravi turns to me and his eyes narrow. "Jayce, are you deaf? Get out of here, man. Back in nine." He holds open the door from the studio to the hallway like it's a gentlemanly gesture, but it feels like a cattle prod. He's asserting his power over me as well.

When we come back in the room, the mood is different. We pick up our instruments, do our takes, and under Ravi's sharp, subtle guidance, things just start to flow.

While I was fantasizing about that Viper Records contract in the first half of the morning, Ravi forces total concentration after the break. He prods and pokes us whenever we lose focus—a little comment, a gesture.

"You're here to *work,* to perform and produce," Ravi says when we hit a snag long after lunch. "We're not here to bullshit or hash out our creative differences. Nobody cares about whether something was your idea or even a good idea. They only care about the sounds that actually make it into your mic."

We run through the rest of our confirmed playlist in the afternoon. I watch Ravi through the mirror as he adjusts and levels, one set of headphones on his ears, another around his neck, and a freakishly large collection of empty Red Bull cans collecting on a ledge next to him.

It looks like Sunday's going to be light duty. When we wrap, Ravi shakes each of our hands in turn and ushers us out.

"Jayce, can you hang around for a little longer?"

Maybe he's just a really flipping good hypnotist, but I hear myself agreeing to Ravi's request even though my brain is begging for

Violet. I need to be with her. I need to apologize. I need to beg her to come with me tonight, to help me. Or at least, I need her to understand if Chief forces me to take someone else.

In a choice between hanging out to see whatever Ravi's got back in his sound booth for me, or going back to the hotel to face the music with Violet, I choose the easy route.

Shit. Why is it I can run at danger, I'm ready to kick a stalker's ass, but the fear of disappointing her absolutely freaks me out?

Ravi flips a few switches and inserts a disc. A mournful woman's a cappella voice fills the booth, midrange and rough enough in the lower register that it doesn't take on that over-trained operatic tone I hate. Her pitch is spot on, and when a guitar and some percussion joins the woman's vocal, it's a magical build. I can almost feel my chest expanding.

"What do you think?" Ravi watches for my reaction as much as he listens for it.

"It's good. Damn good. Who is she?"

He shakes his head. "It's not about who she is. It's about who she could be. For you. Darren Bishop reached out to me, asked me to show you what's possible at Viper."

My jaw goes slack. "What? Who?"

"You don't have to play that game. I'm a free agent, but I know what's going on, both here and back at Viper. Darren thought you needed a little convincing."

"You can't tell anyone—"

Ravi rolls his eyes. "Give me some credit, Jayce. I've been testing stuff for you for a week, and you've only just met me. I played the part today, and we'll wrap this album for Tattoo Thief successfully. It'll be a great transition into your solo career."

I step back, reevaluating him for the third or maybe fourth time today. "I'm sorry. I misjudged you."

"Yeah, whatever. Don't judge a book by its cover, or reputation, and all that. I get that a lot, but it's not really a problem for me. I'm not the public face. Thing is, Jayce, you are. And we're going to have a bit of a packaging issue on our hands if you make the jump."

I raise my brows and Ravi clarifies.

"The women. The playboy life. You're going to have to decide pretty quick whether that's the image you're gonna stick with. Unless you're Madonna, artists have very few opportunities to reinvent themselves. This is one of your moments. Better grab it."

CHAPTER 34: VIOLET

"I'm not going away." Stella bangs on the door of my suite again. "Violet, let me in before security gets pissed!"

I mute *Say Yes to the Dress* and reluctantly pull open the door.

"Finally. What are you doing in here?" Stella strides inside, a couple of shopping bags dangling from her arms. She sees my guilty pleasure on the TV and rolls her eyes. "Oh. Perfect time for an intervention."

"None needed."

"Says the girl who dragged me to the land of pancakes when *I* needed an intervention."

"Seriously, Stella. This isn't your problem to fix."

She narrows her eyes. "Look, Violet. I helped you with the story on Willa. You're not going to bag out on me for this party and leave me and Beryl with the Wicked Witch."

I can't help it. The thought of Kristina, her face painted green and her nose hooked and warty, makes me giggle.

It's contagious. Stella's giggle becomes a laugh, my laugh turns into a cackle and suddenly we're cracking each other up with each new snort and peal of laughter.

"I *seriously* can't go to that party," I say when I catch my breath. "You don't understand. I don't want to—I can't be in the media. Look at what you got dragged into."

Stella sobers for a moment. "Yeah. It sucks. But I wouldn't change it. It's worth it, being with Tyler."

"I'm still not going."

"That's why I brought something to change your mind." Stella fishes in her bag and pulls out a black ball of hair. It looks like some furry critter died.

I wrinkle my nose. "It's a wig."

"It's a disguise. It's perfect! You don't tell anyone your name, you wear a wig, and you'll be fine. Nobody's going to recognize you. Problem solved."

"But what if I just don't want to go?" I wrestle with telling Stella the real reason, the thing that could blow up my world, but bite my tongue.

"Then do it for Jayce. Because if you don't go, he's going to have to take someone else. And you can't throw a rock around here without hitting some girl with bigger boobs and bleached-out hair and a burning ambition to screw a rock star."

The threat stops me cold. I have nothing to say about that; I'm not his girlfriend. If the band has to go to this party and every guy is expected to bring a date, Jayce is going—with or without me.

"Let's try this thing on."

***

Stella's right. The wig's heavy bangs and soft layers around my face channel Zooey Deschanel, making my green eyes and pale skin even more dramatic. Stella layers thick liquid liner on my eyes, very retro glamour, and foundation that practically erases my freckles.

I look like a totally different person.

And that, coupled with the fear that Jayce might pick someone else, gives me just enough courage to let Kristina, Beryl and a mad genius stylist called Cole into the suite a couple hours later. We go through the dresses he's brought and the three girls eventually settle on theirs—flirtier and more colorful than New York, but just the right tone for summer in LA.

"I already picked your dress," Kristina says, daring me to challenge her. Cole hands me a slinky green thing that tries to shimmy off the hanger. I take it to my room to try it on.

No. Way.

No way in *hell*. The neckline plunges halfway to my navel, revealing more cleavage than most of my bras. Which, by the way, are not going to work under this dress. Nothing can.

"I'm not coming out," I say through the door. "This dress is too much."

Stella opens the door to my room without knocking. "Oh, no, honey. It's perfect. You need a totally different look."

"What, slut circa nineteen-sixty-one?"

"No. You're going for bombshell. And trust me. In that dress, nobody's going to be looking at your face." Stella gives me a naughty wink.

"That's because they're going to be watching to see when my nipples pop out!"

"And would that be such a bad thing?"

"Open up, girls!" Cole, flanked by Kristina and Beryl, enter my room too. So much for privacy. "Oh. That's magnificent. Be sure to tell them you're wearing a Giustiniano."

"Justine-a-who?" The polysyllabic name sails straight over my head.

"I'll write it down for you. He's going to be so in love with this look," Cole gushes.

I'm swept away in a sea of shoes, clutches and jewelry. Stella presses a handful of pewter lace into my hands. "Trust me. When Jayce gets a load of that dress, he's going to be dying to know what's underneath it."

I squeeze my eyes closed, like I'm nearing the top of a roller coaster. I know what's coming. The plunge is unavoidable. The question is whether I go down screaming or thrilled.

I take another glance at the new girl in the mirror, black locks and expressive cat eyes. It's so exotic and so unlike my everyday vanilla look that I shove every ounce of sense out of my head and nod.

I'll go. I want to be thrilled.

***

Beryl and I are working on a little champagne buzz by the time the limo pulls up to the party with the four of us inside. We're somewhere in a hilly, rich neighborhood, maybe Hollywood, and the guys are supposed to meet us here.

I've been in New York long enough not to be impressed much by celebrity, but this is insane. The mansion has landscaped terraces, a pool *with a waterfall,* and paper lanterns strung up everywhere. I count four full bars set up for maybe two hundred guests.

"Is this Kiki Kennedy's place?" I whisper to Beryl.

"No, stupid," Kristina scowls, shooting me a try-to-keep-up look of disdain. "It's Abraham Swift's."

I'm drawing a blank but I don't want to look stupid. Beryl rescues me. "Who?"

"Kiki's boyfriend. The director. Didn't you see *Bent on Annihilation?*" Kristina looks annoyed so I nod, at least recognizing last summer's big action movie. "God, do you even watch television?"

"Shut up, Kristina," Stella hisses. "We can't all be as shallow as you."

"What the fuck did you just call me?" Kristina takes a step toward Stella and I swear there's going to be a girl fight, right here in some director's backyard.

"I said you were shallow," Stella says, slower and clearer this time. "And throw in stupid, because you have no right to call Violet that. And basically a Grade-A bitch, if you want to know the truth."

"I know the truth," Kristina hisses. "I know where *all* the bodies are buried. Gavin's, Tyler's, even perfect little Violet's."

I gasp just as Beryl's champagne flute twitches and Kristina shrieks, the arc of wine forming a stain right down the front of her blue raw silk dress.

Beryl apologizes immediately but there's mischief in her eyes, Stella mutters something like "see you next Tuesday," and Kristina shouts at a passing waiter to bring her a towel.

"You shouldn't have done that, Beryl," Kristina snarls. "I've got so much dirt on Gavin, there's plenty to drag you down, too."

CHAPTER 35: JAYCE

Walking through crowds is always tough when the band does an appearance, and tonight is no different. Just moving from our limo to the terraced garden where most of the party is happening means dozens of hands to shake, cheeks to kiss, and people to pretend I remember.

I don't, but Gavin and Dave are in their element, subtly reminding me of who's who. I don't know how they remember that shit. I can barely remember groupies' names.

I'm edgy and tense, anxious to get this party over with and go back to the hotel to see Violet. Chief said he'd get me another date, no problem, but I don't want another date.

I want Violet.

God, I want her. But this party is the last place she should be, and I get that. I was stupid to even ask her to come.

I spot Kristina and Stella on a lower level garden terrace, hissing and spitting like territorial cats. Beryl flicks her champagne glass toward Kristina and Kristina shrieks, liquid spilling down her front.

Bullseye. Beryl might look harmless, but she's got good aim. I jog down a flight of steps to reach the girls before things really get out of hand, disappointment churning in my gut that Violet isn't here with them.

Serves me right. From day one, she's made it clear that she's not a groupie. Not easy. Not interested in the rock-star lifestyle. I promised to protect her and the very *first* thing I did was undermine that.

I'm a selfish bastard, or at least a spineless one, letting Gavin and Dave and Chief bully me into being here with some random girl I've never even met.

I paint on a wolfish grin and butt in right as Stella looks like she's winding up for a punch. "So where's my hot date?" I say, immediately locking my eyes on some magnificent tits, barely packaged in a green dress with a plunging V-neck that points straight to her crotch.

It takes me a moment to peel my eyes off the boobs on display. When I do, I can barely see a pale face fringed in thick, black bangs. The girl's staring at her shoes, but then her eyes flick up to me. Sparkling green. Alive. And fucking angry.

"No new groupie for you. You have to put up with me." Violet's voice trembles with rage.

"Violet! I didn't recognize—"

"Obviously. You were too busy looking at my breasts."

Shame floods me. She's right, but hell if I'm going to let her bitch me out in front of the rest of the girls. Kristina's busy with a towel supplied by an overly attentive waiter and Beryl's whispering to Stella.

I take Violet's arm to lead her away but she wrenches it out of my grasp. "Don't touch me."

"You're making a scene," I growl. "Follow me."

I stride away from her and glance back when she doesn't follow.

"Do it, Violet." The command in my voice sets her feet in motion. When we're safely away from the crowd in a quiet corner of the garden, I stop and square my shoulders to face her. "I'm sorry."

"For what?"

Being an asshole. Failing to protect you. "For forcing you to be here."

"You didn't force me. I *chose*, Jayce. I came because I didn't want you to be here with some groupie. But obviously I chose wrong, because you don't want me here after all."

"That's a lie," I grab Violet's shoulder and this time she doesn't pull away, just stares at me with green eyes full of hurt and fury. "I wanted you here. Hell, I just *want* you. But I never want to force you to do anything you don't want to do."

"You want to control me." Her voice is softer, more timid.

"Maybe I do, but that's different. Force is taken. Control is given. I'll never have control of you unless you give it to me freely."

"And if I do?"

I see her pulse flutter in her neck, a delicate flush rising between her breasts and coloring her skin. "If you give me control, I won't take it until you're sure. You have to be sure of what you want, and sure of me. You have to trust me."

"I do."

I drop my hand from her shoulder, studying her face as her eyes burn with intensity. "You what?"

"I do trust you. I want you. But I don't want to give you control unless I know you're not going to treat me like some groupie. Like the way you just *did.*" Her breath hitches. "I'm not disposable, Justin."

The hurt in her voice is worse than a sucker punch, worse than a scald from hot steam. She thinks she's one of them, and I have to find a way to prove that she's not, and never will be.

I do the first thing my brain supplies—I haul her against me and kiss the breath out of her. I crush her body against mine, as if that connection could somehow show her I want her for so much more than a one-night stand.

When I finally release her, she's panting.

I frame her face with my hands, the fury gone, gentleness in my touch. "You are precious to me, Violet. Don't you get that? I don't want a groupie. I want you, for every minute you'll have me and more. You're exactly who I've been waiting for."

Violet blinks, her lips swollen from my kiss, and I see desire replace fury. "Then what are you waiting for?"

***

We can't get away. I've only just arrived and a few sharp words from Chief remind me that I need to circulate, see and be seen, and fulfill my obligation before I'm allowed to leave the party.

Dave's managed to calm down Kristina and he and Tyler do a good job of steering their girls away from each other. I escort Violet to the bar and struggle to focus on getting through the next hour or two, now that the promise of what's possible is out there.

She's willing. It crackles in the air like a lightning storm.

I hear a trill behind us and Kiki Kennedy's bubbly laughter floats above the crowd. She's in a silver dress that's so short and tight, I swear that either her boobs or her ass cheeks are going to pop out of it at any moment. Silver platform sandals make her taller than Abraham Swift.

Not that he's complaining. He's short, a little paunchy, and could easily pass for her father. I decide now's the moment for introductions.

"Mr. Swift, thanks for inviting us." I extend a hand and he grabs it for a two-handed politician's shake. "Jayce McKittrick. From Tattoo Thief."

"No introduction necessary for you, Jayce. Your music speaks for itself. I'm a bit of a guitar man myself. But I do need an introduction to this lovely creature."

He reaches for Violet's hand and his hooded eyes scan her not once but twice. Right the fuck in front of me. Instead of a handshake, he twists her wrist and plants his thin lips on the back of her hand.

"Do you have a name?"

I clear my throat, fighting my urge to shove him back and scrub the filth off Violet's hand. "Uh, Alyssa," I offer, supplying the first name I can think of that starts with an *uh* sound. "This is my girlfriend, Alyssa, and this is Abraham Swift."

"Call me Abe, babe." He winks, apparently amused by a line that's so tired it should be put to sleep. Forever.

"Jayce! I just saw Gavin and Beryl!" Kiki trips over to me and throws her arms around my neck in greeting. It could be the sandals, it could be the booze, it could be her general ditziness, but suddenly I'm chest-to-chest with some perky silicone that Abraham probably paid for.

I gently extract the birthday girl and introduce her to—shit. What did I call Violet?

"Alyssa." Violet makes the save, introducing herself to Kiki.

"Are you an actress or a musician?" Kiki's blunt, but her question carries no malice.

"Neither," Violet says. "I'm a photographer."

"Oh! I just got some new head shots and my photographer was ah-*mazing*. Who have you shot?"

"I just shot Tattoo Thief," Violet says. "And I'm working on some other projects right now."

"Tell, tell." Kiki's all cozy with us like we're BFFs.

"Well," Violet hesitates. "There's this artist in New York. She does street art, but it's not like regular graffiti. I'm building a photo feature to sell to a magazine."

"Street art?" Abraham's interest is piqued. "That shit is hot right now. They sold a piece at Christie's for, like, three mil. Guy who painted it doesn't even get a cut, but the owner of the building where they cut it out made out well."

"They cut it out?" Violet's tone sharpens. "They sold it?"

"Well, yeah. Whatcha gonna do? Some guy paints it on your building without asking, then that brings out a bunch of looky-loos and some guys who just want to mess it up. Pain in the ass. Best thing is to get rid of it. Sell it." Abraham shrugs as if it's that simple, but Violet's unconvinced.

I change the subject to Kiki's latest movie and we listen to her gush a bit. Violet cuts in and excuses herself to the restroom. Before she gets away, I grab her wrist.

"You sure about what you want? About giving me control?" I whisper in her ear.

She nods once, the black wig feathering across her cheeks.

"Then prove it. Bring me your panties."

"My—?"

"You heard me. They'd better be in my pocket ten seconds after you get back from the bathroom."

Violet's green eyes darken and she licks her lips. "Yes, sir."

I release her and turn back to Abraham and Kiki, scolding my dick to behave. I doubt Violet's ever done anything this risqué in her life.

CHAPTER 36: VIOLET

I sit on the toilet, eyeing the tiny scrap of pewter lace currently strung between my knees. Jayce wants it in his pocket, but I'd rather sing the national anthem right in the middle of this party than go without undies in this ridiculously short dress.

Except that this is a test.

He knows it. I know it. Jayce is testing whether I trust him, how far he can push me, and how much control I'm willing to give him.

Give. That's the operative word. The fear that ruled me and made me fight him even while he tried to help me is evaporating, replaced by the knowledge that he can only have as much control as I'm willing to give.

Or none at all.

I stand up and pull my panties back in place, sliding my dress down over my thighs and the stocking-and-garter-belt contraption that Stella thought should go with my new retro bombshell look.

"Jayce will love it," she said, and I confess I hoped she'd be right.

I step out of the stall and wash my hands, feeling guilty I can't fulfill Jayce's request. I was raised in a conservative family. I've never worn any dress as remotely revealing as the one I'm wearing now. And I'm already feeling more than a little exposed by tempting fate and coming to this party in the first place. I let jealousy take over for good sense when I decided to come, just so he wouldn't spend the night with some groupie.

A couple of girls push into the bathroom as I reapply deep red lipstick.

"You're with Jayce McKittrick!" the blonde girls squeaks.

"Um, yeah." I try to look busy stuffing my compact back in my clutch.

"Girlfriend, groupie or escort?" the other, raven-haired one asks.

My mouth drops open.

"Shut up, Kylee," the blonde girl says. "Sorry. It's just a game we play. You know, like you pick a star and say whether you'd 'screw, marry or kill' him? At parties, we play the guessing game—is he with a girlfriend, a groupie or an escort?"

"I guess groupie," Kylee says, sizing me up. "But that's one fucking fantastic dress."

"It's a Just, ah, a Justina-something." I hopelessly mangle Giustiniano, may the fashion gods forgive me. "But you're wrong. I'm not a groupie."

"Oh! Girlfriend?" The blonde's face lights up. "He's, like, *so* famous for being a player. Girlfriend is *serious!*"

I shake my head again, and both girls' eyes bug out. Then I realize what the final choice is: escort.

I hold up my hands. "Oh, no, it's not like that. He's not paying me to be here. We're just friends."

"Says the girl who was sucking on his tongue an hour ago," Kylee says.

"You saw that?"

"Me and a hundred other people. Not subtle, girl. If you were a tree, he'd be the dog who pissed a mile-wide mark on his territory."

I giggle at the visual. His territory. Jayce is controlling and pushy, but he's also fiercely protective. And we're definitely not just friends—the way my skin heats with Kylee's description of our not-so-private make-out session is proof of that.

I excuse myself and go back inside a stall, reaching under my dress before I can overthink it. I slide the stretchy lace over my hips and down my legs. I curl the panties into a ball in my fist, then fly out of the stall before anyone can give me the stink-eye for not washing my hands again. Kind of hard to do that while clutching a wad of lace.

Jayce is still chatting with Kiki and Abraham when I return, and I creep up next to him to try to unobtrusively stuff the garment in the pocket of his slacks.

"I got you more Champagne," Jayce grins, a naughty twinkle in his eye, and extends it to my fisted hand. I force a smile and a word of thanks and reach for the flute with my other hand.

He leans to my ear for a quick whisper: "Ten, nine, eight …"

I try to play the part of a tipsy girlfriend, snuggling up to Jayce to find his pocket, but he steps slightly to the side.

He flashes me a grin and mouths the words, "Seven, six, five …"

"Jayce, would you mind helping me find Stella?"

"Sure, Vi—uh, Alyssa. In just a minute." His wicked grin tells me he's not going to make it easy, and the seconds are evaporating.

Flustered, I glance around desperately and see a black circle protruding from a tall, shiny hedge that flanks all sides of Abraham's property. It takes less than a second to register. "I think I just saw a camera through there!"

All three heads turn in the direction I'm pointing and my hand darts into Jayce's pocket to deposit the panties. He squeezes my hand, a sly smile playing on his lips.

"You made that hard," I whisper furiously.

"No, *you* made it hard," Jayce says, his voice husky with intent. "Now just imagine what I can do to you—"

"Where'd you say you saw the pap?" Abraham breaks in, his phone pressed to his ear as he directs his security team. He says *pap* like *pop*, short for paparazzi. I point again and he barks something about the southwest corner, lower terrace.

"Paparazzi are *so lame*," Kiki whines. "I used to go swimming naked because we've got all these fences and hedges and stuff, but they got through that. The pictures came out a few months ago."

"How did you cope with that?" I worry that my voice is a little too keen to know the answer.

Kiki shrugs, "What could I do? *I* wasn't doing anything wrong, I was on private property. Of course we sued them, but it's hard to make it stick, especially since they paid off a neighbor to get access."

I feel Jayce's hand on my hip, pulling me closer to him. Maybe for comfort. Maybe he's listening as closely as I am.

"Weren't you embarrassed?" I ask.

Kiki grimaces like I've asked if she sleeps on nails. "Of course not! I kill myself in the gym practically every day for this body. If you've got it, flaunt it, you know? It's not the naked part, it's the fact that I had no control over who was taking the pictures and what they'd do with them."

I can't help it. My eyes rocket to Jayce and he locks on them, hearing the same meaning I do. It's not the *naked* taboo, or even the bondage, that's so wrong with my pictures online. It's the fact that I've lost control.

And as the images make their way to every sleazy corner of the Internet, that control slips further from my grasp.

***

Jayce's hands rest on the dimples of my lower back, just above my butt, as a ballad has me swaying in his arms.

Under cover of darkness on this terrace, with my wig and the so-not-me dress, I can almost forget the stalker nightmare and the fact that I'm playing with fire by even being here.

The DJ fires up a fast-paced song and Jayce dips his head for a slow, soft kiss before he lets me go, shoving his hand in the pocket where I *know* my panties are. "It's time, Violet. Let's go."

We wave to a few people and slip into a limousine out front. I haven't seen the rest of the band or their girlfriends in a while, but I was wrapped up in my own little world dancing with Jayce.

In the limo, Jayce raises a privacy barrier and then his hand goes to my knees. Gently, he pries them apart, his eyes on mine. He drops his chin and blows, a warm air current that drifts between my thighs and electrifies my skin.

"It was torture knowing what wasn't under this dress," Jayce says, and pushes the hem of my dress up my legs just enough to see the tops of my stockings and their garter attachments. "And now that I see what *is* underneath, it's even better."

Jayce licks his lips and I shudder.

His fingers trail up my arm. "Are you sure, Violet?"

I nod, but my insides quake. The last time someone had power over me, he abused it, and the threat that Brady could do worse still hangs over my head.

Jayce seems to sense my hesitancy.

"Think of this like a game. Like cards, like we're playing Go Fish." His fingers reach the top of my shoulder and then they descend, following the neckline of my dress. "You ask for a card and I give it to you. I ask for a card and you give it to me."

"And if I can't?" I'm not thinking cards, I'm thinking panic. What if he does the things Brady did? What if they make me feel filthy instead of free?

"Go fish." Jayce smiles, a tiny shrug in his shoulders. "I'm new at this, too, Violet. But I know I want it."

CHAPTER 37: JAYCE

I breathe on the back of her neck, watching fine hairs stand up. We've got about ten seconds before the elevator door opens on our floor, so I trail my hand up the back of her thigh and around the curve of her ass, just close enough to her center that she's reminded again that her panties are a wad in my pocket.

The elevator dings open and I take her hand to walk her to the door of our suite. She won't meet my eyes and I'm afraid she's having second thoughts.

Me? I'm horny as hell, but I try to contain it, worried that I'll scare her off.

I've seen some groupies do weird shit, and some even throw their panties at us—well, mostly at Gavin—while we're on stage. But I've never had a girl do *this*, simply because I asked her to.

It's a small thing, and the biggest turn-on wasn't the fact that I had to think about her bare pussy beneath her dress all night. The biggest turn-on was that she gave me that power.

I asked and she gave it. Control.

With groupies, there's no such thing as control. Even though you're the star, you don't control them. That's because they're focused on what they can get *from* you, whether it's a great lay or a story to tell their friends or a shopping spree on your platinum card.

I don't remember Violet asking for anything from me, ever. When she was scared, I protected her. When she was hungry, I fed her. And now, when I see the need in her eyes, I want to give her release, too.

Hell, I want to do more than that. I want to give her a toe-curling, earth-shattering orgasm.

But we'll get to that. First things first is talking her down off that ledge she's on. Because she might *say* that she's into this power exchange and that she's willing to give me control, but I can *see* that she's not all in, not yet.

She's scared out of her mind, but it's clouded by lust, too.

"Stand here." I point Violet to a space in front of a small desk that faces the floor-to-ceiling glass windows overlooking LA. "Take off the wig."

Her fingers shake a little as she reaches into the wig and pulls a dozen hairpins out. Then she slides it off, revealing a flat bun where her real hair's been hiding. I unravel the bun so her hair falls softly over white shoulders. It looks even more fiery in contrast with the cool green dress.

I tell her to place her palms flat against the desktop. She hesitates but then follows my directions. It has the delicious effect of making her bend slightly so her ass sticks out toward me.

My semi springs to full attention as I walk in a little half-circle around Violet, adjusting the lights, turning on music. She's watching me.

God, what I wouldn't give to get inside her head and put her fears to rest. But if I force things, if I move too fast, I'm going to be just like *him,* that guy who took pictures of her. And I know she'll run.

"Close your eyes." When she does so, I wait a beat, then close the distance between us and trail a feather-light touch across her cheek. She leans into my hand. "I want you to anticipate my touch. But I also want to keep you guessing. Wondering."

I bend down and one at a time pull her feet from her shoes, hearing her sigh as she loses a few inches in height.

Unfortunately, now her ass isn't displayed as prettily, so I take the hem of her dress and peel it up her thighs, until her ass is bare, just the silky ribbons of the garter belt running down the sides of each ass cheek.

I brush my thumb over one cheek, seeing her skin flush even here at my touch.

"Violet, are you OK?"

Her eyes still closed, she nods.

"Do you want more?"

Another nod, this one firmer.

My hand slides down the back of her leg and up to her center. She's wet. *Very.*

"Your body says you're ready for me, Violet. But I intend to take my time making absolutely sure that you get everything you need tonight."

Her dress is bunched around her waist and I find a hidden zipper under her arm, tug it down and dispense with the dress.

No bra, either. God, this woman is going to kill me.

My sorceress, my fairy princess, is equal parts Rapunzel and the witch. She remains absolutely still where I've commanded her, on display for me—nothing but a garter belt and stockings, her breasts taut and nipples in tight round buds.

I breathe on her shoulder and brush my fingers through a strand of hair. Her face is a mask of concentration, but I don't know if she's focused on me or the fear that I'll use her the way someone else did.

I let my fingers explore her soft skin, trailing my hands over her back, shoulders, breasts, thighs. I drag my fingernail up the back of her calf and she lets out a squeak of surprise. When I bend and flick her nipple with my tongue, she moans.

But through it all, she remains precisely where I positioned her: bent at the waist, hands on the desk, legs spread just enough.

"You're doing very well following my directions. Shall we try something more?"

Violet nods her head vigorously, her eyes still closed. I move my hand between her legs deliberately, but just before I reach the apex of her thighs, I touch the top of her stocking where the garter attaches.

Violet whimpers in frustration.

"I'll warn you, Violet, I'm very, very thorough." I kneel on the carpet behind her, her perfect ass inches from my face, and I unfasten the back garter straps. Then I move to the small space in front of her, between her legs and the desk, and I unfasten those garter straps as well.

Violet's legs tremble and I breathe across her pussy, stroking one finger down the delicate red-blonde hair. I grasp her hips and touch her with my tongue, slow strokes that flood my mouth with her taste.

Milk and honey.

Violet's quaking more violently now, as if it's taking all of her concentration just to remain upright. I wriggle out from under her and stand again, still dressed for the party.

I step a few feet away from her and remove my shirt, watching her breathing hard as she grips the desk. I drop my trousers and shove my boxers down over an epic hard-on that's begging me to quit torturing this girl and *do it*.

It's this very thing—not torture, but control—that has me about ready to explode even though she hasn't laid a hand on me. And what I *really* want to do to her is not something I've ever asked a groupie. I'd get slammed in the press for being kinky faster than I could pull my pants up.

I slide a finger between Violet's thigh and stocking, slipping the silk down her leg and off her foot. I repeat this with her other leg, then dispense with the garter belt altogether. Now I have what I need.

And I hope I can give her what she needs.

I get a couple of pillows from the bedroom and return to the living room. Violet still hasn't moved. It's surreal—Los Angeles lit up and sparkling forty floors below us, and Violet's naked form braced on the desk for whatever I ask from her next.

I pick up her hands, brushing her knuckles to my lips. "This is where it gets real," I whisper. "You can go with me as far as you want to. And you can open your eyes."

Her emerald eyes knock me back a step when they open, smoldering in intensity. I see surprise register in her face that I'm naked too.

I pull the desk a couple of feet from the window, thankful that we're not close enough to another building where people could see what we're about to do. The pillows go on top of the desk, then I direct Violet to resume where she'd stood, only this time, her palms don't go on the desktop.

I bend her over the desk on the pillows, her ass in the air, her arms dangling down over the other side. I take one of her stockings and tie her wrists together, then anchor them to a crossbar between the legs of the desk.

She whimpers, but doesn't protest.

I walk around the desk, brushing her ass with the back of my hand. I use the other stocking to anchor her ankle to one of the desk legs, and I grab my belt from my slacks to finish off the other leg.

Bound. Exactly where I want and need her to be.

CHAPTER 38: VIOLET

I gasp when I feel his fingers dig into the flesh of my hips. I feel like an acrobat, swinging on a thin rope between two platforms—utter panic and total bliss.

When I told him I'd give him control, I never said I wanted to be tied up. I probably vowed a million times while I was trying to get my stupid pictures off the Internet that I'd never let it happen to me again.

And yet here I am, skin on fire, my core throbbing with need, and my wrists bound tightly enough that I'm sure I won't get out of this by myself.

Fear seizes me and my breath comes in short, desperate pants as Jayce's hands slide up my ribcage to caress my back. I imagine some poor housekeeper discovering me tomorrow. I think of what Jayce could do to me now, with his body or with a camera. I don't even have a pair of panties covering me the way my Internet pictures did.

Panties. That's how this started, this playing with fire. No, it was before: when I teased him by sucking on his finger, and then made good on that promise by taking him in my mouth.

I'm afraid to speak, that my voice will betray my fear. Jayce works his fingers into my skin, massaging my ass, my thighs. He reaches to the front of me to find that bundle of nerves that makes me gasp. My brain feels like it's in a swirling cauldron of conflicted emotions that are so vibrant, they drown out all rational thought.

I could tell him to stop. I could tell him thanks for the walk on the wild side, but I prefer plain vanilla. I could tell him that something, *anything* would be better than tying me up—that power exchange doesn't have to be bondage, right? *Right?*

The voice in my head that whispers to me to take risks and reach for what I really want stuffs the rules-following girl into a closet and locks the door. My risk-taker is afraid if I stop this now, Jayce might never touch me like this again.

Worse, I might never try again.

Brady will win. He'll have delivered a poison pill that makes me never want to be this way—or this free—with someone again.

He'll have tamed the wild part of my heart forever.

I feel Jayce's touch evaporate and I shiver, immediately missing the heat of his body. I listen for his soft footfalls on the carpet, see him come into my peripheral vision, his broad, muscled body golden in the dim light.

He kneels, so his face is even with mine, his normally hard jaw softening.

"Violet, I have to know you're here with me." His fingers trace my cheek and jawbone, and he studies me with brown eyes flecked with copper and gold at their center. "Where did you go?"

I bite my lip and close my eyes, arrested by the softness in his tone when I expected that he'd be inside me by now.

"No. Open your eyes, Violet." His tone takes on a harsh edge. "Giving me control isn't the same thing as just giving up. You can't go hide somewhere inside your mind. You have to be *with* me."

"I am."

"No. You're not. I know your body. I know how you respond to me, and just now, you went cold. Limp. What happened?"

"You tied me up." My voice trembles. "That's what he did. And I'm just—afraid."

Jayce pales and immediately he reaches for my wrists to untie me. "God, Violet, I'm so sorry. I didn't mean—I didn't realize this would trigger…"

He trails off as he tugs at the stubborn stocking, but the knot seems to grow tighter. "I feel like such an ass. I just had this picture of you in my head."

Jayce stops, looks at me, and the guilt radiating from him shocks me. It's bigger than just tying me up.

"Tell me what you mean."

Jayce gives up tugging at my wrists, still on his knees in front of the desk.

"I'm making such a mess of this," he says disgustedly. "I just meant that I wanted this, and I thought, maybe if you'd let me, you'd like it too." He mutters something about cutting off the stocking and moves to stand, but I stop him.

"Wait. Justin, I'm fine." And even though I'm bent over and tied in this weird position, I really am. The fear has evaporated. "Tell me what you mean about the picture."

"I looked at your pictures. When you were gone in Ithaca. I looked at them a lot. And I wanted that." He hangs his head, guilt or shame twisting his features. "I'm sorry."

"You mean you wanted to tie me up and take pictures and put them on the Internet?" I'm trying to get him to see the ridiculousness of why he's feeling guilty, but he's not ready for it.

"No! God, no, Violet. I'd never do that. It's just, I wanted that control that you gave up for those photos. I wanted you to give it to me."

A smile forms on my face, and he looks slack-jawed with surprise that I'm not angered by his admission. "Then you're in luck, Justin. Because I never gave up control for those photos."

His head tilts in question.

"I'm tied up there, yes, but I never wanted to be. I didn't give him control; he took the power from me. My ex wanted those photos as protection, to be sure I'd never smear his name, so he made sure he could smear mine if I ever talked."

"Violet, please forgive me. I never meant to—"

"Shut up!" I can't keep the scream from tearing out of my throat. "Stop it! Stop apologizing for something you wanted."

"But it's something I never should have asked for!" Jayce looks buried by self-loathing, and the slice of the secret that I've been afraid to share with him cracks wide open, begging me to reveal it.

If I don't, this is the end. Maybe not of us, not yet, but it's the end of my opportunity to tell him this secret. This is my window. Take it or lose it forever.

"You can ask for it if you want it," I sob. "You can ask for control, you can ask to tie me up, you can ask for any sort of pleasure if you're brave enough." My tears come hot and heavy and he's pulling my face against his, our foreheads touching, his hands deep in my hair. "I wasn't. I never asked for this—not then and not now. But the truth is, with you, I wanted it."

There. That's the messy truth, and at first I think Jayce hasn't heard me or doesn't understand the full weight of what I'm saying. The shame of my pictures is bad enough, but the shame I carry for actually *wanting it* enough to let it happen, even though I never asked for it, drowns me.

Jayce takes a breath, tipping his face away from mine enough to look in my eyes.

"You wanted this?"

I nod. "Not with him. With you. But I was too afraid to ask."

"I just hoped, well, if you were willing to give me control, and I took care of you, you might be willing to give me more. Like this." Jayce fingers my bindings, the stocking still anchoring my hands firmly in place.

"Are you up for a round of Go Fish?" I ask. "Can we try again?"

Jayce nods. "I'll start with an easy one. Would you give me a kiss?"

I comply, letting his lips settle on mine and his tongue sweep through my mouth.

"Would you let me kiss you there?" My eyes dart to his erection, and he stands, close enough that I can take the head in my mouth.

After a minute, he groans and steps out of my reach. "You're killing me, Violet. This does not bode well for my endurance. My turn. Would you let me lick you?"

I nod.

"Anywhere?"

His question sends a delicious tremor through me. "Yes."

CHAPTER 39: JAYCE

I move behind her, my tongue seeking her folds, her wetness, her warmth. The taste of her explodes on my tongue, tangy and rich, and I probe for more.

I hear her moan, this time pure pleasure without a hint of fear. My tongue reaches deeper inside her, sucking her into my mouth, then I work the bud that makes her buck against the desktop, begging me for more.

I grasp her thighs, bringing her closer to me. I trace the crack of her ass down to where my tongue strokes her, and then up again past the tight entrance of her ass.

"Yes," she whispers. "Touch me there."

I'm alive with hunger, electrified by her invitation. I gather moisture from her and work it up her seam, swirling it around her rosebud and testing her resistance. She's quaking above me, and I move my tongue faster, flicking across her clit until I feel her body seize and stiffen, her climax rushing into my mouth.

Her moan becomes a wail, and I hold her there, my fingers stroking, moving, probing for what she wants. "I want you inside me," she begs, and I dive for my pants, grabbing a condom and rolling it over my cock.

I'm throbbing with need, too eager, but even as I approach her, I have to be sure. The dim light of our suite reflects in the window so I can see her, see the *yes* all over her face, and I position myself at her entrance.

She's wet but I press into her carefully. Her hips jerk back, her legs straining against the restraints I created, and I give her the full length of me, inch by inch, as I grasp her waist and guide us together.

"Justin. Yes." It's all she can manage, and everything I need. I draw back and thrust into her, building a rhythm that forces the air from my lungs. I rub her back, her waist, her ass and then the crack, pressing a finger against her bud until it flowers open for me.

"More," she pants, and I thrust harder, my cock buried inside her and my finger stroking her other entrance. We're moving together, each thrust met by a counter thrust, each stroke making her clench harder around me until I am pushed to my limit.

Our skin slaps together at each contact, and I explode, feeling my cock pulse with release. Violet's body stiffens, twitches, twists and goes slack as another orgasm crests and recedes. When I'm sure she's through it, I drape my chest across her back, my lips working to plant ten thousand kisses across her shoulders.

***

I'm not sure how I managed to get those knots apart after the most intense orgasm of my life ripped through me and left me hollow.

And content. I curl around Violet as I see dawn color the sky, her hair fanning across the pillow in front of me so I can smell its heady fragrance. I pull her close to my chest, my tanned forearm in stark contrast to the pale skin of her waist.

I can't resist. I kiss the freckles sprinkling her shoulders and she stirs.

"You seriously don't know how to keep your hands to yourself."

My hand covers one of her breasts. "Can you blame me?"

There's a smile in her voice. "Not really. I *am* pretty cute."

"No." My tone is serious. "Not even close. Beautiful, exquisite, breathtaking. But not cute. That just doesn't cover it."

She giggles as I plant more kisses on her shoulder. "Don't you need sleep?"

"After…" I plant my lips on another part of her shoulder. "I get to kiss…" I give her another. "All these freckles."

She laughs and rolls toward me, tucking herself into my chest. "Come here, Justin. If you've got some weird freckle fetish, I'm game."

***

Ravi grins when I walk into the recording studio with Tyler, each of us carrying a massive cup of coffee. Dave, Gavin and Chief are already here, and from the looks on their faces, they're not pleased with what we laid down yesterday.

"It needs more polish," Dave says, and makes Ravi jump to the first transition into the bridge for "Can't Fall for You." "I think you should splice in a different take here, and pull back on the bass."

Ravi pulls on his headphones and adjusts the mix, but I think I catch an eye-roll. Good. Then it's not just me wondering where Dave gets off micromanaging our *producer* who has a jillion more hours in the recording studio than he does.

While Ravi's remixing the track, Dave continues spouting off about the need to get things just perfect, and he bitches about a whole slew of faults with each of our work, even Gavin's. Chief keeps sucking down his coffee, but I think Dave's enough for the both of them.

Ravi pulls off his phones and punches a button. The remix is sharper, but it lacks the emotional build we had with the first, un-dicked-around-with one.

I know better than to fall
Know my heart and build a wall
Been through the forest and been misled
Been down that dark path to your bed
And I can't fall
Can't fall for you

"This is shit," I say. "You can't stitch together a bunch of tracks and call it right. Maybe we're more technically perfect here, but I don't hear the truth of the song."

The guys stare at me like I just declared an alien invasion.

"What?"

"He's right," Ravi mutters. "We can engineer the hell out of this, but that first take is the realest thing we've got."

"Don't you two have ears? Gavin's voice goes ragged at *misled*," Dave says, his annoyance evident.

"And that's what makes it work." I catch my voice rising and I struggle to keep my temper in check. Now's not the time to have it out.

Nobody looks convinced.

Ravi clears his throat. "Dave, you want it more perfect. Gavin wants it simpler. Jayce wants it more complex. But guys, this is art, not science. I can mix the hell out of it and it'll get different, but not necessarily better. It's like getting Picasso to color in the lines. Perfection isn't the thing to strive for. It's passion. It's the perfection in the *moment*, not in the song."

The intensity of Ravi's little speech stuns me. Finally, Tyler breaks the silence. "OK. Let's go with the first version." Thank God he's got my back.

"Maybe there are just too many cooks in the kitchen right now," Chief says and stands. "I'm going to make a call. You guys get in the studio and nail down the last three songs and then we'll talk."

Gavin, Tyler and Dave follow him out of the sound room to get warmed up, but I hang back. "Thanks for that," I tell Ravi.

"No thanks needed. You have good instincts."

"Dave can be a jerk when he takes charge. And the less he's in charge of, the more he tries to force the issue."

Ravi leans back in his chair, eyes unblinking. "And how about you?"

"Me?"

"What are you like when you can't be in control?"

My mind flashes back to the night with Violet, the war between what she's willing to give me and what I want to take. All of her. I'll take everything she can give me and more, but unlike her bastard ex, I'll keep it safe. I *need* to protect her.

And that's when it hits me, that this thing with her—all my lust and protective instincts—they're nothing compared to what's really driving me. Love. I love that girl like I'd lay down in the street for her. Take a bullet for her. Give my life for her.

"Jayce?"

My head snaps up, realizing Ravi asked me a question that I failed to answer.

"What are you like when you can't control everything? Because if you go solo, it means less control, not more. You can't do it all yourself, and you're going to have to find people you trust to make it happen."

"I'm a pain in the ass," I admit. "But when I know someone's got my back, like Tyler, it's all good. I don't have to run the show."

Ravi nods. "Good. Then you need to figure out who you can trust. Once you're crystal on that, then you make your decision." He puts out a hand to shake. "Either way, it's a pleasure working with you."

I grasp his small hand in mine, nodding. This guy might seem insubstantial, young and slight, but he's got sense where it matters.

He's also got a hell of a backbone. We play through the next three songs and he coaches us through them, focusing on tempo and timing. His instructions are sharp, clear, and cut down each of our egos in turn. I fuck up just as much as the rest of my band mates, and each time, Ravi doesn't let it slip.

By mid-afternoon, I'm sweating and spent. My fingers are on fire, the pads raw and tender from playing my heart out. But Tattoo Thief has never sounded better. Even Dave looks like he's shrugged off his pissy little mood as we exit the studio.

"That was hot," Tyler says, giving Gavin a playful punch. "You made that last vocal scream sex. Beryl's going to flip."

"Maybe I'll make her scream," Gavin answers, chuckling at a dirty thought. "Chief, where are the girls?"

"Already en route to the airport," he says. "We'll meet them there. You guys were so into it that we don't have time to go back to the hotel."

We load our instruments into a black SUV and cruise to the airport, my mood darkening by the mile. We're going back to New York. Back to the stalker and Violet's nightmare. Back to the reality that I can't protect her forever.

CHAPTER 40: VIOLET

It's been three weeks since I came home from Europe, and my life has changed, utterly and completely.

I'm no longer coaching eight graders on the finer points of drawing with perspective and scaring them with the realities of unplanned pregnancy. I'm taking pictures of street art and a rock band, hiding from a stalker, and living in fear of paparazzi who might associate my name with Jayce's.

And things are starting to come apart.

I've holed up in Jayce's apartment for three days since our return from LA and each time he asks me to go out, I refuse. The stalker is just one guy, but the paparazzi could be anywhere. Everywhere.

I remember watching the old movie *Arachnophobia* with Katie in high school. It's a horror flick that's full of spiders chasing people, and the thing that makes it really scary is that there's not just one villain chasing you, like Freddy or Chucky. You're running from everything, and nowhere is safe.

Nowhere is safe for me but this apartment. And so I stay here.

My phone rings and I lunge for it, eager for some human contact while Jayce is away at practice and secret meetings with a lawyer. He says he hasn't made up his mind about splitting from the band yet, but I think it's coming.

It's Katie, not Jayce, on my caller ID.

"Sister!" I sing. "How much trouble are you in, and how long are you grounded?"

Katie laughs. "Just because I call you to complain whenever I get caught breaking curfew doesn't mean I did it last night. Or, at least I didn't get caught."

"You're going to give Dad a heart attack, Katie."

"Not if he's drooling in an armchair when I sneak in."

Katie's so bad. If I'd pulled stunts like that, I'd have been grounded for a month.

"Seriously, Katie. He's working hard on the campaign stuff. Give him a break." I don't know why I'm sticking up for my father, considering the rift between us since he asked me to reconcile with Brady. Call it growing up. "Anyway, this will all be over in November."

"It better be. I don't want to do my senior year with a million rules when my friends can get away with pretty much anything."

She has a point. My folks have always been strict.

"So, the real reason I'm calling is not that I'm in trouble. But you are."

My heart plummets. "What did you see?"

"Did you see *People?* New issue just came out."

Of course I didn't see the magazine. The last thing I want to read is garbage about people who are unlucky enough to be sucked into the spotlight. They could have been me.

"Hang on a sec. I'm sending you a picture." I hear Katie rustling in the background and then my phone chimes with a text. The photo in the text is a picture of a page from the magazine, and that page features a large picture of Kiki Kennedy, boobs thrust out, hand on her hip, with Abraham Swift's arm snaking around her waist.

"So?" I ask. I don't want to admit I know Kiki, much less that I was at her party. Katie would ask me an avalanche of questions.

"Look in the corner, over Kiki's right shoulder. That's you, Vi."

I toggle my screen back to the text and holy cats, that *is* me. It's a grainy shot, probably taken with a cell phone by one of the party guests. I'm in the background, my arms locked around Jayce's neck as we dance.

My sister knows what's up. She reads *People* the way my parents read the bible, so I shouldn't be surprised that she spotted me with Jayce.

"That wig is so wild," Katie gushes, not waiting for my confirmation. "I wouldn't have even believed it was you, but I've been looking at you for seventeen years. Is he really your boyfriend?"

"I'm not sure," I confessed. "He might be. We're—close."

"I thought you said you liked a guy named Justin?"

"That's his name. He just goes by Jayce, like, short for JC."

"A nickname for a nickname. Weird." Katie shrugs it off. "So can I come visit? I want to meet him! I'm lifeguarding but I'm off Mondays and Tuesdays, so I could take the bus down Sunday night and stay with you."

"No!" I choke out, then try to moderate my voice so she won't hear the fear in it. I can't let her come to the city until the police catch that stalker. Until then, Jayce has commanded me to stay at his place. "I mean, not yet. Give me a couple of weeks to figure stuff out, then we'll plan it."

"OK." Katie's tone is wary. "What are you not telling me, Vi?"

"What?"

"Something's up. Why are you so afraid of people knowing you're dating a rock star? If it were me, I'd tell everyone I know. Especially that Tierney bitch who stole my prom date."

"I can't talk about it right now," I say, putting an officious note in my voice. "I'm sorry, I'm just on the way out the door. But I'll tell you everything once things calm down."

"Promise?" Katie's sweet request makes it hard to lie to her. Of course I can't tell her the whole truth about Brady's pictures.

"Yeah, I promise."

"Don't leave out the juicy parts. He's gorgeous!"

"Katie," I scold. "Can you promise me something? Promise you won't tell anyone about this, OK? I'm just not—I mean, Jayce is a really private guy."

Katie snorts. "Not buying that. He's in *People* like every other month with some new bimbo." She halts, realizing what she's said. "Wait. Not you, Violet. I didn't mean that you were one of his bimbos. Sorry."

"You're forgiven if you promise not to tell anyone. Maybe Jayce isn't all that quiet about his dating life, but I'm not ready for *my* life to be public yet, OK?" There. That gets as close to the truth as I'm ready to tell her right now.

"Fine. But remember, you're already kind of public. I mean, with all the campaigning you've done for Dad and Butthead—don't you think that's a better name than Brady?—you've got to have a pretty decent presence online."

I gasp, afraid that this thought will send Katie's fingers to Google. The only thing I have going for me right now is that my name's not in the picture caption in *People.* They don't know who I am, and the black wig makes it unlikely anyone else will recognize me.

"I really have to go, Katie," I say, hating the words. "But we'll talk soon, K?"

"We'd better. Miss you, big sister."

"Miss you too, little sis."

***

I call Neil and beg him to bring me some more stuff from our apartment. I buzz him in when he hauls it over on his lunch break, grumpy as usual.

"More shit from your secret admirer." He flips a bag on Jayce's kitchen counter with several envelopes inside. None are stamped, but all are addressed to me. "He's not going to stop until he gets to you, Violet."

I press my fingers to my temples, my head pounding as blood rushes to my brain. "I'm trying. Jayce found me a lawyer who's trying to work something out with the porn sites."

"That's not going to make any difference with this guy," Neil says. "And you can't just hide here forever."

I nod miserably, feeling every bit like Rapunzel in her tower. I need more than just a prince to climb my hair—I need him to slay dragons: the stalker, the revenge porn sites, and the media vultures.

It's too much to ask of anyone.

"I'm all out of options," I tell him. "The police still haven't called with news and I can't go out without risking being seen and linked to Jayce. And then everything will blow up."

"So they've won," Neil says. "Brady. The stalker. They've backed you into a corner and it's like you're building your own prison."

"What can I do? There's no magic formula that will get me out of this."

"It's true. You can't un-ring this bell." Neil steps up to me, toe to toe, our eyes at the same height. "But you *can* live your life. Starting now. I was closeted for five years from the time I admitted to myself I was gay, and the time I was willing to tell anyone. The only thing worse than the shit that'll rain down on you from going out and being yourself is the shit that suffocates you when you're in hiding. There is *nothing* worse than that."

I open and close my mouth, at a loss for what to say.

"Those pictures aren't the end of the world, Violet." Neil takes my hand and his tone softens. "You didn't do anything wrong, but *he* did. Brady took a private moment and threw it out there for the world to see. So go get your suit of armor, find a sword, and quit waiting for someone to rescue you. The only way you're going to win is if you fight this yourself."

***

Neil planted a seed and as I shower, an idea takes root. I might not be able to fight the revenge porn sites, but I can fight the man who caused this hell.

Brady.

I blow dry my hair and dress, mentally rewinding the ten months we were together. He was careful, but not careful enough. In the weeks after he tied me up and took those pictures—in the time it took me to gather the courage to break up with him—he let things slip through the cracks.

I flip open my laptop and log in to my email. I dig through dozens of messages between us, messages I should have deleted long ago, until I find the clue I need: the picture he sent me of his dream car. I couldn't remember the name of the Lotus Evora, but I know he types it daily.

And then I commit my own cybercrime. I log out of my email account and attempt to log into his. I try LotusEvora, lotusevora, and finally break through with L0tusEv0ra.

I search for the words *Sexy Bitches* and find nothing. But when I search the word "upload" I find dozens of messages. And after combing through one dull political message after another, I finally hit pay dirt.

In his sent messages folder, there's an upload to a site identified only by ISP numbers. Attached to the message are three photos—mine. Fire floods my veins as I hit "forward" and send the message to my own email. Even though Brady all but confirmed his crime in the foyer of my parents' house, this is proof.

He did this.

With this first taste of blood, ratting him out isn't enough. I want to ruin him, so I poke through other folders, searching for something worse, tastes I know he has for girls far younger than me.

In an email folder labeled "Term Papers - Grad School" I find the sickening truth. Emails exchanged with a handful of people bearing photos of girls in bondage. They're bent and bound, humiliated, stripped bare, contorted and covered in God knows what.

There's no way these girls are eighteen. I wouldn't just card them for cigarettes. I'd card them for a PG-13 movie.

My stomach rumbles with revulsion. Cringing, I forward three of these emails to myself as well.

CHAPTER 41: JAYCE

I ask her every day, and every day she says no.

Finally, I've found the girl I really want to be with, and she doesn't want to be seen with me. No dates. No dinners out. Nothing but hiding in my apartment.

I'm sick of it, but I can hardly blame her. I can't risk what we have right now simply because I want more.

I pumped weights hard tonight after practice, working out the anxiety of being stuck hiding her but unable to help.

Gus has made some headway on takedown orders, but it's still less than half the sites he dug up with her pictures splayed across them. In a roundabout way, he even suggested hiring a hacker to try to take down the sites, but I wouldn't know where to start to find someone who could do that, and of course Gus has to cover his own ass and avoid anything illegal.

I swing by a market and pick up stuff for dinner—fresh pasta, herb salad, and chicken breasts that I'll pound flat and turn into a wicked parmigiana. At least I can cook for my girl.

When I swing open my door, Violet's at the kitchen bar tapping on her laptop with a glass of wine beside her.

But oh, holy hell, she looks good. She's wearing a clingy black dress with sleeves that sit below her shoulders, displaying every inch of that freckled collarbone I love to taste. Her hair is fresh and curled, falling softly over her shoulders, and her makeup makes her green eyes pop.

I dump the groceries on the counter and circle her waist, pulling her off the barstool and against my chest. "You look amazing," I manage, before taking her lips with mine, exploring that soft crease in her lower lip, tasting apricots and sweet white wine.

She takes my tongue between her teeth and I feel myself go hard immediately. It's a shame she looks so good, because I want that dress off her in three, two, one...

"Go get ready to go out," Violet says, and pushes me away slightly, but with a smile.

I look down at my chest, T-shirt still damp with sweat and my shorts looking pretty ratty next to her polish. I didn't know she had this dress with her.

Wait.

"Did you go to your apartment?" My voice is harsher than I intend, but fear for her safety puts me on edge.

"No." She scowls. "I had Neil bring me some stuff. And then he talked sense into me, said I can't hide here forever. So we're going out."

"Even if you—even if we're seen?"

"I figured out a place where that shouldn't be a problem," Violet said, one of her brows arched. "Get ready. We've got a reservation at eight."

I dive for the shower, wishing I could coax her to follow me, but knowing we'd probably be here another hour if she has to re-do all the girly shit like hair and makeup if I get her wet.

Wet. God, my cock throbs at the promise of it. Since we've been back, I haven't tried anything as kinky as tying her up again, but even normal sex always carries this charge with us, this give-and-take power exchange.

I've had her in every room, in every position, and on practically every surface in my apartment. But there's one thing we haven't done since we've been back from LA.

"Are you curling your hair, or what?" Violet's in a sassy mood as she comes into the bedroom, watching me as I dress. I practically fall over pulling on nice jeans when she deliberately crosses her legs and I see a flash of creamy flesh above her stockings.

Stockings. Damn. The last time she wore stockings, I almost pushed her too far. But maybe these are an invitation for more.

I call a car and she gives the driver an address in the East Village I don't recognize. We pull up outside a place called Crif Dogs with a low ceiling and brick walls. Violet's way overdressed for this place. Past the arcade games, vinyl barstools sit beneath a skinny ledge. At the back, an oversized sign advertises the weirdest hot dog toppings imaginable.

She tugs me into a phone booth, and there's barely enough room for one person, much less two. Not that I'm complaining as I mold her body into mine, her back to my front.

Shit. Not a good idea if I don't want to walk without a tent pole in my pants. Violet picks up the phone and says a few words, then the wall at the back of the phone booth swings open, revealing a hidden room.

It's dark, the kind of place where mob bosses would make deals under smoke-clouded air. A hostess leads us to a booth beneath some freaky taxidermy and I slide in next to her.

The menu is hot dogs and high-end cocktails. Violet winks at me. "Your night's about to get a lot more interesting," she says, and her hand snakes up my thigh to my crotch, ensuring I might never get up from this table with all the blood rushing to my dick.

"You're trying to kill me, woman."

"No, I'm just feeling a lot more brave," she says, and strokes me through my jeans. Holy shit. If she gets any braver, I'm going to come undone.

Violet keeps up the tease through our meal, and true to her promise, the hot dogs are fantastic. I pick something called the Lil' Ma, which is pretty much everything a pregnant lady could wish for—pickles, peanut butter and crushed potato chips on a hot dog wrapped in bacon. All that's missing is the ice cream.

I'm flying by the time we finish our date, pawing Violet in the town car, grinning like an idiot as I hold her hand and walk her through my apartment lobby.

I grab her boobs in the elevator, slam the apartment door behind us, and bend her over the back of my couch because the bedroom is too damn far away.

Violet's hair tumbles around her and I slide up her skirt to get a look at her ass bracketed by the garter belt's ribbons. My mouth has been watering for her taste all night.

I drop my pants and let my fingers explore her, coaxing her into the position I've imagined all night: legs spread, ass up high, chest draped down over the couch, hair spilling across the cushions. The tip of my cock nudges her ass and she shivers.

I snap the garter's elastic against the tender flesh of her thighs and she whimpers, but when I pause to be sure that I'm not pushing her too far, she tilts her ass and grinds harder against me.

I pull away from her and she whimpers again with need. I go to the kitchen and fill a glass with ice and whisky, savoring its rich aroma as it slides down my throat. I walk back to the couch where she's still bent and waiting for me, the rise of her rib cage and quiver of her legs telling me exactly how much she's anticipating my next touch.

I pluck an ice cube from my glass and hold it above her ass, letting droplets fall on her milky skin. Each drop makes her quake and I stoop to follow them with my tongue.

"Is this a test?" Her voice is breathy.

"It can be. What are you willing to give me?" I hold my breath, waiting, watching, wanting.

"Everything."

The word electrifies me. I've been afraid to go back to that dark place that almost tore us apart, when I bound her and it was too much for her to take. And since then, I've never taken the full measure of what I wanted.

But tonight, Violet gives me control. She gives and I take, but I'm not just taking pleasure for myself. I'm taking her to the place she wants to be.

I peel off her stockings, my lips and tongue and teeth caressing her flesh as thoroughly as my fingers. I bind her wrists again, holding her dark green eyes captive as I anchor the stocking to the leg of the coffee table.

I take her mouth greedily, my hands pulling at her dress to strip her bare as we kiss, as our tongues writhe and dance.

And then I take the rest of her body—with my tongue first, and then my sheathed cock slides into her. I feel the rippling of her body as she clenches me inside her, the vibration of her chest as she moans with my strokes, the twitches of pleasure as I torture her clit, flicking it faster as I increase our pace.

I push her harder and higher. Her wrists strain against the stocking bindings, her legs tremble from this position and each time I slam into her. Our bodies slap together and I can feel the energy gathering, the fuse lit inside me.

I grit my teeth to hold it back, bearing down on her clit with one finger and circling her ass with another. Three more seconds, two, one, and I know the *exact fucking moment* when Violet's world explodes.

Her scream rips through my ears as my climax rips through my cock. The surge shatters my vision and in my moment of blindness, I don't see stars, or God.

All I see is Violet. Perfectly.

***

Pounding on my door wrenches me out of deep sleep, and I extract myself from Violet, whose body is tucked into the curve of mine. I grab boxers and a T-shirt and hustle to the front door. Chief's on the other side.

"What the fuck?" My clock reads six a.m.

"That's pretty much what I've got to say to you," says Chief. "Look." He thrusts his iPad at me and I read a news story with mounting horror. It's everything.

Violet's pictures, her nipples and crotch barely covered by a black bar. A sharper, enlarged picture of us dancing at Kiki's party. Another picture of us coming back from our date last night.

"Jayce McKittrick's latest lady," the headline screams, "… or is she?"

The story goes on to crucify Violet, with details about how she was fired from her teaching job for unprofessional conduct for posing for porn. The article trashes her for playing the role of family-values icon in her father's campaign, and does a side-by-side of her tied up next to one of her looking like a Sunday School teacher while speaking at a campaign event.

"Which is she—the saint or the sinner? Jayce might not know his new girl's past, but it's catching up to both of them," the article concludes.

"Fuck. Me." Bile rumbles in my gut and I want to puke out the filthy accusations. "Where did this come from?"

"That's what I've been trying to run down for the last hour," Chief says. "The reporter called me to get a comment from you, and I pushed as hard as I could. All he'll say is a source close to the band tipped him off to the photos of Violet. Like, really close."

"Nobody knew about those pictures but Jayce," Violet says, and I jerk around to see her dressed. "I never even told Stella."

"You should have told me," Chief growls at me. "I can't do damage control unless I can see what's coming."

"He had no right to tell you." Violet says. "They're my pictures. *My* secret. And he would never—"

She whips her gaze to me and I swallow. *It was me.* I may not have told the reporter or my band mates, but I handed the information to the worst possible person—Kristina. A girl who seems to hate Violet and Stella more with every passing day.

Violet's eyes widen as she sees guilt wash over my face. "Did you? Did you tell someone about those pictures?" She crosses the room and wrests the iPad from my fingers, flicking through the article as color drains from her face. "You gave away my secret?"

"I didn't mean to—" It's all I can manage before Violet's eyes flash with fury and hurt and betrayal.

"I don't care what you *meant*. I care what you *did*." She moves like a whirlwind, grabbing her purse and her phone. "You promised to protect me and now you've ruined any chance I have to get those pictures destroyed before our relationship is public."

She spits the word relationship at me, and I flinch like she's hit me, my heart ground to dust for what I've done, for sharing a secret that wasn't mine to tell. "Violet, I swear, I never went to the press. I'd never do that to you."

"But you *told*. How can you treat my life so casually? Maybe you don't care if your sex life hits the tabloids, but *I* do!" She shoves her feet into shoes by the door.

"Give me a chance to explain. Please, Violet."

"I gave you a chance and you ruined it. You ruined *us.*"

She slams my apartment door before I can go to her, hold her down and tie her up if I must, just to talk some sense into her. The slam echoes in the stillness of my apartment and my chest heaves like I've had the wind knocked out of me.

"You're going after her." Chief's not asking. He knows what I need.

"Yes. But first, I'll tell you what you can tell that fucking reporter."

CHAPTER 42: VIOLET

I'm blind with fury as I hail a cab in the early dawn emptiness of the street, as I punch into my apartment lobby and pound up the stairs. I unlock my apartment door but Neil's thrown the chain, so I pound on it and yell at him to get his ass out of bed and open up.

The chain slides back and I stomp inside, whirling around to tell Neil about Jayce's betrayal. My mouth opens to pour out the hurt but the words freeze, cemented to my tongue.

A pair of dark, watchful eyes stare back at me. Not Neil's.

He's taller than I remember, with brown hair shaggy over his ears. His charcoal gray shirt drapes over a thin chest, his fingers resting lightly on his jeans-clad thighs. Without breaking our gaze, he throws the chain back into place.

"I knew you'd come home, Violet." His voice is slithery-smooth, cold, and focused. He takes two steps to the side as if he's a lion circling his prey. "I've been waiting for you."

I know him. *I know him.* I see him nearly every week at the bodega on the corner.

He crosses to my kitchen. "Would you like a drink?" I shake my head no but he ignores me, each movement deliberate as he cuts foil from a wine bottle, inserts the corkscrew, and pours a glass.

He comes at me with the glass, and I back up so fast the couch takes out my knees. I sit as terror shoots up my spine and he deposits the glass in my hands. *Think, Violet. Be your own prince for once. Figure out how to save yourself.*

I lift the glass to my lips and tip the barest sip, vinegar on my tongue. Struggling to keep the tremor of fear from my voice, I say, "Thank you. Would you have some with me?"

He smiles, his face relaxing with my invitation. "Perfect." He takes the other glass from the kitchen and sits across from me. He takes a sip.

Yes. That's good. Maybe he just wants to talk. Maybe he'll leave fingerprints and DNA. Maybe he'll drink and get relaxed and I can find a moment to run.

"I—I don't think we've been introduced properly," I say. "You've sent me flowers and letters, but you never signed them. What's your name?"

"Ah, we'll get to that. I do want you to know my name. I want you to know what to scream when I'm finally inside you."

I choke, his matter-of-fact words bearing no hint of possibility, only finality. Determination. He's been after me for weeks, and I was a fool to think he'd lose interest when every step toward me has only been an escalation.

Messages from afar. Messages that proved he was close. Flowers. The letter in my camera bag. The pictures of his naked, hard penis gripped in his hand as he stood in my room.

No, it's clear he'll take his fantasy all the way to its conclusion.

"You told me you loved me," I say, trying another tack. "But you're scaring me."

His eyes flicker with greed. I've given him what he wants. Power, the ability to sway my emotions with his actions.

"It's OK to be afraid in the beginning, Violet. I was scared to admit my feelings at first. But once you confess them, once you *own* them, everything becomes so much easier."

He takes another sip of wine and I follow him, then sputter, struck by the horrible though that he might have drugged mine.

"I know what you're thinking. It's just wine, sweet Violet. I want you alert and focused on everything I intend to do to you." He stands and crosses my small living room, positioning himself on the couch next to me. I think of self-defense maneuvers, of clawing my way to the door, but he's too close and power radiates from his body.

Just like Brady. The power of his presence wrapped itself around my throat and kept me from screaming or fighting when Brady tied me up. It's a subtle threat, but clear all the same.

My stalker places his wineglass on the coffee table and takes my free hand nearest him, the one that isn't gripping a glass so hard it could shatter. He trails his fingers up my inner wrist, to the crook of my elbow and up my arm to the sleeve of my T-shirt.

I swallow, then I see an unfamiliar gym bag across from me. It's open and inside there's a coil of rope.

"You like my toys?" he asks, and crosses the room in a flash to display them. The rope. A blindfold. Some kind of gag with a ball in the middle of it. A knife. He flicks open the hunting blade and rests it on the coffee table by the wineglass. "I brought them to play with you."

My fear is gone, replaced by icy terror.

I could scream, but he'd silence me, and likely with enough force that I'd lose my chance to escape. I force my body to be still as his finger trails down the side of my breast.

I shudder and my nipples peak, my traitorous body signaling that he's found a button to press.

His mouth curves up, eyes on my breasts, and he squeezes my nipple painfully. "You like that. I knew it wouldn't be long, Violet. I knew you'd find a way to respond to me, to show me you can love me, too."

Love. On his lips the word is blasphemy. Love isn't about force, it isn't about taking power. Love isn't surrender, either. I could give up and let him use my body so I can get through this without him using the knife.

Love is the opposite of fear.

Even in this roiling pit of terror and desperation, that thought shines clearer than anything. *Love is the opposite of fear.* In everything I've been through with Jayce, in every moment we've been together, I've had nothing to fear from him or with him.

He's shown me love at every turn, love in each little sacrifice he's made for me. Even when we were deep in the moment and he tied me up and I *knew* he wanted to be inside me, he sensed my fear, stopped, and cared for me.

The stalker picks up the knife, testing its weight in his hands. "This can be a good toy if you know how to use it, Violet," he says. I hate the way he speaks my name, another violation. He slips the blade between my arm and my T-shirt, a quick thrust up and a flick of his wrist, and the sleeve splits like curtains.

I gasp. Each touch is a splinter of ice, his caress washing me in fear until I'm drowning, paralyzed with the reality of what is happening, and what will happen next.

"Maybe you'll like it if I take you like this," he says, the tip of his knife playing with my sleeve again until he slips it through the hole on a path to my throat. Another thrust and flick and my shirt falls away from one shoulder, sliced from the collar so it drapes down my chest and reveals my bra.

"This next cut will be fun for both of us, beautiful Violet," he says, and I see his erection forming through his pants, his eyes darkening as he licks dry, thin lips. His knife point reaches for my bra strap and I flinch.

Hot red blood seeps from the wound even before I register the pain of the cut.

"Oh, now you've done it, Violet. I didn't mean to hurt you, but I will if I must." He bends his head and licks the trickle of blood above my breast, near where my bra strap attaches to the cup. His tongue lingers on my skin before he straightens and smiles. "I will if you're uncooperative."

"Can I—can I touch you?" I force my voice to be steady, low with hunger instead of fear. Slowly, I move my hand toward his pants, watching his eyes widen and the knife go slack in his hand as I stroke him through his jeans.

As much as my stomach lurches and I want to throw up, I thrill with the effect, as if I've just found a light that can lead me out of this darkness.

"Very good, Violet. You're doing so well." He moans when I stroke him harder, then he straightens and swallows. "Let's see what's next."

The knife springs to life in his grip, and I freeze as it comes near the cut that's still trickling blood. He finds the small space where the curve of my breast pushes the bra strap away from my body, inserts the knife, and flicks. The elastic springs away and the bra cup sags, but the lace remains covering my breast.

"I've seen your breasts a thousand times in pictures, Violet, but to touch them … yesss." He peels the lace cup down and my nipple springs free. His face is a burst of elation and avarice, and he licks his lips as if he's ready to taste me. I move my hand in his lap again, eager to distract him.

"Touch me," I choke out, hoping he'll hear need instead of loathing. "Please."

I see the indecision on his face as his eyes flick between his knife and my nipple. I stroke his penis harder through the denim, begging his hormones to cloud his judgment.

"All right. Since you asked so nicely."

I watch as he places the knife on the coffee table, both hands free now to touch my breasts. He rolls my nipple between his fingers, his other hand working to push my T-shirt down under my other breast.

My far hand grasps the wine glass, my only weapon. "Taste me," I beg. "Now."

I hear him take a ragged breath and bend toward my nipple. Just before his lips close over it, I slam my hand with the wineglass into his face, driving shards into his eye.

The scream sears my brain as he grabs his face. I grab his knife and plunge it into his shoulder. His hand swings out wildly and knocks me to the ground.

The knife flies from my hand and I scramble to grab it again, feeling his fingernails dig into my calves as he comes after me. Broken glass slices my knee. I kick back hard, my shoe connecting with his jaw.

He lets go. I grab the knife. I hear a crunching sound as I turn to this bloody, howling animal, ready to stab it a thousand times and put every one of his victims out of their misery.

"No, Violet!" A hot hand clamps down on my wrist and I whirl around to stab the new intruder.

CHAPTER 43: JAYCE

Her eyes are wild, her teeth clenched, and I know what she's ready to do. The howling man clutches his face, writhing on the floor from the kick I saw Violet land as I burst through the door.

I hold her wrist tight while she has a death grip on the knife, willing her to release it. I finally pry it from her fingers and press her down into a chair.

Waves of red hair mix with the blood from a slash just above her breast and her nipple is exposed, jutting out from translucent skin. She's blind or disoriented, a thin pant squeaking from her throat.

I deal with the man next, hog-tying him with a rope that lies on the coffee table next to a ball gag. *That rope was meant for Violet.*

When I'm sure he's not going anywhere, I dial 9-1-1 with bloody fingers.

Violet stares at her front door that hangs open at an awkward angle. Chunks of molding are gone from where the chain was once attached to the frame. When I heard that scream, I raced up the stairs and used my shoulder like a battering ram.

And now I'm here. Almost too late.

Violet's skin is blue-white and a tremor rocks her. She's bleeding on her chest and knees, but the cuts look superficial, so I direct her to her room to get the guy out of her sight and I wrap her in a comforter to combat the chills that shake her body.

The police arrive and I tell them what little I can guess about what happened. I lead them to Violet and a female detective sits on the bed next to her, talking softly as she asks the kind of questions I never wanted Violet to have to answer.

Another cop steers me away from her bedroom but I want to know. I *have* to know. How far did the stalker go? How much of Violet have I failed?

The stalker screams again as paramedics cut off my ropes and load him onto a stretcher. I demand he be restrained, telling the police that this is the stalker who's been haunting Violet for weeks, for which she's already made three police reports.

They put on grave faces and nod and try to placate me, but it's not enough. Rage bursts through me and if I had the knife in my hand—the one a cop has just placed in an evidence bag—I'd do what I suspect Violet was getting ready to do when I burst through the door.

The female detective comes out of Violet's room. "Will you stay with her?" I nod. "She's in shock and she's going to need a look at that knee, so take her to the hospital. But she's not going to need a rape kit, so she can have a shower."

God, it's all so clinical. So matter-of-fact. The woman I love has just escaped with her life and they're talking to me about a rape kit.

I am fucking *done.* I might not be able to hurt the stalker, but I know the guy who started it. Her ex-boyfriend.

I send Violet to the bathroom and tell her to take the longest, hottest shower possible. I don't go in there because—well, because I'm afraid that betraying her by telling her secret still hangs between us. She's mute, just nods and follows my instructions.

I pull a change of clothes out of her drawer and take it to the bathroom while the cops wrap up their inspection of the living room. I take Violet's purse to her bedroom and pull out her phone.

Her last call is to Katie Chase.

"Hey, sister." The girl's voice is a shade of Violet's, but younger and softened by sleep. I remember she's in high school, and I know they're close. Close enough to know what I need.

"Katie, hi, sorry to call you so early. It's Jayce."

There's silence on the line. "Jayce? As in, Jayce McKittrick? Like Tattoo Thief? The *band?*" With each question, her voice rises until it's an excited squeak.

I laugh. "Yep, that's the one. I'm calling because I need some info on your sister's ex-boyfriend. I have to talk to him." From researching Violet on Google, I'm pretty sure it's Brady Keller, but I have to be sure.

"That's the stupidest idea I've ever heard," Katie says, and I swear she's scowling. "Why would you want to talk to him? They're history. And why are you calling me with her phone?"

I blow out a breath and sit on Violet's bed. It's confession time—I have to tell Katie about the pictures Brady took and splashed across the World Wide Web. The story is live, and as the city wakes up, it's just a matter of time before Violet's family hears about it. I even confess the part I played in exposing her secret. Then I tell Katie about the stalker and the fight in Violet's apartment.

"You're an idiot." Katie says, her voice choked with emotion after I assure her that her sister is safe now. "You think talking to Brady is going to fix anything? It's not like he can un-publish the pictures. They're out there."

"I know. But I want him to pay for what he did. I want to ruin him. I want to strip him of everything he took from Violet, starting with his name."

Katie tells me to wait and I hear shuffling in the background, then she rattles off his phone number. I write it down with shaking hands on a notepad on Violet's desk. "You're really going to do this?" Katie asks. "Because he'll retaliate. His name is the thing he values most."

"Well, Violet is who I value most."

"Then you wake up Brady, and I'll go wake up my dad."

By the time we hang up, I'm fully armed and dangerous, ready to detonate a bomb in the middle of this man's campaign.

***

The calls start coming while we're sitting in the emergency room waiting area, back to the hospital too soon for my taste. Violet's barely said one word to me, just followed me silently as I checked her in.

This is where it all started—the connection that flared between us and utterly changed me from a guy whose dick twitched just watching her take pictures of the band, to the man who wanted to protect her after a stalker's texts drained the blood from her face and put fear in her eyes.

She leaves me to sit in the waiting room as she gets her knee patched up and I duck into one of the offices to talk. Chief. Gus. Her father. Reporters.

Each conversation is like taking another bullet, but I'd gladly take these for Violet if it means protecting her and the last scraps of dignity she has. She's being shredded like that first story, shamed for her nakedness and the kinky bindings, taunted for going to church one day and posing for porn the next, reviled for teaching sex ed to kids when she's clearly a deviant.

But there's one message I have through all of this. I love her. I fucking love that woman, and my heart could bleed every drop before it would give up beating for her. And as I repeat this fact over and over to anyone who will listen, I'm struck by the stupidest thing I've done so far in twenty-five years of living.

I haven't told her.

Yet.

I stride out of the conference room with purpose, finding her talking with a discharge clerk near the front of the waiting area.

"Violet!" I sprint to her side, her mouth dropping open in surprise with the urgency in my voice. "I'm sorry, but this can't wait," I tell the nurse, and then I drop on my knees in front of her, clutching both of her hands to make her face me. "Violet, I love you. I love everything about you, every part of you, the good and bad, the light and dark. Everything I've done, even the screw-ups, were because I love you. And everything I am is here to protect you."

She blinks, and twin streams fall down her cheeks.

"All this stuff that's happening, even what's about to happen, I can take it. I will gladly take all the hurt if it means I can take it from you. I know your heart, Violet, and I know what's true and good about you. And I intend to spend the rest of my life proving it to the world."

I'm panting with feeling, with this speech that somehow roared out of my throat, and I'm terrified she'll turn away. But she doesn't. By some goddamn miracle, she doesn't turn away from me. She lifts me up, pulls me against her and buries her head in my chest.

CHAPTER 44: VIOLET

I have no words for Jayce, who treats me like I'm breakable, or maybe like I've already shattered.

He barely speaks to me after his declaration in the hospital. Maybe my reaction was less than he wanted, but I'm still processing everything: the stalker, Jayce's betrayal, and the gossip article that ripped me to shreds.

Jayce takes me home—to his home—and feeds me. He holds me. And each time his phone rings, he excuses himself to his room and shuts the door between us.

He's shutting me out of fixing this. And as I dress for the press conference, I know I can't let him.

"Are you ready to go?" Jayce leans in the doorway of the bathroom as I dab concealer on the dark circles beneath my puffy eyes.

"Almost. But, Jayce, we have to talk."

His expression slams closed and he crosses his arms. "I told you, Violet. I'm doing everything I can to protect you."

I pull a brush through my hair, measuring my words. "You can't fix this."

"I can sure as hell try. I've got Gus and a PR guy working like crazy to figure out anything I can throw at Brady. Chief's issued a statement to every site that's run the story."

I leave the brush and walk toward the doorway, standing as tall as I can to look straight into his eyes. "It's not your fight, Justin."

"It is. It has to be. I can't let this happen to you."

"Look at me. *You* didn't let this happen to me. I did. I can take responsibility for being with Brady. Even when I knew better, I stayed with him because everyone wanted us to be together. Brady, my father, even the campaign planners. We made a great story."

"And now you're a horrible story." Jayce's eyes are pinched with worry. "They're crucifying you right now, Violet. I don't want to see you hurt."

I cup his cheek in my hand, feeling the coarse stubble in my palm. "You didn't hurt me. So stop owning this. You can't rescue me."

His jaw is set. "I can try."

"Justin, I know you want to. That's who you are—a protector. But if you shut me out of this, if you try to be my knight in shining armor, you're taking away all of the power I have to fight this. I want to have my own sword, slay my own dragons, and cut down Brady and the stalker on my own terms. I'll give you control, Justin, but not the power. I need that for myself."

Jayce is silent, but gives me a slight nod. He understands me.

I walk out of the bathroom and track down my laptop, then open my email. "Let me show you something."

Jayce hovers over my shoulder as I pull up the emails I forwarded to myself from Brady's account. They're more than enough to ruin him.

Jayce gives a low whistle. "How ... how did you get these?"

"I hacked his email. Didn't even hack it, really, just figured out the password." After I take these to the police, Brady will be lucky to find a job slinging burgers and fries.

Jayce shakes his head and smiles. "Remind me not to make you mad."

"Too late for that."

"OK, then, remind me to quit trying to play knight. You stabbed the stalker who cut you, and now you're gonna take down your ex with his own sleazy online pictures." Jayce cups my face in his hands and plants a kiss on my lips. "You're like the best kind of fairy tale, Violet. You're the kickass princess."

***

My father has flown in from Ithaca to make a statement with Katie in tow. In the few minutes between when his town car pulls up and when we have to take our places at the podium, I shut out everyone—Jayce and Chief and Katie—and force him to listen.

We huddle in a hallway out of their earshot.

"I know I've disappointed you," I start, and I bite my lip, watching my father's green eyes and the controlled set of his jaw for some gentleness or a sense that he's on my side. "And I'm sorry for what this might do to your campaign. I didn't do it to hurt you."

"How could this happen?" His strained question is rhetorical. He's talked to Jayce, heard precisely how Brady sent my photos to the revenge porn sites. He's seen the pictures, a fact that horrifies me. He knows what the tabloids are saying. "I know I raised you better than this."

"It doesn't matter how you raised me." I struggle to keep a scream from piercing my lungs. "You controlled everything about my life when I was a kid, but you can't control what happens now. I'm an adult."

My father takes a step back, as if he's reassessing me. "Why, Violet? Why would you let Brady do that to you?"

I shake my head. "I never let him. He used me." I touch his elbow, silently pleading with him to get past the photos and see who's really guilty here. "I have absolute proof that Brady did it. Say what you need to say out there in this press conference. Make me the scapegoat if you have to for your campaign. But I'm not going to apologize for my choices."

"Violet—"

I cut him off. "Even though you pushed me toward him, I *chose* to be with Brady. And I chose to leave him. Now I'm choosing to fight him and the stalker and the websites that post these pictures, whether you're with me or not."

My father shakes his head. "I'm—"

"Senator Chase? Violet? It's time." Chief beckons us to the conference room.

Paparazzi and gossip bloggers stand side-by-side with reporters from the local news channels as my father steps up to the mic. Jayce ghosts to my side and squeezes my hand, and his quiet support begins to heal what he hurt when he told Kristina my secret.

My father clears his throat, and I wish I could plug my ears and sing at the top of my lungs to avoid hearing what's going to come out of his mouth. That I've sinned, but we should forgive sinners. That I'm confused, or a victim, or that I should be pitied.

"I am proud of my daughter."

My knees buckle at his words.

My father stands tall in his suit, staring intently at the sea of cameras assembled. "I am proud of my daughter, and who she chooses to love, in whatever way she chooses to love him."

A whisper threads through the room as he continues. "I am proud that she's a fighter, and that she fought off an attack by a stalker who pursued her for several weeks. He knew precisely where to find her because of pictures Brady Keller took and posted on the Internet, together with her name, phone number and address."

More muttering. My father continues, "I am proud that Violet's taken legal action against the despicable sites that shared those pictures. This is a crime, and a real problem called revenge porn, and I'll stand by her as she sees it through."

My father reaches for my hand and I send him an ocean of gratitude with my eyes. "No parent wants to see his child grow up, but becoming an adult means testing your boundaries, and sometimes making bad choices."

Another whisper, and my heart plummets. I stare at my shoes, ashamed. Now comes the lecture. Will this become another speech about conservative values? And I'm the object lesson on what not to do?

"But Violet never chose this. It was taken by force, and shared with the intent to harm her. And that's why I'll fight—as a parent, as a state senator, and as a congressman if the people of my district choose—to create legislation that punishes both those who share revenge porn and the sites that host it."

The surprised murmur in the crowd matches my racing heartbeat. A reporter rockets from his seat, hand waving. "Senator Chase, how does standing up for this reflect the family values of your campaign?"

"Family values?" His tone is hard, bordering on angry. "Family values aren't just part of church and marriage. Family values are respect and fidelity and protecting the people you love. There is *nothing* in the world that could make me love my daughter less, and nothing that she can do that will make me fail to step up to protect her at every turn."

I squeeze my eyes shut, feeling the flood of love from my father whose strict rules and conservative ways were always—*always*—meant to protect me.

"And I'm not just doing this for her. I'm doing it for your sisters and girlfriends and daughters. I stand for all of the young women who've been caught by some sleazy ex or hacker, only to have their faces and names dragged through the filth."

***

After twenty minutes of questions, most handled deftly by my father, we climb into a black SUV to go to Jayce's place. He's in the seat by my father, talking in hushed tones. Katie and I huddle in the back, and thank God she threw the mother of all tantrums to come with Dad. I needed her today.

Jayce starts cooking while Katie *oohs* and *ahhs* over his apartment, then demands he take a selfie with her so she can show her friends, "or it didn't happen."

Dad sits with me on the terrace couch. "I blame myself for this," he says, scrubbing his hands across his face and through his hair.

"How could you? It was my stupid, embarrassing mistake."

"I trusted Brady. I trusted him to be part of my campaign, but worse, I trusted him with you." He takes off his jacket and tie, unbuttons his shirt collar and rolls his sleeves. "I'm so sorry, Violet. And I'm sorriest of all that you didn't feel like you could tell me."

"It wouldn't have helped," I mumble. Now that the story of Jayce's kinky girlfriend is out, my pictures will never be reined in. Gus will keep dogging the original sites that posted them, but it's futile.

The Internet's memory is infinite, and its tentacles are everywhere.

"Violet, it can always help to share the burden," my father says. "The most important thing is that you know your family loves you no matter what. No. Matter. What."

"Even if I do something stupid like this?"

"Especially if you do something like this," he says with a smile, and I notice he dropped the word stupid. "You're young. You get to test your own boundaries now that you're an adult and you don't fall under mine. And I'll tell you a secret."

I wait, watching a smile twitch on his face.

"I am very, very glad that social media didn't exist when I was your age," he says. "Because if it did, I can assure you, I wouldn't have a future in politics."

My mouth drops open in surprise and I giggle. His chest rumbles with a laugh and pretty soon we're cracking each other up with the horrible hilarity of this situation.

"What's so funny?" Jayce comes out on the terrace and hands my father a beer and me a martini.

Katie trails him with a glass of lemonade. "You've got to let us in on the joke."

"Daddy just gave me the *best* ammo against your next broken curfew," I tell Katie, and she grins wide.

"Don't start with me." He pulls his brows together in an attempt to look stern, but laughter still dances in his eyes. "I've already got one wild child, so Katie, you'd better not give me another."

"Too late, Dad." Katie winks at me. "Do you think now's a good time to mention I have a new boyfriend?"

***

I kiss and hug Dad and Katie a million times before they leave to go home to Ithaca. Dad shakes Jayce's hand, two strong men united. "Take good care of my daughter."

"Always, sir."

The door closes and he turns to me, indecision on his face. I wait a beat and then go to him, squeezing him around the middle so tight I might squeeze the breath out of him.

Jayce's arms are around me instantly; he drops his chin and kisses my forehead, breathing into my hair. Soon his hand is tangling through the strands, combing through it the same way he first comforted me.

"Violet, I'm sorry. I told Kristina your secret and I had no right to. I did it because I wanted to take you with me to LA to protect you."

I feel his heart pound against my chest, his wall of muscle curve around me to pull me close.

"I know. I know you, Justin. I know you did what you thought would help me. Thank you—" my voice breaks. "Thank you for fighting for me. For not giving up."

Jayce chuckles and I look up at him. "Looks like you were pretty good at rescuing yourself. I did some checking while you were in the ER and you put that guy *down*. He's going to be in the hospital for a couple more days before jail, and they don't know if he'll ever be able to see out of his eye again."

I shudder. Even though Jayce didn't rescue me from that guy, he rescued me from myself. In my bloodlust I might have stabbed him again, and again, and taken self-defense to the point of murder.

I never knew I had it in me.

"You told me I couldn't keep you locked up in some tower like Rapunzel, and I get that, Violet. But now you're free. There's no stalker and no secrets hanging over you. You're free to go and free to stay with me. But I want you to stay with me. If you're willing."

"I'm willing." I reach behind his neck and pull his lips down on mine so he can't mistake my meaning. This time, I take the lead, my tongue brushing his lips, then darting inside his mouth to taste him.

Beer and chocolate, the last of our dinner with Dad and Katie. And beneath what's on his tongue, I taste *him*—musky, slightly salty, pure maleness that makes me rub my chest against his just to feel the hardened planes of his stomach and thighs.

Another thing hardens between us, but I'm not ready to give into the carnal pull of fantastic make-up sex just yet. "Remember that thing you said in the hospital?"

"What thing?" Jayce's eyes are hooded with desire, and I confess I might be giving a bit more friction to a certain area. "About how I'm going to spend the rest of my life proving to the world your goodness?"

"Mmm, I like the rest-of-my-life part. But before that."

Jayce's hand drops to cup the curve of my rear. He hitches me up against him, my legs around his waist, and he walks us back toward the bedroom.

"The part where I told you I loved you?" His voice is husky as he lays me down on his bed and lifts my hands over my head, trapping them. "Because I do. I love you, Violet. And I'll do everything I can to prove that to you."

I thrill with this promise, thrill with the absolute certainty of his intent. *The opposite of fear is love.* I have no fear of Jayce, but even more, I have no fear of anything else. The secrets are out. The stalker is done. I can finally love this man freely.

And so I do.

CHAPTER 45: JAYCE

I have a decision to make, but first, It's up to Dave.

Based on what he says, I'm in or I'm out.

The contracts are done—all but my signature. Viper Records is pestering the hell out of me to make it happen. I'm still not sure if Tyler's in with me, but the contracts leave the door open, a guaranteed place for him if he comes with me.

If I leave and the band dissolves, he'll be forced to choose sides. Me, his best friend, or Gavin and Dave? He sure as shit better choose me.

I pause at the door to Tyler's loft, ready for the tough conversation that might mean Wednesday's practice was my last one with Tattoo Thief, ever. I skipped yesterday's for the press conference with Violet.

Hell, I'd skip breathing for her.

Tyler's alone, and when he sees the look in my eyes, he starts shaking his head. "Don't do this, man. You don't have to decide this now. You're still angry about Kristina. I get that. But don't make your decision to leave just because of that."

I set my jaw, unwilling to hear him. He's been my best friend since high school, when I was playing football and pawing cheerleaders and he was this too-tall gangly guy who couldn't get a date. He got me through math and out of trouble more times than I can count.

"Jayce, you know I've got your back. Always." I nod, and he continues. "And so I'm telling you not to do this. Don't break up the band, don't leave us over this. If I've got your back, that's got to count for something." Tyler's pleading, seriously freaking out.

"It counts, Ty. But it's not enough."

Gavin bursts through the door and stops cold, sensing the dark mood. Maybe sensing danger. Dave's on his heels and I look, but Chief's not behind him.

Good. Then it's just the four of us. That's how it should be.

"Ready to practice?" Gavin asks, but it's a half-assed attempt. We all know shit is going down.

I stalk to the couches, three set up in a U-shape. I sit, Gavin sprawls on the couch next to me, and Dave squats on the third, directly across from me. Tyler takes the other half of my couch. I send Ty a mental note of thanks for siding with me, even on something so small.

"This is the end of something," I start, and panic fills Tyler's eyes. I hold up a hand to prevent his interruption. "Kristina did something unforgivable. To Violet, and that means also to me. She betrayed my trust and shared a secret that I never even told you guys. Violet never told Stella or Beryl. And Kristina gave it to a reporter to hurt Violet."

There. The facts are out, and I stare at my band mates, daring them to contradict me.

No one speaks.

"So I see two choices. Either you cut Kristina out like a cancer—cut her out of your life forever, so she never gets near any of us or our girls—or you choose her. But if you do, you're against me and Violet. And I'm out of the band. Period."

Dave narrows his eyes. "So we're taking sides for our girls? What the fuck, Jayce? Where's your 'bros before hoes' macho shit, or does Violet have you pussy-whipped now?"

I lunge across the space between the couches and grab his shirt, my arm drawn back for a punch that never lands. Tyler hooks his arm in my elbow so I can't smash my fist in Dave's face, but I've still got him by the shirt.

"Calm down, you fucknugget!" Gavin's still seated, his voice patronizing. "Kristina took a secret to the press. Keep in mind, Stella threw my song out there, basically stole it from Beryl, and you didn't get in Tyler's face and tell him to leave *her.*"

"She did that before I met her," Tyler growls at Gavin. "And it wasn't malicious. She wasn't *trying* to hurt you or Beryl. And she's apologized, up, down and sideways, trying to make it right."

"Fine. So this is different. What are you going to do about it?" Gavin's hard gaze challenges me.

"That's what I want to know from Dave."

His lips thin and he pulls back from me. I let go of his shirt and he sits, raising a brow as I tower over him, challenging me to sit, too.

I do. I wait for an explanation. This better be good. No, this better be fucking *poetry* with the kind of hurt I want to throw at Kristina, and at him if he defends her.

He puts his elbows on his knees and rests his head in his hands, rubbing his face like he's trying to wake up from a nightmare. "I didn't go home last night."

He means home to the Brooklyn townhouse he shares with Kristina. The one he's bought and paid for, but that she lives in and controls like its hers.

"I didn't know what to think when Tyler called me," he continues. "I didn't want to believe she'd do that to Violet or any of us. But the truth is, she could do it to all of us. Especially to me."

Tyler's loft is silent as blood rushes in my ears. What is he saying?

"What could she do?" Gavin's voice is cold and hard.

"For you, it's Lulu," Dave says. "Kristina saw what was happening, saw her wasting away and spiraling into junkie madness. She saw you give Lulu drugs. You think that story's behind you, but she could bring up more. She knows things Lulu's family could use for a civil suit that would kick your ass to next Christmas."

Gavin's face is a mask, but I smell fear.

Dave turns to Tyler. "For you, she could corroborate enough of Kim Archer's timeline to make you look like a heartless bastard, even if you aren't the father."

Tyler shrugs. "Doesn't matter. Kim lost her moral high ground the minute she got arrested with drugs in her baby girl's diaper bag."

"I don't think you're hearing me, Tyler. If that's not enough to cut you, she'll go after Stella. Something about a pregnancy when she was a teenager, and the father being a famous director."

Tyler visibly pales, and I know Dave's hit the mark.

I'm next, and I brace myself.

"How many groupies have you been with, Jayce?" Dave asks.

I shrug, not wanting to admit the number. It's a lot, a hell of a lot more than any of them, and I'm thankful Violet's never forced me to share it with her.

That's behind me now. I hope.

Dave snorts. "I don't really want to know, either, but Kristina knows. She's got most of their names and numbers. You think she can't get Shelly and Teal to do a tell-all piece with a tabloid for ten grand? She *saves* their numbers, buddy, and calls them when you dump them, letting them cry all over her shoulder and pretending to be their friend."

My jaw goes slack, stunned by Kristina's duplicity.

"Hit me, Jayce." Dave stands, takes a couple steps toward me, squares his shoulders and tilts up his chin. "Hit me if that's what it's gonna take to get it out of your system. Hit me like you want to punish Kristina, but don't fucking break up the band. You guys are all I got."

His voice wavers in that last sentence, and suddenly I get it. "She has something on you, too."

Dave's nostrils flare but he stiffens with resolve. "Hit me, Jayce. Do it."

"Is it worse than Gavin's secret? Or Tyler's? Or mine?"

He closes his eyes and nods, a tiny tilt of his head. His whisper is choked. "Hit me so hard I can feel it. Because I can't feel fucking anything right now."

I stand and see Dave brace himself. Tyler's eyes are wide and fearful, but I shake my head to tell him to stand down. I reach for Dave, a hand on his shoulder that makes him flinch like I just sucker-punched him in the gut. His eyes fly open.

"You don't kick a man when he's down, Dave," I say. "What do you mean, we're all you got? You've got a fucking great record we're about to put out, a sweet place in Brooklyn, and an evil bitch you've got to kick to the curb."

I grab both shoulders and shake him, trying to force him out of this daze of self-loathing.

"I can't. If I leave her, she'll bury me."

"Then let her try. It'll be four against one," Tyler promises.

"Cut her loose." Gavin agrees.

Dave looks at me hard before he gives an answer. "If I do, do you promise to stay? With the band?"

I work my jaw, debating. "Will you stop being such a controlling jackass?" I say it in jest, but Dave hears me. He's always been pain-in-the-ass pushy, but that's what made him a great manager when our band was starting out. It's just the last few months, especially when Gavin was gone, that turned him.

Made him different. Harder. More demanding. Angrier.

But maybe it wasn't Gavin's absence. Maybe it's was Kristina's presence. "You found out the dirt she had on all of us while Gavin was gone, didn't you?"

He nods. "She's always had something on me, but it was our secret. Just a horrible thing that happened when we were young and fucked up and stupid. But when I found out she was ... collecting ... on you, I realized how much she knew about Lulu. How much she could prove about Gavin."

"Fuhhhhhhhhhk," Gavin groans. "And you stayed with her to *protect us?* Because, Dave, that's like giving her insider access to get even *more* shit on us!"

"I know!" Dave explodes. "But what could I do? If I dump her, she'll ruin me. She'll try to ruin all of us."

Gavin's voice drops to a snarl. "Then let her try."

EPILOGUE: VIOLET

The air feels different here, and it should. We bid the oppressive humidity of early August adieu and launched ourselves into the crisp, thin air of Steamboat Springs, Colorado, elevation 6,695 feet.

That's more than a mile high, and more importantly, it's nearly two thousand miles west of the crazy fallout in New York City.

Now I'm *that girl* in the naked pictures.

That girl dating a rock star.

That girl whose father is running for congress. (And it turns out my naked pictures didn't ruin his shot at this election—if anything, they've helped him.)

But here in Steamboat, I'm just Violet.

Jayce has shed every shred of being a rock star. He's back where he grew up. He's Boot, or JC. He's my Justin.

We stay at a condo meant for skiers but it's way out of season, so the place is dead. That's good, because Jayce likes to walk around the tiny downtown holding my hand like we're a normal couple.

He drags me into a bakery bursting with every form of carbohydrate that makes me drool. The older woman behind the counter recognizes him immediately. "It's on the house, Boot." She hands us a pair of scones. "You tell your parents hi for me."

On our second night in Steamboat, Jayce tells me he has a surprise. He pours wine into a stainless water bottle, rolls up two towels, and stuffs flashlights in a backpack. He drives our rented Jeep top-down, bumping along the gravel for a couple miles until we find a lot dotted with cars.

"A late-night hike?" I study him in the light from the dash.

"Trust me."

I follow Jayce down a zigzag path that curves around a series of wide pools of water, each cascading into another. The stars are bright, saturating a velvet sky like I've never seen in the city.

A few people are wading waist-deep or sitting in the water, but they're far enough away that I can't hear their voices.

Jayce strips off his shirt, unlaces his shoes and drops his shorts. He stands, his naked body gilded by moonlight. "Come with me, Violet." He waits until I'm naked too, then takes my hand and we ease ourselves into water that's just right, the temperature blending with my skin so perfectly that I feel like I'm weightless.

"Lie back." He supports my neck as I float, one hand in my hair and the other by my hip. Water feathers across my body as he moves me in it, a trance, a dance, with stars scattered above us.

I hear him humming, a rumble in his chest, and I strain to recognize the melody. He swirls me through the water and I close my eyes, my skin tingling with sensation.

When I recognize the song, Tattoo Thief's driving rock anthem, "Sweet and Wild," I lift my head. Jayce sits on a ledge beneath the water and I curl up on his lap.

"You changed it up. That song. You made it a ballad."

Jayce chuckles. "You caught me. Sorry."

"Don't apologize. I like it when things are unexpected."

"Like us." He dips his chin and touches his forehead to mine. "You're deliciously unexpected, Violet."

Our shoulders are exposed to the air and the tops of my breasts pucker with gooseflesh as a breeze ripples through stands of aspen. I press myself closer to him.

"I love you, Justin," I say, and let his soft lips take mine. His tongue curls and flicks and his hand cups my breast. "I never thought I'd find ... this."

I don't have words to describe our unique mixture of connection and control. It defies everything I thought I knew about the *one right way* to love or be loved.

"I think I've always been searching for this," Jayce says and presses his hand to my heart. "It's just like that song."

I pull my head back in question. "Changing it up?"

"Making it whatever you want it to be. I think love is like music—whether you play it sweet and gentle or hard and wild, what matters is that you get to choose what speaks to you."

AUTHOR'S NOTE

This is not entirely a work of fiction. Revenge porn is part of our real world.

Violet's nightmare was inspired by a series of articles detailing the victims, activists and owners of revenge porn (RP) sites.

In some cases, nude pictures and sexts are posted on a site together with a person's real name and photo, often culled from Facebook. *Gawker* called it "a new generation of amateur erotica: stalker porn," and noted that nude photos taken with a cell phone are often submitted to these sites by vengeful exes.

A *Jezebel* article stated that RP might include identifying information such as the victim's full name, address, workplace, boss's email address and parents' phone number. Harassment of the victims, their families, and their employers has led to firing, ruined personal relationships, and at least two women have killed themselves over RP.

When Facebook took legal action against one RP site, "I replied with a picture of my dick," Hunter Moore, the site's then-25-year-old founder, told *Gawker*. "I'm not a virgin to cease and desists—I get about a million a day. I think [Facebook] is under pressure from users to do something about me ... I don't give a fuck. I'm never going to stop."

Jezebel published an article by Charlotte Laws, whose 24-year-old daughter Kayla took pictures of herself posing in lingerie in front of a mirror. She sent her cell phone photos to her email, which was hacked, and the hacker forwarded her images to an RP site.

Laws also wrote about a kindergarten teacher in Kansas whose pictures were posted on an RP site. Viewers promptly bombarded the principal with messages such as "fire that slut," and "you have a whore teaching your children."

While I was writing this book, Hunter Moore was indicted in a federal court in California following an arrest by the FBI on charges of conspiracy, unauthorized access to a protected computer, and aggravated identity theft. According to the indictment, many of these crimes were committed in an effort to obtain nude images of people against their will.

Also in January, Israel became the first nation to classify RP as a sex crime. In the U.S., the Cyber Civil Rights Initiative launched a campaign to end RP, which includes anti-RP legislation. At the time of this writing, just seven states have RP laws: Arizona, California, Idaho, New Jersey, Utah, Virginia and Wisconsin.

ACKNOWLEDGEMENTS

Huge, heaping gratitude goes to my critique partners Emma Hart and Katie Ernst. From the kernel of the idea to egging me on to *land the damn plane* (in other words, finish the story), these insanely talented ladies make writing a delight. We plotted future books together in a Paris apartment fueled by wine, laughter, and fabulous French carbs.

Every writer needs a team, and I have wonderful people in my corner. My developmental editor, Jim Thomsen, guided four novels and helped me grow by leaps and bounds. He ensures the mistakes I make are opportunities to hone my craft.

Cynthia L. Moyer kills it with copy edits (hundreds!) while wrapping her red pen in truly encouraging feedback. Amy Duryea is my proofreader who picks up on the tiniest details, including my penchant for mistyping *than* as *that*. She tells me I tend to skip words during the hot scenes. (What can I say? I get caught up in the moment.)

I write with fantastic writers' groups: *80k Words, NaNo in Feb* (aka 4evNo), and *Anything Goes*. Thanks for the sprints Emily R. Pearson, Annisa Tangreen, KK Hendin, Lex Martin, Brianna Lee, Claudia Bradshaw, Tami Carter and Kerry Taylor (and many more!).

Diana Peterfreund is incredibly generous with advice and ideas, so you'll spot a tribute to her next book in my last chapter.

Melanie Harlow has been a tremendous ally—thank you for inviting me to the WrAHM Society! These kickass women who wrangle words and kids (stole that line from Gen) have wonderful NSFW commentary on writing and life.

My husband gives me time and space to write, edit, and take glorious "research" trips, while tackling far more than his fair share of housework.

Although my kids are too young to read, I adore their enthusiasm. My three-year-old stands on our coffee table, proclaims, "My mommy writes books!" and then jumps down with a dramatic, "Thank you!"

My parents' encouragement means even more considering I don't write PG books. Their unwavering support inspired Violet's father's press statement.

Finally, I am grateful for the bloggers, readers and reviewers who cheer for my characters and share my books. I am especially humbled by the enthusiasm and feedback from Lisa Reeves, Sam Stettner, Hetty Whitmore Rasmussen, Naomi Hop, Holly Baker, and Chelcie Dacon-Holguin, whose kind words make me fall in love with these stories all over again.

After typing 76,000 words, these two are the most heartfelt: *Thank you.*

COMING SOON

Dave and Willa's story is the final novel in the Tattoo Thief series.

Dave faces an ultimatum—dump his toxic girlfriend Kristina or break up his band Tattoo Thief. But Kristina won't go quietly. She has enough dirt to ruin each member of the band, and enough on Dave to send him to jail.

This stinking, bloody threat has haunted him for years.

As Dave hangs in limbo, a new star emerges: Willa, dubbed "The Lady Banksy" by the modern art world. When a magazine feature article catapults the graffiti and tattoo artist to sudden fame, she must cope with the spotlight when all she's ever known is the shadows.

Life as a runaway jaded Willa, and it leaves her deeply in doubt of her fifteen minutes of fame. Nothing good lasts forever. Especially not love.

It seems like *everyone* wants a piece of Willa now. Except Dave. When their music and art worlds collide, she finds the one person who isn't trying to take something from her, and who might have something to give.

As Dave's secret is laid bare, a mystery unravels, pointing to his guilt and its dangerous intersection with Willa's old life on the streets.

Both must risk their success and the intense connection to each other to prevent their pasts from defining their future.

ALSO BY HEIDI JOY TRETHEWAY

TYLER & STELLA (Tattoo Thief #2)

When aspiring music journalist Stella Ramsey gets insider access to America's hottest rock band, she's torn between selling a story and telling the truth. Celebrity gossip swirls around Tattoo Thief's bassist Tyler Walsh, forcing Stella to reveal her own secrets to save him from his.

TATTOO THIEF (Tattoo Thief #1)

When 22-year-old Beryl leaves her sleepy hometown to become a house sitter for New York's richest residents, her first client is Gavin Slater, lead singer for the rock band Tattoo Thief. He trashed his penthouse, abandoned his dog and fled the country, leaving Beryl to find out why he's running and what can bring him back.

WON'T LAST LONG

Can two people who are totally wrong for each other ever be right?

Opposites attract, but friends think sly, feisty Melina and steady, laid-back Joshua can't possibly last. When crisis throws their world off its axis, Melina must confront her history and the destruction of her pristine image.

A HANDFUL OF GOLD

A new fairy tale adventure with an un-princess twist.

If there's just one thing Audrey wants, it's an adventure. When she travels through the forest to see the kingdom castle for the first time, she must rely on kindness and courage to outwit bandits, rescue a girl and help a prince.

Read more at www.heidijoytretheway.com.

Made in the USA
Charleston, SC
16 August 2014